PRAISE FOR RICHARD DUE'S
MOON REALM SERIES

Moonbeam Children's Book Awards
Gold Medal Winner

THE MOON COIN

Book One / A Moon Realm Novel

"*The Moon Coin* is a fine and adventurous read for young adults, highly recommended."

—Midwest Book Review

"*The Moon Coin* is a beautifully written fantasy novel, perfect for middle graders to pore over themselves or as a bedtime story for younger kids. The descriptions of everything, from Uncle Ebb's electronic fish-bird hybrids to the fanciful creatures Lily meets in the Moon Realm, are so rich that the action instantly comes alive for the reader. The story's tension builds slowly but the excitement is constant, with Lily asking the same questions puzzling the reader. *The Moon Coin* has all the elements of a great fantasy: a unique, complex world, a battle between good and evil, and creatures that are a mix of comical and terrifying."

—ForeWord Reviews

"So begins a beautifully descriptive, cleverly written, intricate story, full of adventure and captivating characters, who draw you into their very lives and worlds. The wider adult reading population will no doubt be entranced by the skill of the author, Richard Due. I just cannot believe that this maturity and skill with the written word comes from a debut author."

—Fiction Books

D0291516

THE DRAGONDAIN

Book Two / A Moon Realm Novel

"Get ready for a wild ride! *The Dragondain* will have you gasping, cheering, and falling in love with the characters all over again. Due's rich descriptive prose and fast-paced dialogue make for a truly exciting read. There were so many "goosebumps" moments I literally could not put the book down. I can't wait for Book Three!"

—S. S. Tamberrino

"Due has just become one of my favorite authors. I love that his books are smartly written. So many YA and childrens books are just junk food for the brain. This book is complex, the characters have some depth, the scenarios faced by the characters are not simple. I read this to see if it was ok for the kids, and it turned out to be a great story, perfect for family reading or for older kids/teen (or even adults) to read on their own. It's excellent fantasy that appeals to both genders."

—CS (Amazon Review)

"This is the 2nd book in the best new series for young and old readers. Middle graders can read for themselves but younger children will enjoy being read to. The pictures are fabulous. There is a new adventure brewing all the time. You will love meeting the characters from the different moons of the moon realm."

—Kindle Customer

TheMoonRealm.com

WILLA SNAP AND THE CLOCKWERK BOY

Titles Available in the Moon Realm Series

The Moon Coin
(Part One: The Rinn of Barreth)

The Dragondain
(Part Two: The Rinn of Barreth)

Richard Due

WILLA SNAP AND THE CLOCKWERK BOY

An Idiot Genius Novel

Illustrated by
Carolyn Arcabascio

Calvert Library
410-535-0291 301-855-1862
calvertlibrary.info

Gibbering Gnome Press
A Division of Ingenious Inventions Run Amok, Ink

Huntingtown

Gibbering Gnome Press, A Division of
Ingenious Inventions Run Amok, Ink
Huntingtown, Maryland

WillaSnap.com

ISBN-13: 978-0-983-8867-8-5 (ebook)
ISBN-13: 978-0-9838867-9-2 (KDP paperback)
ISBN-13: 978-0-9996071-0-7 (CreateSpace paperback)

First Gibbering Gnome Press, A Division of Ingenious Inventions
Run Amok, Ink ebook and print edition December 2017

To my mom,

who showed me how to tilt my artwork on the refrigerator at a jaunty angle . . . because, you know, it just looks better that way.

Vivian Rosslyne Due
"Viv"

ACKNOWLEDGMENTS

In order to preserve our home's fragile sanity, we established a rule to end all rules: thou shalt have no more than one all-consuming mammoth writing project at a time. It's a good rule! It's an important rule! It's a rule we've thrown out the window of a speeding MiniDirigy.

I've decided to take the low road on this one. That's right, I'm blaming everyone but myself. First, I'd like to blame my lovely wife and editor, Liz, who, after I foolishly pitched her the idea of Idiot Genius, blurted, YOU HAVE TO WRITE THAT! Next, my alpha beta readers, Meredith and Clare Prouty-Due, for begging me to *write faster, Dad!* For the heinous crime of encouragement, I blame Emily Bakely (editor), who, after reading the beginning in a coffee shop, scooped up the rest of the MS, clutched it to her chest, and ran out the door with it. For their patient scrutiny, I blame my beta readers: Jessi Wood, Jared Jiacinto, Jimmy Humphries, Bridget Evans, and Sharon Grummer. I blame Carolyn Arcabascio, the illustrator of this work, for capturing my characters so beautifully—how dare she! I blame the people who contributed IG idioms and exclamations: Tricia Rightmire, Jessica Western, Lenny Lind, Christine E.P.V. Culver, Alyson Griese, Georgi Ridgway, Danny Paul, William Wolfgang Allen, Sari Benmeir, Gerald Smith, John Verrico, Susan Hanson Turfle. And, lastly, the cherry on this ice cream sundae of blame, John Verrico and Yeşim Nuri Clark, for helping me with Nimet's Turkish.

CONTENTS

A Note on the Text

When Willa Snap's first highly illegal memoir landed on my desk (I have since received two more), I must say I was intrigued—and after the first read, fearful for my life. Would proceeding with publication be wise? It was a fair question. But after a long talk with Nimet Simit, all my fears seemed to magically vanish.

As to the text, a little clarification is in order. First, I have no doubt Willa wrote her first drafts in the field, as events unfolded. However, it appears that while redrafting, she was unable to resist adding occasional asides that referenced later adventures. While these interjections at first seemed jarring, I have decided to leave them intact, as I believe the information they contain is as droll and unpredictable as Willa herself. Eğlenmek!

— E.A.P.

Somewhere South of the Flatiron

Building, Manhattan Island

"Genius is not measured by a number alone, but by the deeds and inventions it brings to our world. To possess the number alone, and to make inventions of wide-scale destruction, is not the hallmark of Genius—it is the hallmark of Idiot Genius. This is why we regard The One Who Got Away [Albert Einstein] as the patron saint of the Idiot Genius."

> —Bartholomew vos Savant, chancellor
> of the Institute of Intellect, speaking
> on the relevance of IQ as a number

History is always older.

—Black Fez axiom

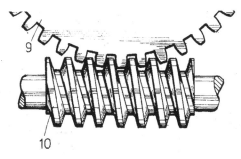

Cat's in the Bag

E VER wonder why some crazy scientist hasn't blown up the world? I used to wonder about it all the time. Actually, I was pretty sure my mom would be the one to do it.

But now I know better. It turns out there's a force working hard to keep the world from going KABLOOEY.

Who are these people? Wait for it:

Idiots. Yep, you heard me right.

How do I know? Well, apparently, I'm an Idiot. At least, according to the Geniuses I am. Confused? I'm not surprised. You're probably an Idiot too. Offended? You shouldn't be—I called you an Idiot, not an idiot. There's a difference, just as there's a difference between a Genius and a genius. Confused *and* offended? It gets worse. There's a third category: Idiot Genius. Those are the ones you really have to look out for. You see, Idiot Geniuses—for some unaccountable reason—are completely obsessed with "improving" the world. Maybe it's encoded in their DNA. I don't know. I didn't get those genes. I have Idiot genes, which means that for an equally unaccountable reason, I'm obsessed with *sav-*

1

ing the world—usually from them.

I must warn you, my story isn't a pretty one: abductions, time-traveling dragons, the Order of the Black Fez, highly verbal cats, a secret invisible city, condescending robots (condescending means they talk to you like you're an Idiot; wait, is it condescending of me to explain what condescending means?), and that's just for starters.

But I digress. Digress, by the way, is a word I learned from my mother. You tend to grow a big vocabulary when someone in your family is a genius. If *your* vocabulary isn't up to speed and you're using an e-reader, feel free to look up *digress* using your built-in dictionary. However, if you're reading an ancient, smelly fire hazard of a book, then take a minute or two and go look it up in an ancient, smelly fire hazard of a dictionary, because I'm not going to waste my time explaining every single word I use just in case you don't know it. But I digress.

It all began on a Thursday at precisely 8 a.m. I was standing in the family room of our lovely two-story house, directly across the street from Squirrel Brand Park in Cambridge, Massachusetts. The same family room that, in a few minutes, I would never ever, ever see again—ever.

Squirrel Brand Park is a small park, but I miss the little place every day. When I was six, my dad swore he saw a squirrel in the park hide a tiny pair of binoculars behind its back. Dad was *so* serious! After, we laughed and laughed and laughed. We are *not* laughing anymore.

Back to the story. My mother had kept me out of school that day so I could attend her big lecture at the Hall of Speculative Science at MIT. MIT is a university in Cambridge, across the Charles River from Boston. Every month they pick someone to give a talk on an invention that could change the world. That month, they'd chosen my mom.

We were due at the hall in less than an hour, and my cat, the Magnificent Lady Grayson of the Silky White Underbelly, or Just Grayson for Short, was mixing up my mother's speaking notes by employing her claws to simulate a Cuisinart. Shredded papers were flying everywhere.

"Willamina Gilbert Snap! Get control of your cat!" screamed my mother.

I ran over to the coffee table, plucking bits and pieces of flying paper out of the air, and lifted the Magnificent Lady Grayson of the Silky White Underbelly, or Just Grayson for Short into my arms. She protested with a loud meow, clawing desperately to reach the last remaining unshredded note.

That's when

my father walked into the room. "Honey," he said to Mom, "can you give me a hand with this?" He was trying to tie his tie, which he should know better than to try and do by himself. If you haven't already guessed, he's an Idiot, too.

My dad's a fun dad. Kindly eyes, quick to smile, built like every guy you ever saw on a pre-steroids baseball card—how did all those guys hit so many home runs when they were so skinny? He doesn't talk down to me. He takes me out to ball games and museums and parks when Mom's busy in her laboratory all weekend, but he's not exactly what you'd call brilliant. Unless he's got a wrench in his hand and a bunch of pipes to play with, which is convenient since he's a plumber by trade. Not that he really has to work or anything, except when Mom loses one of her paychecks, which happens kind of often. She uses them as bookmarks, or writes grocery lists on them. Once, we found one in the freezer. It's like she doesn't understand how money works.

Grayson plunged her claws deep into my shoulders. The resulting bolts of pain loosened my grip. Out she flew from my arms. In a single bound she crossed the room and plastered her face against the front window, paws spread-eagled on the glass.

"What's the matter with you—"

She glanced over her shoulder at me, a look of horror on her fluffy face. That's when the doorbell rang.

"I'll get it," said my mother, finishing up my father's tie.

As my mother made her way to the door, I watched Grayson's eyes dart back and forth between whoever was outside and Mom. The cat sprang into action, racing up the back of a chair and leaping into the air. (This wasn't the first time I'd witnessed this kind of behavior. The Magnificent Lady Grayson of the Silky White Underbelly, or Just Grayson for Short arrived on our doorstep using much the same maneuver, only she was swinging off a nearby tree branch the day she tumbled into our home. If you told me she was a runaway from a flying trapeze circus family, I would say to you: ya think?) Lucky for Mom, I anticipated this, catching Grayson and balling her up in a jacket before she could land on my mom's head. I dropped to the floor, tied the arms in a knot and—voilà!—instant bagged cat.

My mom looks like one of those movie stars from way back. Today, for example, she'd styled her blonde hair in a sleek updo and was wearing a white swing skirt with a wide red belt and a short red bolero jacket covered with big white polka dots. It's the kind of outfit that makes strangers stare and mumble. So whenever she answers the door and I want to know what's what, I stand right next to her. It's the only way to get the firsthand scoop.

"Good morning," said a woman wearing a black fez emblazoned with a big red *G*. "My name is Heather Peaceout, and I'm with the I.O.I. Would you be Dr. Audrey Snap?" This lady was *not* mumbling.

Except for the bright red tassel attached to the top of her fez, she was dressed all in black. Black clothes, black fingernail polish, black sunglasses. She wore no makeup that I could detect, a plus in my book. If she hadn't been standing so close to my mother, I would have said she looked pretty.

"Can I help you?" Mom asked.

"Are you Dr. Audrey Snap, inventor of the pac-a-purse?" persisted Heather.

"Yes, that's me. Say, that's an unusual style of fez you're wearing, isn't it?" Grayson began struggling inside the jacket like she was warming up for an Olympic gymnastics routine. "You say you're with the eye-oh-eye?"

"Yes, the Institute of Intellect. It's a private concern."

Grayson growled loudly. Heather, suddenly alert, dipped her chin and peered over her sunglasses at the growling jacket in my arms. Her eyes were sky blue, and unruly tufts of blonde hair rimmed her fez. I looked down at the squirming bundle and made a *this couldn't be helped* face. Heather gave me a wink and pushed her sunglasses back into place. All business, she tapped her wrist, and a computer thingy strapped to her forearm appeared out of thin air.

"Totally bean!" I whispered. Mom and I say that when we see something unthinkably amazing.

Reading from her computer thingy, she asked, "Are you still planning to give your talk today at 9 a.m. in the Hall of Speculative Science at MIT?"

"Are you with the press?" asked Mom coyly.

"No. I'm with the Institute of Intellect. Don't you . . . remember?"

Mom flinched and touched her hand to her forehead, the way she does when one of her headaches is coming on. "I'm afraid I really don't have the time—"

"One quick question," said Heather. "Then I'll be out of your hair forever." This is standard Black Fez procedure, designed to plant an image in your brain of them walking away. This dramatically reduces the chances of you instead imagining something unpleasant, like being tasered, or hit with a tranquilizer dart, or rolled up in the rug you're standing on and carried off. "Is it true that the principal technology behind your device can be easily scaled up?"

Mom brightened at the mention of her invention. "Why, yes.

That's the beauty of it, you see. Because my discovery uses a heretofore little-understood quirk of quantum mechanics—"

Heather held up her hand. "One more question. Could it be used on something as large as a city?"

My mother placed a finger next to the adorable dimple on her chin and thought for a moment. "Well, I suppose . . . but all I want to use it for is a purse! You see, I'm always leaving something at home that I wish I hadn't." Heather examined her fingernails and waited for my mother to stop talking. "And so one day I thought if only I could store everything I wanted in my purse, then I'd always have it. Get it?" Mom was excited. Geniuses always get excited when they're explaining how something they invented will change the world for the better.

Heather looked bored. "I see. One final question. If this new technology of yours were used on say, oh, Washington, D.C., what would happen to the city during the time that it was . . . in the purse?"

My mother gave Heather a funny look. "That's crazy! Who would want to carry around an entire city in her purse!"

Heather looked at me to see if Mom might be kidding. I sighed and shook my head.

"Please, ma'am, what would happen to the city?"

"Well, it would exist inside the purse, of course." Heather clearly wanted more. You see, the problem is that geniuses—both capital G and small g—either think you understand everything they've said as perfectly as they do, or that you're as dumb as dirt. It's one of their biggest flaws. "In a perfect state of stasis until it was taken out again," added my mother, now getting a little annoyed.

CHAPTER ONE

"I see. One final, final question. And *please*, I beg of you, think *very* carefully before you answer. All right?"

"O-kaaaay." My mother was now using the voice she reserves for kindergarteners and puppies.

"Do you see *any* problems with that?"

I knew what Heather wanted to hear. Dad, listening from the living room, knew what Heather wanted to hear. Heck, from the gyrations going on inside my coat, you'd think even Grayson knew what Heather wanted to hear.

I often wonder, if Mom had had an "aha!" moment that day, would that have called off the abduction? Lucky for me, she snorted out a laugh and said, "Do you mean like . . . would fewer bad laws be passed?"

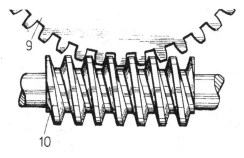

Abduction!

MOM closed the door. The Magnificent Lady Grayson of the Silky White Underbelly, or Just Grayson for Short went limp inside my jacket.

"Fez is kind of a funny word, isn't it?" I asked.

"It's a type of hat."

"I know, but where does it come from?" My mom's an instant-on dictionary. Watch and learn.

"Well," she began. "Let's see. One day in 980 CE, in a brilliant piece of marketing, a clever haberdasher decided to hawk his new hat to a bunch of students. Not only did it turn out to be a flashy fashion statement, but it was also instantly associated with braininess. Before you could say Judah ben David Hayyuj, the entire north coast of Africa was wearing them."

"Let me guess, the hatmaker's name was Fez?"

"Noooo," she said, as if what I'd said would have actually been funny if only I had more brainpower than a canary. "But the city he lived in was."

"There's a city named after a hat?"

My mom laughed. "I can see how you might think that, but no. The city of Fez was doing plenty well all on its own long before the hat came along."

"What do you think that big red G stood for?"

"That I don't know. But I do know that, traditionally, a woman's fez is smaller than the one she was wearing. And they're usually colored a shade of red made from a particular berry that, for a very long time, Fez held a monopoly on."

"More great marketing!" Geniuses love it when you pipe up and show that you've been paying attention.

"Yes! But all that changed after synthetic aniline dyes were invented in the nineteenth century." Sadly, geniuses never know when to stop explaining stuff. "The shade of red made from that berry represents the supreme height of practical wisdom. Isn't that fascinating?"

"Erm, not so much."

"You know, honey," said Dad, scratching his head. "That woman did kind of have a point."

"How's that, dear?"

"Well, the whole bit about what could happen if you applied your invention to something as large as a city. I mean, call me crazy, but I think a lot of people would probably get a little antsy about being tossed in stasis for a week. Don't you think?"

Mom dismissed Dad's concerns with a wave of her hand. "Don't be silly. That woman was being kooky."

"But Mom," I said, jumping in, "don't you think placing millions of people's lives on hold could be confusing? Yay, it's Tuesday! Whoa! Now it's Thursday! Hey, where did Wednesday go?"

"But that would never happen!" she insisted. "It's for a purse."

I looked at Dad. "She's not getting it. Why isn't she getting it?"

"Hey, guys! Lighten up, will ya?" said Mom. "Who's the genius in the family?"

"You are," Dad and I said dejectedly. Geniuses have been using this technique on Idiots for centuries, and with good reason—it's devastatingly effective.

Before we left for the lecture, I placed the jacket containing the Magnificent Lady Grayson of the Silky White Underbelly, or Just Grayson for Short on the living room floor, loosened the arms a bit, and ran for it. The instant I was out of the house, my dad slammed the door shut and peeked through a little porthole of a window high up on the door.

"Did she get out?" I asked.

Dad frowned. "Are you sure she was still in the jacket?"

"Positive. Can I see?"

Dad lifted me up. Sure enough, there was the empty jacket, but no sign of Grayson. Then, all of a sudden, I heard a gallop, followed by silence. A second later, Grayson's face appeared plastered to the other side of the little window. As she slowly sank from view, she let out a long, plaintive meow. Her claws sounded like nails on a chalkboard.

"Ooh! Looks like I'm going to be painting this weekend!" I said.

Dad rearranged some of his tools and plumbing supplies so I could sit in the back of his work van. Just as we were pulling out of the driveway, I heard a loud thump on the roof but didn't think anything of it. Later, I would learn that Grayson had run upstairs to Mom's laboratory, hurled a glass beaker through a window, and then launched herself into the big maple tree out front. From there, she leapt for it, attaching herself to the big snapping fingers on the van's roof. (Get it? *Snap!* Snapping fingers? Our last name is Snap? Try and keep up.)

We didn't discover Grayson until after we'd parked near MIT. Dad gave her a poke. She was like a frozen furry statue. "Should we leave her up there?"

He wasn't serious . . . I'm pretty sure.

"Um, can you get her down?" I asked.

He pried her from the giant thumb while I dumped out one of his tool bags and held it open.

"If you don't want to lose her, I suggest you don't open that bag again until we're back home," he cautioned.

But we weren't ever going home, and that's how Grayson ended up being with us the day we were abducted.

The Hall of Speculative Science was smaller than I'd imagined. It consisted of a podium and about thirty folding chairs. A crisp-looking woman sat my father and me in the wings behind a little curtain, like she didn't want us to be seen or heard. Dad pulled a book out of his pocket. He's a voracious reader: mysteries, historical fiction, memoirs, fantasy, plays, science fiction, you name it.

Right at nine o'clock, Mom started her presentation to a full house. I'd seen her rehearse it a bunch of times. It was full of boring scientific jargon that I couldn't pretend to understand. After what felt like an hour—okay, maybe it was only five minutes—I peeked out into the audience for the thousandth time and noticed a man in black sunglasses, dressed all in black, and wearing, you guessed it, a black fez with a big red *G* emblazoned on its front. I tried to get my dad's attention, but he was too into his book. The next time I looked, there were five more black fezzes, all in the front row. As an experiment, I looked away really, really quickly, then looked back. There was another one! I looked away and then back three times fast. *Fip-fip-fip!* Now there were ten black fezzes in the audience. The most disturbing part, though, was that I couldn't figure out how the normal people were disappearing.

By the time Mom finished her presentation and everyone in the room stood up to clap, they were *all* wearing black fezzes, most with red tassels, but a few with black.

Walking back to the car, Mom couldn't stop talking. "I think they liked it!"

"Um, Mom? Did you notice anything strange about the audience?"

"Strange? Not that I remember. But I really think they liked it!"

"You were great, honey," said Dad, reading and walking at the same time.

Then an odd thing happened.

"Hey," I said. "Isn't that Heather?" Dad's tool bag growled.

The light changed and we started walking toward each other.

It was Heather all right. I looked around. Somehow, we were the only people on the street.

"Maybe she wants to interview you again," said Dad hopefully.

But she didn't. As we met, she raised her arm and threw something to the ground. There was a flash, followed by a weird, low-frequency noise. A shimmering bubble seemed to grow around us, first ten feet around, then twenty, then thirty. Then a whole lot of things happened at once. A few feet to our right, a strange-looking bus appeared out of thin air. Big purple letters scrolled across a screen on its side: "E-X-P-R-E-S-S T-R-A-N-S-P-O-R-T-A—" Its doors flew open, and people in black fezzes poured out and surrounded us. One of them, looking at his wrist, announced, "Let's move it, people. Fifty-five seconds to temporal harmony!"

In a bored monotone, Heather announced, "Do *not* attempt to leave the time-bubble. If you attempt to leave the bubble, terrible things will happen to you. Remain calm. You've done nothing wrong." *Done nothing wrong?* The Black Fez tell lies like this *all* the time. "We're simply relocating you under the Revised Planet Safety Act of 1926. Do not panic. Please enter the transport peacefully. I repeat, don't panic."

"Forty-five seconds," called out the timekeeper.

My Idiot father threw his hands in the air. "I always knew something like this would happen!"

Mom rested her hands on her hips and gave him her best *Oh, really!* look.

"Oh, come on, Dad!" I said. "You did *not* see this one coming!"

Mom pointed at me. "From the mouths of babes," she said.

"Snaps!" said Heather, snapping out of the monotone. "I'm not joking around here! Please enter the transport—"

"Thirty seconds!"

"I most certainly *did* see this coming!" said my dad hysterically. "Since before we were married! I would say 'Just promise me you aren't going to blow up the world one day by accident. Can you *just* promise me that?'"

ABDUCTION!

The Black Fez got all extra agitated. A particularly twitchy-looking one pointed at Mom and started shouting. "Code Tesla! Code Tesla!"

Heather made a growling noise. "Bhattarai, Castillo, get Little Boy Blue here into the transport. And make sure no satellite strike-forces are being called down on this location, will you?"

"Twenty seconds!" called the timekeeper.

"Last warning, Snaps!" shouted Heather.

I looked at Mom incredulously. "Hey, I wasn't trying to defend you! I was pointing out how incredibly unlikely it was that Dad could have possibly seen this *exact* thing coming! I mean, people running around in black fezzes, an invisible bus—what are the odds!"

Mom opened her purse and pulled out a box of tissues. "I hate it when you two gang up on me."

The world outside the bubble wobbled.

"We're losing bubble integrity!" someone shouted.

"Ten seconds!"

"All right, round 'em up," ordered Heather.

"Aw, honey!" said Dad, taking Mom in his arms. "I'm so sorry."

"Me too," I added, joining the group hug.

The Black Fez converged on us all at once, whisking us into the transport and down a wide aisle between facing seats. Doors slammed shut. Outside, in the window of the beloved Cambridge cafe E = More Caffeine², our reflection wavered and vanished. It was like we'd gone invisible or something.

"5 . . 4 . . 3 . . 2 . ." counted the timekeeper.

The bubble outside started collapsing.

"Henderson!" Heather yelled to the driver. "Punch it!"

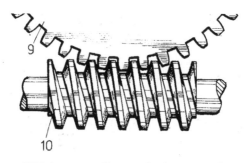

The Order of
the Black Fez

THE engines roared. I grabbed onto a pair of safety bars. Something told me this was no ordinary invisible bus (my biggest clue being the billowy white clouds racing past the windows). We were flying! Across the aisle, looking very relieved and happy, Heather smiled at me.

My dad clutched his safety bars in a death grip, his eyes squeezed shut. "We're all going to die, we're all going to die," he chanted.

My mom, by contrast, seemed very alert, even calm. Every once in a while she glanced through her wide-framed librarian glasses at the pilot working the controls. I could almost hear her voice in my head: *There's always something to learn if you're willing to learn it.* Already, for example, they'd shown her how to take off and fly the thing. By the time this ride was over, she'd probably know how to land it, too.

I usually find myself taking my social cues from my dad.

Don't get me wrong. I really love me some Mom, but Dad and I take to new people more easily. Mom, well, she tends to lead off with a pretty unnerving stare, which is sometimes followed up by a barrage of intimidating questions.

Right now, though, Dad was making little frightened-kitten sounds. Oh, dear. Well, I guess there comes a time when you just have to be your own girl.

I climbed out of my seat and stepped across the aisle. "Excuse me, Ms. Peaceout. Have you seen the tool bag I was carrying? I had my cat in it."

She whipped off her black sunglasses. "What? The cat's missing?"

"Got her," shouted a Black Fez in the back. "Got her right here." He handed me the tool bag. As I wrapped my arms around the bag, I felt the Magnificent Lady Grayson of the Silky White Underbelly, or Just Grayson for Short shift her weight. She was okay.

Heather fell back into her seat. "Oh, good. We never leave a family member behind."

"Is that your motto?"

Heather's eyes crinkled at the corners when she grinned. "You bet it is, Willa. The Order of the Black Fez always gets its family." She stuck out her hand. "We haven't been properly introduced. Heather. Heather Peaceout, Black Fez, Second Order, at your service. You were cool as an ice cube on dry ice today. You've got Black Fez written all over you."

"Um, I'm eleven," I said.

Heather looked at the Black Fez sitting next to her. "She's eleven," she said to him. He chuckled. His fez had a black tassel.

"Great, now you're making fun of me?"

Heather eyed me cautiously. "Peace, young Snap. It's just . . . when you're tired of being eleven, you let me know."

Outside, the view had turned into black space and bright stars. The blue-glowing curvature of Earth made an appearance.

"Oh, wow! Are we going into orbit?"

Heather glanced over her shoulder. "Hm? No, we're just making a little bounce out to the Southwest. We'll have you safe, sound, and on the ground in ten. Feel free to walk around. Just try not to touch too many of the buttons up front." She winked.

A repetitive thudding filled the compartment. I turned to see my dad pounding his fists on the exit doors, wailing something about going home.

"Don't worry," explained Heather, "your Idiot father doesn't have a prayer of opening those doors."

"Hey! He's not an idiot!" I didn't know then that most everyone in Grandeur is classified as either an Idiot or a Genius. "I mean, not all the time, anyway. Very little of the time, actually."

"Oh, he's an Idiot all right. I'm an Idiot, you're an Idiot, even Drew here is an Idiot," she said. "Isn't that right, Drew?"

"You betcha!" he said, taking off his black sunglasses. He was a big muscular guy with an incredibly pale complexion. "There are three basic types of Idiot. You got your Real Idiots, like you and me. You got your Stupid Idiots, like your dad over there."

"Hey!" I said.

"I know, I know," he said. "It's not polite to call somebody Stupid, and I apologize for any offense. Please believe me when I say I'm not trying to make any judgments. Your father's *probably* a Real Idiot, too . . . only not when he's being abducted." Drew held out a massive hand. "Please allow me to introduce myself: Drew Loader, Black Fez, Special Ops." His hand felt like warm carved stone.

"What's the third type?" I asked.

"Oh, those would be your Complete Idiots," said Heather.

Drew grinned. "Not your best decision makers."

"Your cousin's a Complete Idiot, right?" Heather asked Drew.

"That would be Clark. He's always cooking up some crazy venture. Right now he's trying to open a bookstore, with real books in it. Can you believe it? What a Complete Idiot."

An odd squeaking noise made me turn my head. Dad's sweaty face was sliding down the glass. When he hit the floor, he passed out flat on his back.

I turned to Heather and made eye motions toward my dad. "You don't think . . . I mean, there's not any chance he could be . . ."

"A Complete Idiot? No! He's just *acting* like one. Happens all the time during abductions. My medics will have him up in a jiffy. Palumbo, D'Amico, help this man back to his seat!"

Palumbo waved something under my dad's nose while D'Amico gave him a shot. I heard it hiss as it went into his arm. At first, Dad seemed to perk up a bit, only to slump back in his seat a moment later.

I placed my hands on my hips and shot Heather a dubious look.

"Sometimes it takes a little while to kick in," she said.

Mom's mind was racing faster than the transport. If she was worried about Dad, she didn't show it. No, she was trying to find a way out of this mess. I was sure of it.

CHAPTER THREE

I tilted my head ever so slightly toward my mom.

Heather gave me a knowing grin and leaned forward. "Don't worry. I got her scoped. She won't get within two feet of my pilot. Never mess with the Fez."

I climbed back into my seat and tried to nudge Mom without Heather or Drew noticing. Out of the corner of my mouth, in a low voice, I said, "It'll never work. They're onto you. Why don't you ask them some questions? They seem pretty talkative."

Mom peered down at me like I was a petri dish experiment gone wrong. It was a look I was familiar with.

"False sense of security," mumbled Dad. "It doesn't matter what they tell us. It'll all end bad."

I patted his arm. "What are you talking about?"

Dad closed his eyes for a second. His face was squished up against the safety bar, and it made his voice sound funny. "Maybe it's best I don't say anything. I wouldn't want to scare you," he slurred.

"What, and leave it up to my imagination? Don't you always say that's ten times worse?"

"Not this time, peanut."

Ideas bubbled up in my mind like an overflowing test tube.

"Really? Okay, how about this? They harvest our body organs for pet food. 'Cause everybody knows a human liver goes a long way—you could probably feed a whole herd of hamsters on mine." My dad let out a little whimper. "Ooh! How about this: They slowly freeze off our arms and legs, then remove our brains and force us to drive their cabs around for all eternity. Wait, wait! They lower us into a big vat of acid, reducing us to a cellular slush-fuel to power their smartphones, and then, as an added bonus, they string up our skeletons to reenact a massive musical stage production of *Les Mis*." I hopped out of my seat, spread my arms wide, and sang, *"You will live, Papa, You're going to live, It's too soon, too soon to say goodbye—"*

My dad smiled. "Come here, kiddo."

I stepped closer. He was drooling a little. "I love you so much," he said, sounding a little stronger. And then, I think because Mom was sitting right next to us, he mouthed the part he always says after: *and so does your mother.* Followed by, and this part was totally through his eyes: *which she would tell you herself if she knew how.*

"I love you too, Dad." I looked around the cabin. The Black Fez were talking amongst themselves like old soldiers. "Hey, Dad, where's your book?"

"Dropped it in the street, I think."

"Where are you taking us?" my mother suddenly asked.

"Grandeur," answered Heather.

"Anyone ever heard of Grandeur?" asked my dad, sitting up a little straighter and sounding more like his old self. "Did they teach you about Grandeur in school, Willa?" I shook my head. "Honey, is Grandeur in your encyclopedic brain?"

Mom shook her head. "Who lives in Grandeur?"

"Geniuses and Idiots, mostly," said Heather.

"How old is Grandeur?"

Heather lifted an eyebrow. "Older than you would believe. Grandeur is the place where people like *you* go to live," she told Mom.

"Me? Whatever do you mean?"

"The pac-a-purse," I said slowly. Dad, Heather, and Drew all nodded at the same time. I looked up at Mom. "Don't you see? It's dangerous!"

"What are you talking about?" Mom snapped, looking at me like I was crazy. "What's wrong with wanting to have everything in your purse? This is insane!"

"You could explain it to her a million times," said Drew, "but she ain't ever gonna take it in. It's the way she's wired."

"We're never going to leave Grandeur alive," dad muttered.

Now I know what you're thinking. Dad's beaten the old paranoid drum a few too many times, and it's addled his brain. But not this time.

I held the tool bag containing the Magnificent Lady Grayson of the Silky White Underbelly, or Just Grayson for Short a little tighter and thought about the way she'd been acting all morning. She knew. I didn't know how, but she *knew*.

Listen, I don't want you to worry too much. I know things look pretty bad right now, but it's all good. The Black Fez had no intention of hurting us—they simply wanted to imprison us for the rest of our natural lives.

"Approaching the Forest of the Big Bad Wolf," announced the pilot.

We all looked out the front window. The transport had completed its bounce, whatever that meant. We were flying high above a vast desert landscape. There wasn't a tree in sight.

"All right, everybody. Hold tight and think good thoughts."

"Almost there," said Henderson. "In three . . . wait for it . . . ."

A terrible feeling swept over me. All I wanted to do was run. I leapt out of my seat.

"We've got a runner," announced Heather.

Suddenly, I was all legs, charging blindly down the aisle. One of the Black Fez reached out and scooped me into her arms. I screamed. I fought to get loose. I felt like a wild animal trapped in a cage. I had to get free. I had to run! And then, just like that, all the bad feelings vanished. The woman walked me back to my seat.

"Relax," she said, tousling my hair. "Everything's fine."

A few seconds later, four Black Fez wrestled my dad back into his seat. My mom, looking disheveled, came walking back on her own.

"What was that?" asked Mom.

"Perimeter security," explained Heather. "You're lucky we have field suppressors on board. If you were on foot, or in an unprotected vehicle, it would have been a hundred times worse."

"But why?" I asked.

"To keep people away from Grandeur," said Drew. "It's important people think it's their idea to turn around. Much more effective that way."

"Fifty-five seconds to visual," announced Henderson. "Slowing velocity. Going into hover-mode."

We stared out the window. There was still nothing outside but rock and sand.

I squinted.

"Thirty-five seconds . . . thirty . . ."

"How high up do you think we are?" Mom asked Dad.

"Hard to say. Maybe a mile. What's that make our visibility, Mrs. Wizard?"

"A mile up? A little under a hundred miles."

"Twenty-five seconds . . . twenty . . ."

Directly ahead an opening appeared. With no point of reference, it looked really strange, almost like it was moving toward us rather than the other way around.

As we passed through, it became clear we were entering a dome—a dome designed to hide something from view. Something huge.

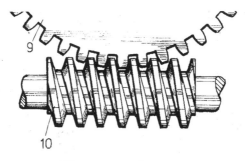

Grandeur

I T was a city! An entire city hidden in plain sight!

"Grandeur," announced Heather. "City out of time."

When we didn't move, Drew spoke up. "All right, Snaps, let's get movin'."

Behind us, the rest of the Black Fez formed a wall. They weren't cracking their knuckles or anything, but we got the message. I hugged the tool bag containing the Magnificent Lady Grayson of the Silky White Underbelly, or Just Grayson for Short extra tight.

"Well," said Dad, taking Mom's hand and putting his arm around me, "I guess this is where we get off."

Out on the platform, we gathered close as the transport lifted off and backed slowly out of the dome. Heather leaned through the open door and shouted, "Welcome to your next great adventure, Snaps!" I watched through the translucent metal dome as the transport disappeared into the blue sky.

We walked out onto the edge of a wide balcony. The only furniture here was a table with four small boxes on it. A mile below lay Grandeur.

"Wow!" I said.

Between us and the city, dark clouds were brewing.

"They have clouds," said Dad, stating the obvious (a wonderful pastime of Idiots). "They have clouds *inside* the dome."

"Cumulonimbus," observed my mom.

"Those are storm clouds, right?" I said.

Mom's eyes brightened. "Very good! We'll make a genius out of you yet!" I made my icky face, which Mom didn't seem to catch.

From this distance, Grandeur didn't seem all that strange. But the more you looked, the more that changed. Three skyscrapers rose out of a central lake, and bus-sized thingies glided all over the place, high above the streets. Sure, there were neighborhoods, roads, parks, fields, trees—but those skyscrapers . . . they just kept going up and up until they disappeared into the clouds, like Jack's beanstalk. Water cascaded down between the buildings, creating rainbows over the lake. There was something else, too, far off in the distance, the size of ten or twelve city blocks and covered with propellers. It was floating above one of the parks and tethered to the ground by masses of spidery ropes.

"Dad, what's that over—"

"What we have here is a classic Buckminster Fuller sphere," announced Mom. "Well, a partial one, anyway." She held out a thumb and squinted through one eye. I could practically see the myriad calculations leaping through her brain. She moved her thumb rapidly from one imaginary point to another. "Given the angle of curvature, it must be—"

"Precisely three miles four thousand sixty-one feet high," said a robot walking toward us. Dad and I jumped, but Mom didn't flinch. "Hello. My name is Ibid-2975 and I'm here to process you, after which I will escort you to your new apartment."

Ibid-2975 was thin and rather unimpressive looking. I'm pretty sure I could've taken it apart with two or three good swings from a plastic baseball bat.

But Mom wasn't finished. "How much of the sphere goes below ground?"

"If it *were* a full sphere . . . about forty percent would be underground."

"Ah," said Dad, "so it won't roll away, right?"

Ibid-2975 stared blankly at my dad for a second, then asked us to take a seat at the table. "I can assure you, the dome surrounding Grandeur is quite formidable. It is in no danger whatsoever of rolling away," the robot said, directing that last bit to me and Dad, like it thought we were Idiots or something.

"I know what formidable means, Mr. Nuts and Bolts." Okay, so I called it a him. I don't like thinking of a sentient being as an it. Lucky for me, most robots in Grandeur make it easy. Even the ones designed by other robots often go for a him or a her look. I couldn't tell you why for sure, but I have a feeling it makes it easier for them to fit in. The ibids, however, had no look one way or the other. In cases like this, I just call 'em like I see 'em.

"Willa!" gasped my mother.

You didn't need to be a Genius to know how this was going down.

"It's perfectly all right," said Mr. Nuts and Bolts, although he didn't *sound* like it was perfectly all right.

My mother wasn't giving up. "Willamina Gilbert Snap! Apologize this instant."

I made some grumbling noises. Mom glared at me until the noises became actual words. This happened grudgingly and by degrees.

The box in front of me had *Willamina Gilbert Snap* written on top. The box next to it, which was smaller, was labeled *The Magnificent Lady Grayson of the Silky White Underbelly, or Just Grayson for Short.*

"Creeeeepeeeeee," I said, under my breath. I could tell Dad agreed with me one hundred percent. I placed the tool bag snugly between my feet.

"Please open your box, remove your WatchitMapCallit, and place it on your forearm—your left if you're right-handed; your right if you're left-handed."

"My whatchamacallit?"

"No," said Mr. Nuts and Bolts, enunciating deliberately. "Your Watch-it-Map-Call-it," he said.

I took the lid off my box. Inside was a long glass oval, like the one I'd seen on Heather's forearm. As I stared at it, the glass darkened and a row of glowing icons appeared. When I held it over my left forearm, it attached itself to me like a second skin.

I shot Dad a gee-whiz look, but he was still staring into his box. When I glanced back to my wrist, the WatchitMapCallit was gone. At first, I thought it must have slipped off my arm. But then, remembering what I'd seen Heather do, I tapped the back of my wrist.

It reappeared instantly. *Totally bean!*

"Your WatchitMapCallit is a wearable, touch-sensitive computing device. You can 'Watch it,' like a TV, navigate with the built-in 'Map' function, or employ the 'Call it' feature to communicate as you would on a video phone. Willa, do you know what a video phone is?"

I looked at my dad and gritted my teeth.

"Yes, I believe she does," he said, before I could say anything out loud. My dad may be an Idiot, but he can be a perceptive Idiot when he wants to.

"What a wonderful idea!" gushed my mother. "It's like a smartwatch, only more useful—it's a smart vambrace! And you beat Apple to market by at least a year. Wouldn't they be jealous . . . if they knew, I mean."

When Mom gets super-excited, she sometimes reverts to a childlike state. If she wasn't so cute when she did it, it would be annoying.

"Closer to a hundred years," huffed Mr. Nuts and Bolts.

My dad made his that's-not-possible-face. "But the first silicon transistors weren't even invented until the 1950s, after World War II." See, my dad's not a Complete Idiot.

Mr. Nuts and Bolts tilted his head back ever so slightly and looked down his metal nose. "Outside Grandeur, yes," he sniffed. "Inside Grandeur, no. In 1819, three years before Charles Babbage presented his pathetic, hand-cranked difference engine to the Royal Astronomical Society, Grandeur was taping out its first silicon chips. Now, all three of you, look at your WatchitMapCallits. But don't panic if you don't see them. Most Idiots have difficulty grasping the concept of object permanence."

My mom tapped her wrist, like she'd done it a thousand times before, and hers reappeared. "Your WatchitMapCallit will adapt to its environment. If you place it over a shirt sleeve or coat and look away, even for a few seconds, it will do its best to blend in. There are many ways to summon it. The simplest is to give it a tap while looking at your wrist. On your desktop you will see several different icons. If you touch the one that looks like a sphere with a red G on it, you will activate Grandeurpedia. Ask Grandeurpedia anything you like and it'll endeavor to answer you in a way that you can understand. The question mark icon will give you more information on how to use your WatchitMapCallit." My mom started tapping things, and all kinds of stuff popped up—maps, diagrams, mathematical equations.

Mr. Nuts and Bolts eyed my dad and me. "I understand the tutorial videos are very helpful should you require them."

"Doesn't mind listening to himself talk, does he?" Dad said to me softly. Mom kicked him under the table.

"The second device is your BrainRent. Please take it out of the box and clip it to your earlobe."

Mom had hers on in a jiffy. Dad and I were more suspicious. They were white plastic discs, each about an inch in diameter with a clip on the back and a circle of ten dots on the front.

"What does it do?" asked my mom excitedly.

"The BrainRent is a multifunction device, but its primary purpose is to earn you easy dolleurs, which you can readily spend anywhere in Grandeur."

My dad raised his eyebrows. "Easy money, huh? Exactly how does *that* work?"

"The device simply scans your brain and utilizes the portions you use the least. It's harmless, I assure you."

"Is that right?" scoffed my dad. "And how exactly does it . . . *utilize* them?"

"Very simple. The BrainRent will access those unused areas of your brain much like a computer does a hard drive. However, if it judges your ganglia to be quick, it may use your excess brain cells as an NPU-node for Source. Earning you bonus dolleurs."

"NPU? Source? Can we have that in English?" I asked.

My mom's arm shot into the air. "Ooh, ooh! Let me try!"

"By all means," droned the robot.

"What this nice robot is trying to say is that the BrainRent can tap into the power of your unused brain cells and use them like a computer's Central Processing Unit, or CPU. The N in NPU, of course, means Neuro, as in Neuro Processing Unit." Mom looked to Mr. Nuts and Bolts for approval and I swear that, even though nothing moved on its face, somehow that thing actually smiled. "And that would make Source the main or central computer system for Grandeur. Basically, Source is tapping into the brains of everyone wearing a BrainRent to give itself more storage and processing power. Am I right?"

"Full marks, Dr. Snap. I couldn't have said it better myself."

Mom actually blushed. Dad and I put on our BrainRents.

"What are these glowing pips on the front?" asked my dad.

"That's just to let you know the device is active. Now, moving on. The Idiot Genius in your family," the robot nodded to Mom, who bounced once in her seat before freezing in place as her mind tripped repeatedly over the word *Idiot*, "will have full access to the research facilities in Laboratorium Tower. Or as it's known in the vernacular"—at this point, if he'd had a real mouth, I think he would've opened it and pretended like he was throwing up—"the Lab." He motioned with a tilt of his head to the three skyscrapers we'd seen rising out of the lake.

Mom's look of confusion vanished, and she screamed out like a game show contestant.

I was happy for her, but all I could think about were the words *Idiot Genius.* Someone had finally done it. The genie was out of the bottle. Up until that moment, I'd've laughed at anyone stupid enough to refer to my mom as anything less than brilliant. But these two words, so seemingly at odds, described her and all her kind *perfectly.*

"There are only two things you need remember, Dr. Snap. One, you are *not* allowed to share the principles of your invention—the pac-a-purse, I believe it is called—with anyone. And two, you may not attempt to build your own laboratory outside of the central towers."

"Seems fair," chirped my mom.

"And you, sir," droned the robot to my dad, "what skills, if any, do you claim to possess?"

My dad folded his arms proudly over his chest. "More than you can count," he said softly.

"Excuse me?" asked the robot.

"By profession, I'm a plumber, but I guess you've got robots for that in here."

"Robots?" sputtered Mr. Nuts and Bolts. "Performing menial labor? You must be joking!" Then he laughed in a way that didn't sound at all amused. "Why would Grandeur waste the talents of a robot on menial labor? Not to worry, though, your services will be in high demand."

"Glad to hear it," said Dad, shooting me a puzzled look.

"Don't you mean *manual* labor?" I asked.

"No. I do not," said the robot. "I said *menial* because I meant *menial*, as in, 'Why would a robot perform a meaningless job beneath its station?'" I rolled my eyes and silently made my *yap-yap-yap-yap* face, tilting my head in time to each *yap*. "Willa, I see from your BrainRent scan that you've tested out as an Idiot."

"Wait, it's already scanned my entire brain?"

"That's correct."

"And I'm an Idiot?"

"The Idiot school in your neighborhood . . . let's see, that would be Idiot School 223, doesn't start for another two and a half hours, so I don't see any problems in your attending today. Good luck to you."

"What kind of a school starts at 1:30 in the afternoon?"

Mr. Nuts and Bolts leaned forward, speaking slowly. "Idiot . . . school, and it starts at 11:30. You're on Grandeur Time now." He then opened Grayson's box and removed a kitty-sized BrainRent. "May I see your cat?"

"Her name is the Magnificent Lady Grayson of the Silky White Underbelly, or Just Grayson for Short, and why?"

The robot glanced briefly at my mother. "All family members must be evaluated. Even cats with ridiculously long names. I assure you, she will not be harmed."

"Willa . . ." Mom began.

I sighed. Against my better judgment, I placed the tool bag on the table and opened it wide enough for the Magnificent Lady Grayson of the Silky White Underbelly, or Just Grayson for Short to poke her head out. Quick as a shot, the robot attached the kitty-sized BrainRent to her earlobe. Then he clipped a kitty-sized WatchitMapCallit onto her paw. What was Grayson going to do with a WatchitMapCallit?

Speaking very clearly and slowly, Mr. Nuts and Bolts said, "And how are you feeling today, little kitty?"

The Magnificent Lady Grayson of the Silky White Underbelly, or Just Grayson for Short looked in turn to each of us and said, "Meow?"

But the sound didn't come out of her mouth. It came out of the little BrainRent device.

"I know you can do better than that. I have your charts. You appear to be an especially smart little kitty. Now try again."

The Magnificent Lady Grayson of the Silky White Underbelly, or Just Grayson for Short looked up at me with her sad eyes, and out of the little speaker I heard, "Me-home?"

I almost fell out of my chair. She hadn't actually said it out of her mouth, but it did appear to be exactly what she was thinking.

"She said home!" I exclaimed. "Did you hear that? *Home*."

"If you say so, dear," said my mom, looking a little embarrassed.

Grayson ducked down and curled into a ball.

"I see," said Mr. Nuts and Bolts. "Well, I suppose that's that."

"What's next?" my mother asked eagerly.

"A MiniDirigy"—he motioned toward Grandeur, and, sure enough, a double-decker bus-sized dirigible was nearly upon us—"will deliver you to your new apartment. Ask me anything you like along the way. After you're properly checked in, I will most likely never see you again."

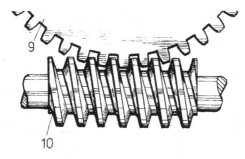

A Ride in a MiniDirigy

THE cigar-shaped part on top of the MiniDirigy looked way too small to lift the passenger area underneath, but that didn't stop it from slowly pulling up to us with little more than a pulsing hum.

I shouldered the tool bag and grabbed Mom's and Dad's hands.

"Please follow me," said the robot.

We walked down a little ramp to where the MiniDirigy had parked. Its lower doors opened as we approached. But instead of stepping inside, Mom let out a scream of terror and yanked me back so fast I thought she was going to snap my arm off.

Inside the MiniDirigy—THERE WAS NO FLOOR! Just about a mile's worth of empty space. Then, to our utter amazement, Mr. Nuts and Bolts walked right on in—ONLY HE DIDN'T PLUMMET TO HIS DEATH, or whatever it is robots do after they go to that big junkyard in the sky.

"Glass-bottomed," he explained. "Perfectly safe."

Dad grabbed a railing, and my mom cautioned him to be careful. He tapped the floor with the tip of his shoe. Solid. He stepped in, turned around, and laughed.

"Cool!" I yelled, ripping loose from my mother's grip. I jumped as high as I could and slammed my feet on the floor. "I bet I can smash it!"

Mom wobbled. Dad leapt to her side.

"Don't look down, honey," I heard him say. "Just—whatever you do—don't look down."

I climbed onto a seat to gain a higher altitude. "Nut Yippee!" I screamed, landing right in front of Mom, coming down as hard as I could with the edge of my heel. But nothing happened. "Dang! What's this stuff made of anyway?"

Nuts and Bolts leaned down and put his face in mine. "It's a clear metal. You would need a jackhammer just to dent it."

"Let me guess," said Dad knowingly. "Transparent aluminum?"

Nuts and Bolts let out a little groan. "You're thinking of a *Star Trek* episode, you Idiot."

Mom rolled her eyes. "Really, Jack, this isn't one of your crazy science fiction TV shows."

"But it wasn't an episode," he said, sounding a little hurt. "It was one of the movies. The one with the whales. You said you liked it." But Mom and Mr. Nuts and Bolts didn't hear him. They were already halfway up the stairs to the MiniDirigy's second deck.

"Can I stay down here?" I asked Dad, while eyeing the immediate area for sharp, heavy, pointy objects. "The view is . . . so awesome." And it was. The MiniDirigy was already descending to Grandeur. My dad gave the other passengers a quick once-over, like he was considering what I might do to them.

"As long as you don't get off without us, it's fine with me."

The second Dad's feet disappeared up the top stair, I ran to a glass box containing a big red ax. But its door handle was missing. Can you believe it? Stenciled on the glass were the words:

SMASH GLASS IN CASE OF EMERGENCY

I threw up my arms. My kingdom for an emergency!

Occasional bouts of poor impulse control are pretty normal in eleven-year-olds. It wouldn't surprise me if—statistically speaking—rates ran higher for ones recently classified as Idiots. Just guessing.

I pushed my shoulder against the glass and pressed as hard as I could without looking like I was doing anything, but it was no good. I prowled the aisle, spying under the seats for a decent-sized rock or better yet a pickax. But my search proved fruitless. Hey, it's not like I wanted to smash the whole floor out. A little hole that I could toss stuff out of would do.

Temporarily foiled, I took a seat and gazed out the window. The skies above Grandeur sparkled like fairy dust—not that I believe in fairies, mind you. As we got closer, I could see the cause: sunlight glinting off of thousands of flying objects. The bulk of them were small, but some were huge. As we passed through a layer of them, I had to look away or duck down below the window a bunch of times, convinced one of the things was going to smash into us. The biggest object in the sky by far, though, was the floating platform covered with propellers that Dad and I had seen from the balcony. I could see now that it wasn't one platform, but hundreds tied together. There was another strange thing I saw, or thought I saw. It was flying over a part of Grandeur covered in billowy white steam. It looked—I know this is going to sound crazy—like a steam-powered wooden ship, with rigging and sails and everything.

The other passengers talked and chatted among themselves, showing not the least bit of concern for what was going on out the window.

We leveled off about a hundred feet above a tree-lined boulevard. After a dozen blocks or so, the sound of the engines deepened, and we changed course, heading for a bunch of landing platforms mounted this way and that on top of a tall tower. It was an open structure, with stairs and an elevator down to the street.

I ran back to the seat closest to the glass box as we pulled up. If an emergency broke out, *I* was going to be the one wielding the ax.

The doors swished open. A woman wearing a beautiful pale-green chiffon party dress with a tiered handkerchief hem took the seat across from me. She looked like a dancer—a flapper—straight out of one of those old black-and-white movies, only she was in color and perhaps a bit plain in the face. When she caught me staring, she gave me a knowing look and unfolded a newspaper between us.

Several others entered, including an old man and a dog. If there's one thing I'm not, it's a dog person. They smell, they slobber, and they're dumb as rocks. (I mean the dogs. As near as I can tell, dog *people* don't really slobber any more than anybody else.) But he—the dog—was cute and happy. I gave him a little scritch behind his ears . . . and told him he was *such a good boy*. But then his doggy odor hit me, and all at once I just wanted to wash my hands and be done with him.

A few minutes later, we were skimming over the treetops again. I caught glimpses of people on the sidewalks below—but all in all, I was getting a little snoozy, and my stomach was rumbling, and this dog next to me smelled all doggy. Bleah!

At the next stop, I was delighted to see the old guy get up to leave. But he walked right past his dog! And the dog didn't budge!

"Hey, mister!" I yelled. "You forgot your dog!" But he didn't even turn around to look at me.

And then a deep woofy voice next to me said, "He is not my master."

I turned toward the voice and . . . there was the dog.

"You *talk* talk?" I said to the dog.

"My master gave me vocal implants," he said—TALKING THROUGH HIS DOGGY MOUTH! "Do you smell cat?" he asked.

I said nothing, opting instead to stare like an Idiot. Vocal implants? I made a mental note to look them up in my WatchitMap-Callit to see how much they cost. Suddenly, I had something to start saving for.

After an awkward pause, he continued, "Because *I* smell cat."

I looked away and caught the eye of the flapper peeking around the edge of her newspaper.

"I am a dog," the dog announced, as if it were a revelatory statement. Sniffing the air, he added, "Did you know there is a cat in your tote bag?" After another long pause, "I am on a chore for my master. He has sent me to the store where they are expecting me. I have a tote bag just like you. Mine is blue. Why do you have a cat in your tote bag?"

I tried not to encourage him, but you know how dogs are. Thankfully, he got off at the very next stop. No sooner had he stepped out the door than a flutey voice started shouting from somewhere below.

"Hold the doors! Hold the doors!"

I searched for a button or something but couldn't find one. The shouting grew louder, and now I could hear heavy feet clanging on the metal stairs leading to the platform.

"Hold the doors! Hold the doors!"

I looked in all the likely places, but I still didn't see anything to press. A boy waving a cane appeared at the top of the stairs and raced toward the MiniDirigy. I say he was a boy, but he wasn't a boy at all. He wasn't even a man. He was metal. But unlike Mr. Nuts and Bolts, he was a symphony of turning gears and pulsating springs.

He wasn't scary or anything, but his reckless charge made me duck for cover.

"Please! Hold the doors! Hold the—"

The doors started closing. At the last second, he leapt ten feet in one bound, landing half in and half out. Bending himself up like a pretzel, he pushed the doors open enough to roll into the car, unfolding and standing upright as he came. He ran up and down the aisle, scanning the passengers' faces with his oversized glass eyes and talking strangely to himself.

"Wobblepot!" shouted a man pointing at the Clockwerk Boy.

"Poor thing just needs a good winding," said a woman pulling her child out of the aisle. "Don't get too close!"

"Oily cogs," cursed a third. "Got no business bein' in Greater

Grandeur."

The Clockwerk raised his hands to his mouth, making a cone. Little bellows pumped erratically in his chest.

"Is there a Willamina Snap on board?" he asked.

My mouth fell open. I dropped the tool bag containing the Magnificent Lady Grayson of the Silky White Underbelly, or Just Grayson for Short. The flapper thrust down her newspaper and craned her neck to get a better look.

"Um," I said, raising a hand.

The Clockwerk Boy spun around and approached me with irregular steps. I quickly snatched up the tool bag and put my arms through its loops like a backpack.

"It's true, just as they foresaw." As he stepped closer, I got a better look at the mechanism of valves and tubes in his neck producing the sound of his voice. It was a marvel of engineering.

"How did you know my name?" I asked.

"The dragons . . . you're all they talk about."

I took a small step backward. "Dragons? Me?"

"*Dracones finis*. It's your fate to decide."

He sounded like he was repeating something. "I don't understand."

"If they are to survive, you must sacrifice yourself to right the wrong."

"Did they send you here?"

"No. But there is no time to explain." He opened a drawer in his belly, pulled out two books, and put the smaller one back. "This is a memory book. Quick, take it! Find me after I'm rewound. Hold the first page before my eyes. Only then will I understand what's going on again."

His framework began to shudder, like an unbalanced washing machine during its spin cycle. I reached for the book, but he pulled it back.

"Wait! Did you test out as an Idiot?"

"Why is everyone calling me an—"

"Good! Time travel is business best left to Idiots." A commotion began on the floor above; people were running for the stairs. "Hide it!" he piped, pressing the book into my hands. "I wish there was another way, but as you can see, I've run myself down trying to reach you."

"Can't I wind you back up? Do you have a key or something?"

"No—time."

"But how do I find you?"

A seizure rattled his frame and he lurched a step closer. "Your timeline is in danger, Willamina Snap! Take my c-c-cane. You're going to neeeeeeeed it."

He wound to a stop and his hand sprang open with a *CLICK!* The cane tumbled out, shrinking to the size of a baton as I caught it.

My mother's legs appeared at the top of the stairs, followed by my dad's shoes and the sound of Mr. Nuts and Bolts' clanking footsteps. As Mom elbowed her way through the crowd, I tucked the book beneath my shirt and pocketed the cane.

"What's going on here?" she shouted, her eyes dancing between me and the now-silent Clockwerk Boy.

"A Clockwerk has run down," said a man in a dapper gray suit sitting where the flapper had been a second before. "Nothing to worry about."

I gaped at him. Where had the flapper gone? I didn't see her get up.

"Are you all right?" asked Mom, pawing my shoulders and spinning me around.

"I'm fine," I protested. "He rushed in at the last stop and just . . . wound down."

"Gangway! Gangway!" said a woman in a blue conductor's uniform, wheeling a handcart. "Happens all too often, but usually not this far out of the burg. And especially not with a model as old as this one," she added, after getting a better look.

I glanced back to the man in the gray suit. The flapper's newspaper lay folded in his lap.

"Can't you wind him up again?" I asked the conductor.

She removed her blue cap and scratched her head. Tapping a plate on the Clockwerk Boy's back, she said. "Now that's highly irregular. Says here his memory reset *just* as he wound down." She pushed the handcart under the Clockwerk Boy's feet, strapped him to it, and wheeled him into a corner. "Show's over, folks! Back to your seats."

Mom gave me a questioning glance. She was worried about me. *Highly irregular indeed.*

"I'm fine," I assured her.

Dad, on the other hand, sensed I was in the middle of something.

"All's well, Audrey," he said. "Willa's fine." Mom's worry visibly lessened.

Best Dad ever.

My parents and Mr. Nuts and Bolts went back upstairs.

Not long after, the MiniDirigy entered the shadow of a storm cloud, and the entire compartment darkened. I looked back at the

Clockwerk Boy, then at the man in the gray suit. He was holding up the newspaper again, but now it was glowing dimly like a paper lantern.

I edged closer. The hands holding the edges of the paper were a woman's.

"Excuse me," I said, wondering who might be behind the newspaper this time. "Are you aware that you're glowing?"

The flapper woman slowly lowered the newspaper, her face alight with that strange glee you see in the faces of far-flung relatives you're meeting for the very first time. It's a look that says *I know so much more about you than you do me.*

"Why, Willamina Snap, how did that Clockwerk Boy know your name?"

"You're back. But where did you go? There was a man—and now—"

"Oh, *him.* Righto, allow me to introduce myself, old bean. My name is Tuppence. I'm a mettle man," she said, whispering the last.

"You don't look metal," I whispered back.

"No. Not metal, mettle, as in M-E-T-T-L-E. The 'man' part's not quite right, as I'm neither woman nor man, but I like the alliteration. Rather sporty, don't you think?"

I quickly tapped my WatchitMapCallit and looked up *mettle* in Grandeurpedia.

met′tle \mĕt′'l\ *noun*

> A person's ability to cope well with demanding situations in a spirited and resilient way. Figuratively, the "stuff of which a person is made."

"It does have a nice ring to it," I conceded. "But *what* are you?"

"Step closer," she suggested. "Watch carefully as I power down my holo-projectors to fifty percent."

Tuppence's skin and clothes became transparent. Her real skin was in fact metal, covered with tiny glowing pinpoints of light. Suddenly, her ghostly image changed to the man I'd seen earlier.

"Remember me?" he said using his man voice, then he became Tuppence again, all bright and real looking, only a little *too* bright.

A flash of lightning lit up the compartment. Rain pelted the windows. The cabin's lights flickered, then grew brighter. Suddenly, Tuppence was as normal looking as anyone else.

"You still haven't answered my question. How did that Clockwerk Boy know your name?"

"He said I'm all the dragons talk about. Maybe if we wound him back up, he could give us some answers."

"You'd need a winding station to do that. Not that it would matter. This one's memory probably resets every two weeks."

"Two weeks!"

"Sentient Clockwerks don't remember things the way we do. You can only make gears so small, after all. And that goes double for old Clockwerks. Wind this one up again and all it will *know* are the few trade skills hard-geared into its BrainBox."

"You mean like how to bake a cake?"

"More like how to repair a set of da Vinci wings, but that's the idea. Can you imagine waking up with virtually no memories, not knowing what you did yesterday?"

"I'd be disoriented," I said, "and a little sad, maybe."

"Sad?"

"Because I wouldn't remember who my friends were."

"Or your enemies. Then again, you wouldn't remember anything to be sad about."

"So, no baggage. Well, in that case, I guess I'd be curious, ready for anything."

I pulled the memory book out from under my shirt. "He said

to show him this."

Tuppence looked longingly at the book in my hands. "Tell me, does it have a title . . . written on the spine?"

I turned it sideways and read, "*An Adventure of My Own.*"

"So he has a memory book . . . of his own," said Tuppence.

"What does that mean?"

"It means that this Clockwerk Boy has become quite clever. Open it. What do you see?"

I opened the book to a random page. "It's just a bunch of numbers and symbols."

"That's his language. What you're looking at are important memories he doesn't want to forget." Tuppence narrowed her eyes to slits. "How much you want for it?"

"I think I'd better keep it."

"I can offer quite a lot," she added, so softly I could barely understand her words.

"No, thank you. He wanted an Idiot to have it. And I'm pretty sure you're not one of those."

"Well, you've got me there." Tuppence's face softened. She seemed impressed. "It would appear he chose well. Now, on to more important things. I have a job offer for you. A real job, mind you. Very important stuff. Fate of the world hanging in the balance and all that rot. You interested?"

"I think you've got the wrong person."

"Do you really? I couldn't agree less. No. In fact, I think you're *just* the right person."

"But we've never met."

"Perhaps you're right," she said, like she was humoring me.

"He said my timeline was in danger."

"Yes. He did," she agreed. "But when you get right down to it, isn't *everyone's* timeline in danger?" I didn't know how to answer that. "You know what I think? Forget about the dragons. Forget the memory book. It's Grandeur's timeline that must be saved. I can't tell you how, or where from, but something evil is coming. A time of great peril is near at hand. The soothies are restless." I tapped my WatchitMapCallit and pulled up Grandeurpedia.

sooth'ie \sōōth'ī\ *noun*

"'A friendly sifter of information,'" I read aloud.

Tuppence blinked. "Does it really say friendly?" I held up the screen. She made a *tsk tsk* sound. "You would be wise to give the soothies a wide berth, Willa. They're forbidden to sift a developing brain like yours, but I wouldn't put it past them, if you knew something they *really* wanted to know."

I looked around nervously. "What does a soothie look like?"

"Don't worry, they rarely leave the burgs. It's highly unlikely you'll ever encounter one. As for your mission: I need you to snoop around. Keep your eyes and ears open at all times. Write things down."

Tuppence reached into the folds of her dress and withdrew a small leather pouch. I suspect what she really did was reach through her holographic clothes and open a little drawer or compartment in her chest, like the one in the Clockwerk Boy's belly.

"Here, take this."

"Wait, what about *my* timeline?"

Tuppence looked curiously at me. "Grandeur, Willa, Grandeur. There's a greater danger here. I'll point you in the general direction whenever I can spare the time. The rest will be up to you."

Inside the pouch were a clean pad of paper, several empty pockets, and two sharpened pencils. Old tech. There's nothing like the smell of paper and freshly sharpened pencil. I pulled out a pencil and wrote: *Tuppence, mettle man: pushy.*

Tuppence looked at me curiously.

"I haven't said yes," I pointed out.

"You'll be looking for something out of the ordinary."

I glanced through the transparent metal at my feet, at the Clockwerk Boy, at Tuppence herself. "Yeah, that'll really stand out here."

Next to Tuppence's name, I added: *prone to wild bouts of optimism.*

"You won't get a better offer."

I let out a deep sigh. It was like talking to my mother, which gave me a desperate idea. "Hey! Wouldn't you rather ask my mother to do it?"

"Would that she could."

More riddles. "How about my dad?"

"Children can go places unobserved that adults can't." Tuppence rose. "This is my platform." She took a few steps toward the opening doors, then paused, tilting her head down and to the side but not enough for me to see her face or eyes. "Willa? Are you with me?" Even though she didn't say it, I could hear the rest of the question: *or are you against me?*

Against! my gut screamed. *Your timeline is in danger*, the Clockwerk Boy had said. *My* timeline!

"I'm eleven!" I shouted.

"You'd be surprised what an eleven-year-old can get away

with."

I wrote the word *trust*, put a big question mark next to it, and circled them.

"How do you know the dragons have nothing to do with this coming evil?" I asked. "And what did he mean when he said time travel was best left to Idiots?" But when I looked up again, Tuppence was nowhere to be seen.

I tapped my WatchitMapCallit and typed in something the Clockwerk Boy had said: *Dracones finis*.

Dra·co′nes fi′nis

Dragons' end.

I turned to a new page and wrote that down, too.

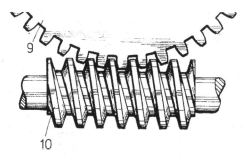

The Snaps' Apartment

A FEW stops later, we exited the MiniDirigy. We rode a glass elevator down to the street and left the station through a wide arch proclaiming *Welcome to Greater Grandeur*. Was there a lesser Grandeur, I wondered?

The stroll to our apartment was short and pleasant. The buildings in this part of town were made of brick, and none of them were more than four or five stories high. Mr. Nuts and Bolts talked the entire way, pointing out conveniences, such as grocery stores, parks, the street leading to my Idiot school. I tried to listen but kept getting distracted by all the stuff flying around in the sky. When I heard the word "burg," my ears perked up. The conductor and Tuppence had both used the word. Mr. Nuts and Bolts was pointing.

"The Biowerks Burg is only two blocks . . ."

I tapped my WatchitMapCallit, and entered *burgs*.

> Grandeur's 237 burgs contain not only vibrant reminders of our past, but also seeds of our future. The largest burg, the Steamwerks, com-

prises more than forty city blocks. Other burgs of note are the Clockwerk, the Biowerks, the Windwerks, the Waterwerks, the Robowerks, and the Dieselwerks.

"Excuse me, but what burg will we live in?" I asked.

"You'll live in Greater Grandeur," the robot said with exaggerated patience. "It is, by definition, *not* a burg. Ah, here we are, Whitehaven Mansions."

The building, easily twice as tall as the others we'd passed, stood out.

"It's beautiful!" exclaimed my mother.

Dad looked up at the towering curved façade. His eyes flickered, and his face was twitchy. In retrospect, that should've been a clue that whatever they'd given him during the abduction was wearing off. Inside, the lobby was filling up with people in formal dress. Waiters served finger foods from small silver platters, and in the middle of the room, under a grand chandelier, stood a glistening ice sculpture of a little short man wearing a hat and a funny mustache.

"What's all this?" asked my mother.

"One of Grandeur's many bizarre or illogical religious cults, I suspect," sneered the robot. "Leisure time . . . it would take a human to think up such a concept."

At the lobby desk, Mr. Nuts and Bolts announced our names to a thin-nosed woman wearing spectacles. She ran her finger down the register and frowned.

"Is there a problem?" creaked Mr. Nuts and Bolts.

"Not *exactly*, but Source has put them in . . . *her* room."

Mr. Nuts and Bolts motioned for the keys. "Hand them over,

please."

The woman hesitated. "I—I think I better call the supervisor—"

"Source has no supervisor, my dear Idiot. Now hand over the keys. I don't have all day."

"I meant *my* supervis—" In one swift motion, Mr. Nuts and Bolts reached over the counter, his mechanical arm telescoping out, and plucked the keys out of the clerk's hands. "Hey!"

Partway to the elevators, I doubled back to the desk. The clerk was talking into a wooden box mounted to the wall. A short cable ran from the box to an earpiece. Slowly, it dawned on me. She was talking into a really, really old phone, like you'd see in a museum. Catching sight of me, she hung up abruptly.

"Can I help you?"

I pointed to the people in the lobby. "Hi. Can you tell me who those people are?"

"You don't know?" She seemed aghast.

My parents were almost to the elevator. I probably only had another ten or fifteen seconds before they noticed I was missing.

"Whose room did Source put us in?" I asked.

But she wouldn't say. I dashed to the elevators just as one arrived.

Mr. Nuts and Bolts pressed the button for the fifth floor. Dad jumped about a foot in the air and let out a little yelp for no apparent reason. This isn't normal Dad behavior, but I didn't have time to tend to him just then.

"Mr. Ibid—" I'd already forgotten the numbers that followed, but I thought I'd make a stab at being polite.

"2975," finished the robot.

"Right. Say, who lived in our apartment before we did?"

"That's unimportant. Source assigns apartments as Grandeur sees fit."

"I thought you said Source doesn't have a supervisor."

Ibid-2975 stared coldly at me but said nothing.

Our new place was only a few doors down from the elevator.

"Ah," said the robot, "here we are. 56B."

He gave us a lightning-quick tour. Everything felt so last century—everything except for the giant black screen embedded in the wall of our living room. Apparently, it was part computer, part movie theater, part phone. Dad was prancing around our new coffee table, bleating unintelligibly, by the time the robot left. And true to his word, we never saw him again. But I did meet many, many more like him.

"Mom!" I said, pointing to Dad. "Do something before he explodes."

Mom quickly surveyed the room before walking over to a glass case mounted on the wall. An open book hung inside.

"Honey," she asked, "you still like Agatha Christie, right?"

Dad's arms flopped down to his sides, and he stopped making the weird noises. "No, dear, I still *love* Agatha Christie."

Mom nodded. "Thought so. Have you read"—she placed her eye an inch from the frame—"*The Murder of . . . Roger Android?*"

Dad cocked his head and scrunched up his eyes. "No. Are you sure it's one of hers?"

Mom lifted the case off the wall, carried it into the kitchen, and placed it in the sink. After opening and closing several drawers, she raised a small wooden mallet into the air.

Smash!

She pulled the book free with a little shake, brushing it gingerly with the edge of her palm.

"Clean that up, would you, dear?" she said to me. Then, reading from the title page, she said, " '*The Murder of Roger Android, by Agatha Christie, Author of The Mysterious Affair at Styles.*' And here at the bottom it says, 'Somewhere in the Southwest of America, Grandeur Press, 1926.' "

"That's her, all right," said Dad. "But I didn't realize she wrote any science fiction titles."

Mom walked into the living room and handed him the book. Dad fell into a chair next to a big curved window. He'd be good for hours.

"Do you think they'd run up a nice pot of hot tea?" asked Dad.

I stopped picking shards of glass out of the sink and opened a few cabinets. "It looks like everything's been newly stocked," I said. "There are lots of teas here. Should I put a kettle on to boil?"

"That would be capital, my dear," said my dad, affecting a slight British accent. "Perhaps you should let your cat out of the bag, as it were. I imagine the poor thing is getting a tad weary, being cooped up in there all this time."

"Oh, no! I forgot!" I'd left the tool bag by the front door. "The Magnificent Lady Grayson of the Silky White Underbelly, or Just Grayson for Short, I'm *so* sorry!"

She squeezed out before I had it half-open, dashing across the living room in zips and stalls, eyeing every piece of furniture as if it might contain a large sleeping dog.

I finished filling the kettle with cool water, placed it on a burner, and had just gotten the sink free of glass when a knock sounded at our door.

"I'll get it!"

Nothing could have prepared me for my next encounter.

Standing in the hallway was a man enveloped in steam. I say man, but honestly, that was up for debate. His leather coat seemed normal enough, but the cloak draped over his shoulders was studded with small steam pipes puffing away at regular intervals. WAS THIS GUY STEAM-POWERED? In one hand he gripped a brass-topped cane, in the other, a clipboard covered with gears. Perched on his head was a top hat mounted with aviator goggles. A monocle—a monocle!—adorned his left eye. He must have had a good twenty pounds of brass gadgets strapped to him. And I couldn't have told you what a single one of them did.

"Good day, young miss." He bowed, lifting his hat and revealing a glass porthole in the center of his forehead, through which I could see his brains—HIS BRAINS!—illuminated by a ghastly green light and bathed in tiny rising bubbles. "Allow me to introduce myself. I am Professor Vander Graaff Farsical the twenty-fourth, but you're welcome to call me the Wondrous Professor Farsical."

Wondrous? I gaped at him.

A ruby red stud embedded in his gauntlet flashed amber and a concerned look crossed his face.

"Aren't you a little young to be a professor?" I wasn't trying to be rude or anything, but his acne hadn't even cleared up yet.

He shifted nervously. "Is your mother home?" I continued to stare. "You see, I'm inquiring for signatures." He held out the clipboard. Gears slowly spun at its corners.

"For what?" I asked.

"It's a petition to have Grandeur completely made over as a Steamwerks society—like the glory days of 1325, when Grandeur Abbey was located but a short pony ride from jolly olde London." He handed me the clipboard and put on a hopeful smile. I won't burden you with the image of what was going on with his teeth.

As I skimmed the document, he bounced his cane on the floor. The brass knob on top bloomed open, creating a concave dish that he swung around furtively. Each time it went past me, an alarm sounded.

I glanced up, and he stuffed the bulky cane under his cloak like nothing was happening. I decided to play along. If he didn't want me to see the cane, I didn't see the cane.

"If your petition was granted, would I have to dress like you?" I asked, choking down a giggle.

He opened one side of his coat and flipped a few switches sewn into the lining. "That would be only one of the great many privileges awarded under—"

Bam! went the door as I shut it in his face. *Snick!* went the deadbolt.

I guess something inside me just snapped. I mean, who puts a glass porthole in his forehead, adds bubbles, and lights the whole thing up? I couldn't decide if it was the creepiest thing I'd ever seen, or the coolest. Creepiest, coolest. Coolest, creepiest. Trying to decide was shorting out my brain. Closing the door had been my only good option.

My one problem? I was still holding his clipboard.

Gah!

I silently slid back the deadbolt, then opened the door super-fast. He thrust his cane back into the folds of his cloak. He'd been scanning again. We both knew I'd caught him in the act.

It was an awkward moment. I needed an opener.

"The bubbles are a nice touch," I said finally.

His face brightened. I got the impression he wasn't setting any records for the most conversations in one day, if you know what I mean.

"Okay, so . . . what are you up to *really*?" I nodded to the cane he'd hastily tucked inside his coat.

He was still considering what to say when something in there beeped three times. Finally, his shoulders sagged.

"Oh, all right. I'm tracking a reverse time-eddy."

"A what?"

He pulled out the cane again and bounced it on the floor. The top folded back into a big brass knob.

"It's like this: when an object travels through time, it leaves ripples in the timeline before and after its 'present' location."

"Are you telling me you're . . . a Time Lord?"

The "professor" snatched back his clipboard. "Don't be a fool! The Black Fez would never allow a Time Lord into Grandeur. Too disruptive. Time-*eddies*, however, can form anywhere. Trust me, I know a thing or two about time travel. In fact, I've built a time machine of my own."

"That seems . . . really unlikely." I didn't mean to say it out loud. The words just kind of popped out when I wasn't paying attention.

The red stud on Professor Farsical's gauntlet started flashing amber again. He leaned forward and spoke in a low voice. "Mark my words: the dragons are up to something. They're planning on sending something or"—he looked me up and down oddly—"some*one* through time."

I looked *myself* up and down. "Hey, what are you trying to say?"

"Don't worry, they only take volunteers."

"Well, you won't find any volunteers here!" Which wasn't at all true, now that I think about it. I mean, given half a chance, I'd leap into a time machine faster than a squirrel could twitch its tail.

Professor Farsical gave me a dubious look. "A reverse time-eddy does not mean, one hundred percent, that you're destined to travel through time. You *do* have free will. Personally, I don't blame you. Traveling through time is a dangerous business. Especially if you've been sent to alter something that *wants* to happen."

"You can do that?"

"I suppose it all depends on how you look at it, but yes, I believe so. Time is more malleable than you might think. I'll give you an example, shall I? In a few seconds I'm going to say a sentence. This is what we call the future, although, now that I'm actually saying the sentence it has become the present. And now I've said it—it's in the past. See?"

"But you didn't change anything."

"Didn't I? How do you know?"

It hurt my brain to think about it.

Professor Farsical took a card from an inside pocket and handed it to me.

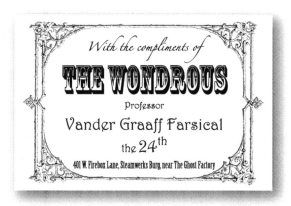

With the compliments of

THE WONDROUS

Professor

Vander Graaff Farsical

the 24ᵗʰ

401 W. Firebox Lane, Steamwerks Burg, near The Ghost Factory

"If the dragons want to send you through time, you can bet it'll be for their benefit. They may try and make it look like it's in your best interests, but they will not hesitate to send you to your death if they feel it necessary. Think about that." He turned and walked down the corridor, disappearing in a haze of white steam.

I closed the door and stared at the card. As I drifted back into the living room, the kettle began to whistle. Without looking up from his book, Dad motioned toward the kitchen.

"Could you . . . get . . . please . . ."

I made him his favorite: Earl Grey, hot. As I set the cup and saucer by his chair, I noticed the Magnificent Lady Grayson of the Silky White Underbelly, or Just Grayson for Short poking her head out of a back room. She made a fist and, using a single claw, beckoned to me.

So that was new.

The room she'd picked was obviously one appointed for a young girl . . . just about my age. Well, someone definitely knew I was coming. And it disturbed me to think they might know my underwear size.

The Magnificent Lady Grayson of the Silky White Underbelly, or Just Grayson for Short stood on her hind feet and pushed the door shut. Huh. I'd never seen her do that before. She leapt up onto a dresser, clapped a paw on either side of her head, and spoke through the little speaker on the BrainRent device clipped to her ear.

"What are we going to do? Nobody escapes from Grandeur! Nobody! Do you understand? We're stuck here FOREVER!"

"The Magnificent Lady Grayson of the Silky White Underbelly, or Just Grayson for Short," I said, "you talk?"

"And that's another thing. Don't you think the Magnificent Lady Grayson of the Silky White Underbelly, or Just Grayson for Short is a bit much? I mean, for the love of Bastet, can't we go with Grayson, or Lady Grayson, or the Magnificent Lady Grayson?"

I—I didn't know what to say. I felt a little hurt, and yet, sure, saying the Magnificent Lady Grayson of the Silky White Underbelly, or Just Grayson for Short *did*—at times—seem a little bit much.

I mulled it over. "All right. Lady Grayson it is. But I still reserve the right to call you the Magnificent Lady Grayson of the Silky White Underbelly, or Just Grayson for Short whenever I'm really mad at you!"

"Deal!" She stuck out a paw. I gave it a little shake. Then she lost it again. "Dogs dancing with cats!" she wailed, throwing her paws wide. "I *knew* this was going to happen! I knew the day I first walked into your house that your mother was nothing but trouble. She had Idiot Genius written all over her! I was a fool to think I could stop her! A fool! A f-f-fool!" She broke down into heaving sobs.

I had a mini-flashback: this morning, Lady Grayson, back when she was still called the Magnificent Lady Grayson of the Silky White Underbelly, or Just Grayson for Short—okay, okay, it's a little hard to let it go all at once; I'm working up to it—shredding Mom's notes. Then a secondary series of flashbacks hit me, going back years. All the wrecked experiments in Mom's laboratory upstairs. The countless laptops pushed off tables. (Dad suggested they were committing suicide, to put an end to all the grueling calculations Mom kept putting them through.) Cell phones in toilets. The answering machines that mysteriously erased ALL their messages.

"You didn't walk into our house. You swung in, like one of the Flying Wallendas. And if you knew this was going to happen, then why did you stay?"

Grayson (see, I did better that time) butted my cheek with her head.

"I—I couldn't leave you all alone, kid," she said sheepishly. "Especially with you being right next to squirrel headquarters . . . and your mother working on the pac-a-purse. CAN YOU IMAGINE WHAT WOULD HAPPEN IF IT FELL INTO THEIR DEMONIC LITTLE PAWS?"

"*Squirrel* headquarters? Mom's pac-a-purse?"

Grayson grabbed me by the collar. "BUT NOW WE'VE GOT BIGGER PROBLEMS! WE HAVE TO GET OUT OF HERE! Don't you see? What's going to happen to the old neighborhood? Who's going to protect the Petrelli kittens from that big stupid Doberman on Clover Court? Who's gonna keep Scruffles and Fluffy, the two meanest toms who ever lived, from tearing each other's eyes out? I've gotta make my nightly rounds! Oh!"—she stood on her back paws and threw a furry forearm over her eyes—"never to leap from tree to rooftop in the black of night again! THE NEIGHBORHOOD WILL FALL INTO UTTER CHAOS WITHOUT ME!"

"Hold on. If nobody ever escapes from Grandeur, how do you know about it? You're just a cat."

Grayson threw off her hysteria like casting off a cloak on opera night. "Just a cat! *Just* a cat! *I* am the *stealer* of breaths, the *walker* of shadows, the *keeper* of nine lives."

"Don't forget spitter of hairballs, chaser of tails, and eater of moths," I added dryly. Grayson's fragile resolve crumbled. Climbing into my arms like a lost kitten, she buried her nose in my neck and burst into tears. I petted her back comfortingly. "Look, if you can't explain, that's fine. Everybody needs a few secrets." *Especially if they involve demonic squirrels and cheating death.* "But since it sounds like we're going to be here for a while, I need you to promise me one thing."

"What," she said, her voice all muffled.

"If, in the meantime, *you* figure a way out of here, we all go."

"Okay," she said, still sniffling.

I opened a few drawers until I found one filled with sweaters.

"Do you think you can hang out here for a little while?" Grayson burrowed her way into the drawer until all I could see were her green eyes staring back. I pulled out the memory book and Clockwerk cane and tucked them in with her. "Guard these as best you can. They're important."

"Willa?" said my mother.

I spun around. Mom was standing in the doorway. She must have been inspecting the closets in her room or something, because now she was wearing a nifty little cape and pillbox hat that I'd never seen before.

"I was . . . talking to Lady Grayson."

Her eyes brightened. "Lady Grayson! Is that what she likes to be called now?"

"Yes. Well, either that or the Magnificent Lady Grayson. We haven't fully—"

"My word, Willa. You make it sound like you have conversations with her."

I bit my lip.

Mom strode into the room and opened the closet door, which was now *my* closet door.

"Listen," she continued, while rummaging through the racks. "I'm heading out. Your father seems to have calmed down for the moment. How about I walk you to Idiot school?"

"I'm hungry."

"You're always hungry."

Mom emerged from my closet with an armful of clothes and a very pleased look. She laid out a short red cotton dress, a light cardigan, stockings, a pair of canvas shoes, and a beige cloche hat.

"Will they feed us at this . . . *school?*"

Mom frowned the way she does when she doesn't want to tell me something. "Dear, it's not going to be like the schools back in Cambridge. Just come home when it's over and tell your father to take you out to lunch."

The clothes were straight out of an American Girl catalog.

"I'm going to look like Nancy Drew's English cousin, fresh off the boat from London," I complained.

"I know! Isn't it fun?"

It wasn't really to my taste, but after viewing myself in the mirror, I decided to enjoy it. And why not? Moping about it certainly wasn't going to improve my day.

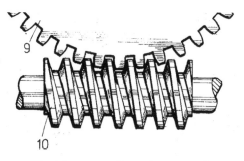

Idiot School

W E opened our apartment door at the same time as our neighbors across the hall. The man was tall, wide in the shoulders but skinny everywhere else. He had thick, dark eyebrows, and he squinted when he smiled, like he was looking into a strong headwind. The boy was the opposite in every way—short for his age, pudgy in the face and around his middle. And he kept his eyes open wide, like he was seeing everything for the first time.

"Well, hello," said the man, removing the hand that a second before he'd plunged into his coat pocket. "I didn't realize this apartment had been let. Please allow me to introduce myself. I'm Dr. Quimby Wudgepuddle, but please—call me Quimby. It's a family name."

"It would have to be," I muttered. Mom pinched me.

"And this is my boy, Heathcliff. I work in the Lab. In fact, I oversee the BrainRent devices you've—" He looked quizzically at my mother's bare earlobes. "Oh, dear. Have you lost yours? I believe I have a spare."

Dr. Wudgepuddle patted his pockets.

"No, that's all right. It's in my purse." Mom fished it out and put it on. "Do you think they're safe?"

Dr. Wudgepuddle pulled back his hair, revealing a BrainRent. "Not only are they perfectly safe, Doctor, but they help make Grandeur a better place to live. They generate easy dolleurs, too."

Mom didn't look convinced.

I couldn't possibly tell you what made me look—dumb luck, I guess—but suddenly I noticed the back of a redheaded girl wearing a purple fez and heading for the elevator. She *had* to have walked right through us. There was no other way. As I continued to stare at her, she turned, and I caught her surprised eye.

I tried to take a step in her direction, but my mother's radar, which may have missed the stranger, didn't miss me. Her hand clamped onto my shoulder and she spun me around toward our new neighbors.

"We just took occupancy today. My name is Dr. Audrey Snap. This is my daughter"—I tensed up—"Willamina."

Nooo! Not the Willamina! My shoulders went limp. It could've been worse, of course; she could've said Willamina Gilbert Snap, thereby causing me to melt into the carpet.

"My husband goes by Jack. And your wife?"

"Dr. Lysteria Kanker." Mom's smile froze. Even I thought it sounded disgusting. "She decided to keep the surname, as her father was very dear to her," said Dr. Wudgepuddle, wincing.

Mom was speechless. A rare event. I slipped away and made for the elevator. Only fools and slackers miss golden opportunities.

I wedged my hand into the elevator's closing doors, triggering the thingy that makes the doors open again. But the car was empty. Where had the girl gone?

"I hope you weren't on that MiniDirigy when the Clockwerk wound down," I heard Dr. Wudgepuddle say. "If it were up to me, they wouldn't allow Clockwerks in Greater Grandeur. They'd keep them confined to the burgs where they belong."

A dour-looking set of dark-haired twin girls entered the elevator, followed by a much younger boy playing with a device that I swear made him occasionally fade in and out of existence.

"Good afternoon, Rufus," said one of the girls in an English accent.

"Mm, Zoe," said Rufus, fiddling with a small probe on an open panel of the device.

"Still can't get it working, I see," chimed in the other twin.

The edges of Rufus's mouth curled up in a crazy grin. "Give it time, sisters Brontë, give it time."

"You'll never get that to work," said Heathcliff, stepping out from behind his father. "Your power source is too small."

Everyone ignored Heathcliff.

Maybe the redheaded girl took the stairs?

As we passed the desk in the lobby, my mother made an excuse to talk to the clerk, allowing the other kids and the Wudgepuddles to continue on without us. Going by the look on his face, I didn't think Dr. Wudgepuddle was any more pleased with the fancy party in the lobby than he was about Clockwerks being allowed out of their burg.

We headed down the street toward Idiot school. Mom asked, "Are you scared, Willa?"

Normally, my mother walks around lost in her thoughts. Not

today. It put me oddly on my guard.

I tapped my WatchitMapCallit and said, "Grandeurpedia: how many murders occurred in Grandeur this year?"

"There have been no murders reported in Greater Grandeur this year," said a disembodied voice.

"How many in the last ten years?" I asked.

"None reported."

"One hundred years?"

"Three."

I gave Mom a thumbs up. "I'm feeling pretty safe."

"That's not really what I meant. I was thinking more along the lines of . . . our being abducted this morning . . . forcibly relocated to a new city . . . one filled with technologies you've never seen before. I mean, what if there are aliens here?"

"Aliens?" I laughed. "Mom! Really? There aren't going to be any aliens here!"

Mom snorted. "I suppose not."

"Now . . . if you'd said dragons—"

"Oh, Willa! The things you think up. Dragons! This isn't one of your fantasy novels, dear. Grandeur is real!"

"Yeah . . . I'll . . . try and remember that." We walked on in silence for a time. "The abduction *was* a bit of a surprise," I confessed. "And I'm going to miss my friends, especially Emma and Ava. But I think Dad's the one you should worry about."

"I'm not worried about him. He'll bounce back," she said confidently while nibbling nervously on a fingernail. "He just needs a little time to adjust. But I'm glad you're okay with it, Willa. I have a good feeling about Grandeur. I don't know what it is, but I feel like we . . . belong here. You know?"

"You certainly have taken to it quickly."

A driverless car filled with passengers rolled past. Mom scanned the streets and buildings with a critical eye and a hint of trepidation.

"It does have a . . . dreamlike familiarity to it. I'll say that much." Then she looked me straight in the eye. "But I think I'd remember a place like this. Don't you?" Her uncertainty frightened me. It wasn't like Mom to second-guess herself.

"This is it," she said softly.

We were standing in front of a sprawling English manor, surrounded by parks, trees, sports fields, and a small lake.

"This is Idiot School 223?" I asked, gawking at the manicured lawn and stately windows. "Maybe it won't be so bad after all."

Man, am I an Idiot or what?

Mom grabbed me by the cardigan and gave me a look that demanded my full attention. "There's one thing I want you to know, Willamina Gilbert Snap. You're a *very* smart girl. Going to this Idiot school does *not* mean you're an idiot."

If living in Grandeur meant Mom acted like this every day—I *wanted* it.

A lump formed in my throat. "I understand what you're trying to say, Mom. Idiot is just a word and all that." I wanted to say more. I wanted to say I was okay with being an Idiot. I wanted to say that, contrary to popular belief, Idiots too had important jobs to do—like keeping Idiot Geniuses from blowing up the world. But I didn't want to ruin the moment. I didn't want the look of worry on her face to change to one of pity. Geniuses always think everyone wants to be like them. So I just nodded and fought back the tears.

"Cheese stick?"

I blinked. "What?"

"A little protein? To help get you to lunch?"

"Where exactly did that come from?"

She tossed it into her purse and pulled out a plated wheel of brie smeared with what looked like raspberry jam and accompanied by an assortment of crisps. I eyed it suspiciously.

"It's still warm," she said temptingly, waving it under my nose.

"They let you keep the purse?"

"You can't kill ideas, Willa. This jinni is out of the bottle. The only way to stop it would be to kill me and everyone who knows—" The plate of brie disappeared into the purse. She closed it with a *snap!* "But that's not how things are done in Grandeur. Here they simply . . ."

She stared into space, an empty look on her face, like she'd just forgotten what she was going to say.

"Are you okay, Mom?"

"Huh? Yeah. Totally . . . bean." Without even thinking about it, she pulled a glass of ice water from her purse and held it soothingly to her temple.

"Headache again?"

"It'll pass."

"You're getting more of those."

"It's been a stressful morning." She dropped the drink into the bottomless purse and put on a smile. "I'm fine, see?"

She wasn't lying. Whatever was bothering her had passed. But something wasn't right. I could feel it in my bones.

Inside the school's lobby, a large screen rose out of the floor like a giant black tombstone. The moment we opened the doors, it glowed to life, revealing a woman sitting behind a desk located who knows where. She looked up and smiled at us. I ducked behind Mom. People inside screens aren't supposed to be able to see and talk to you unless they're on your phone or computer. A disturbingly few questions later, I was enrolled in Idiot school. "Down the hall," said the woman. "Second door on the right."

"Do you want me to walk you to—"

"No!" I said firmly. "I'm good. You can go now. Thanks."

"All right. I'll be going to the towers to check out my lab. I'll be home in time for dinner. Maybe we'll carry something in."

As she left, three students entered. I followed in their wake. The Brontë twins were already in the classroom, and the redheaded boy, Rufus—still fidgeting with his invisibility device. Heathcliff was here too, surrounded by a crater of empty chairs. While spinning in place, looking for the mysterious redheaded girl, I suddenly came face-to-face with the handsomest boy I'd ever laid eyes on. In fact, if I were to draw a line in the sand of my life, I could easily say, "Here, on this side, is where I'd never looked twice at a boy, but there, on that other side . . . that is where I first imagined running my fingers through a boy's lustrous . . . raven . . . locks." You're not allowed to repeat that, of course. And if I catch you telling anyone what I just said, I will punch you in the mouth.

The boy's clothes were an explosion of storm-black tweed. Tweed vest, tweed jacket, tweed hat. He eyed me like a puzzle that needed figuring out.

"Do you make it a habit of wearing other people's clothes," he asked, in a crisp English accent, "or is this a special occasion?"

"I—I—" I was surprised I could get even an *I* out.

Suddenly the redheaded girl in the purple fez was standing by my side, her eyes instantly locking onto the mysterious boy's.

"Do not stare directly into his eyes!" she warned, in an accent I couldn't place.

"Why not?" I said, but she was already too late. I was staring directly into his eyes too.

"Because they are dreamy, and endless, and magical. And then when you learn what a terrible boy he is, your heart will turn into a black husk of doom."

I blinked off the spell of the boy's eyes.

"Wait, what?"

The girl continued to stare. "They will suck out your soul, forever ruining you for other boys for so long as you may live."

"You know he can hear you, right?" I whispered.

"Why, hello to you, too, Nimet Simit," said the boy.

Nimet clapped her hands over her mouth and slunk away.

The boy offered me his hand. "Ravenlock Sward, at your service."

My Idiot heart pounded in my chest, and I yanked my sweaty hand back. How my hand got in his I have no idea.

"Wu-We-Willa Snap," I said.

He smiled at me, and for the first time I understood—really understood—what the creators of the word handsome must have had in mind when they thought it up in the first place. Also, at about this time, I forgot how to breathe in.

"Nice to meet you, Wu-We-Willa Snap."

"I'm new here," I said. Turns out speaking isn't advisable when you've forgotten how to breathe in. Who knew? The edges of my world grew a little sparkly.

"I know." He crossed the room to a chair several rows away, speaking as he did so. "You arrived this morning, by way of Boston, or near about. While traveling in a MiniDirigy to your new flat, you met and talked to a dog, after which you were accosted by a Clockwerk Boy. But what did he want with you?" My mouth opened to answer, but he didn't pause. "You're an only child. As for family, your father is an Idiot, also from Boston. That leaves your mother as the Idiot Genius in the house. Source has placed you in Whitehaven Mansions, where your cat is getting more stir-crazy by the minute. Your father performs some form of strenuous labor, something that involves heavy tools. Plumbing, I would wager."

He slumped down in a chair and sighed as though bored.

"That was amazing! Would you mind telling me how you know all that?"

Ravenlock whipped his head around, his eyes now cold and dismissive. "Yes!" he said, sounding put out. "I most certainly would. If you really must know, figure it out for yourself! And take that stupid BrainRent off your ear!"

I took in a deep breath. My heart rate returned to normal. I felt shaken but was pretty sure I'd passed the test. This boy would not turn my heart into a black husk of doom, at least not today. Still, something told me my dealings with Ravenlock Sward were only just beginning.

I sat down next to Nimet. "Did you see the way he looked at me?" I asked.

"You mean as if you didn't exist?"

"Worse. It was like . . . like I wasn't even a girl."

Nimet frowned. "What do you expect? You're what, twelve years old?"

"Eleven."

"Wu-We-Willa—"

"It's just Willa."

"Willa, Ravenlock is fourteen. How could you possibly exist as a girl to him? Besides, he hardly notices girls his own age." Nimet's eyes got all dreamy again. "Mysterious, charming . . . O şeytanın tüyü."

"How's that?"

"He's the devil's feather," she said, snapping out of it. "Look how shamelessly Dashia throws herself at him. Does he pay her any mind?"

I looked up. A strikingly beautiful girl, several years older than me, was fawning over an obviously uninterested Ravenlock. A wave of uncontrollable jealousy raged through every part of my being. What was *that* all about?

"But it's not fair," I said. "It'll be years before I have . . . I have . . ." I looked down helplessly.

"That is true. And by the time you do, some unlucky girl will have snatched him up. It is the way of things . . . when you're eleven. But even if you could get his attention, what would you do with him?"

I drew a blank. "I'd . . . I'd . . . probably nothing."

"You see?"

"Yeah, but . . . I bet it'd be a pretty spectacular nothing."

A robot clunkier and dingier than Mr. Nuts and Bolts thudded into the room. He wrote *Professor Pedagogue* on the chalkboard, then clanked to his desk and half-sat on its edge. I happen to live with a pedagogue, so this word wasn't new to me. It's a teacher who goes on and on in great detail without a care in the world about whether or not you're capable of following along. Or have the slightest bit of interest.

"I understand we have a new student today," he announced. "As she is new to Grandeur, I would ask you all to help make her first day a pleasant one." He looked around the room until his eyes fell on me. "Ms. Snap, will you please come forward and introduce yourself?"

I'd been dreading something like this. I made my way to the front. There were about two dozen people in the class. The youngest looked to be about six, the oldest maybe fifteen.

"Hello," I began. "My name is Willa Snap—"

A boy dropped a spanner (as they call wrenches in Grandeur) and gasped. A second before, he'd been spinning it in his fingers, like a rock star twirling a drumstick. Now his eyes were wide, and he was staring at me like he was seeing a ghost.

"I'm eleven years old," I began, then paused to see what effect this might have on the class. It had none.

"And where are you from?" asked the robot.

"Cambridge, Massachusetts."

"All right then. We don't have a lot of time, so everyone please stand briefly and tell Willa your name and something about yourself."

I must warn you. You're about to hear a lot of names. It's okay if you can't remember them all. The important thing is that some of the people in this room will become my best friends, some will never be more than acquaintances to smile and say hello to, and several will . . . well . . . try and kill me.

Oh, and you may recognize some of their last names. You may even think—as I did the first time I heard them—that the people attached to these names are closely related descendants of their Genius namesakes. But more often than not, they're only *distantly* related, either from many generations before, or many generations after.

Rufus, from the elevator, the one with the faulty invisibility device, stood up and waved happily to me. "I'm eight years old, I was born in Grandeur, and my name is Rufus Feynman."

Okay, perfect example. Perhaps you've heard of Richard Feynman? Famed theoretical physicist, won the Nobel Prize, wrote lots of books, gave lectures, played the bongos? No? You really should read more. You're missing out. There's a whole world out there. Put this book down and go get one not written by some Idiot—AND THEN READ IT! You'll still be an Idiot when you finish, but not quite so much of one. Now, where were we? Right, Richard Feynman. *He* was not the Idiot Genius who got Rufus's family stuck in Grandeur. That was Caractacus Feynman, born half a dozen generations before our zany bongo-playing Genius ever thumped a drum. However, it's worth noting that Richard Feynman *was* on the Black Fez watch list for his entire life.

A girl stood up next. She was cute as a newborn squirrel, and trust me, the *only* cute squirrel is a baby squirrel. "CeeCee da Vinci," she said with a slight Italian accent, "and I'm also eight years old."

You'll notice she didn't bother to say where she was born. That's because her surname is legend. (Um, you do know who Leonardo da Vinci is, right? If you don't, skip this chapter and remember that I met a bunch of people ages eight to fourteen—*yad-*

da-yadda-yadda—some of them will try and kill me. That's all you really need to know.) CeeCee's ancestral Idiot Genius was actually relocated back in 1372, three years before *this* version of Grandeur opened for business. Through the ages, there've been a lot of different Grandeurs. The one before this is commonly referred to as Grandeur Abbey and was located Somewhere Northeast of London. No one seems to know what happened to it or what it looked like. But I've heard plenty of stories. A Nano prince once told me Grandeur Abbey was never completely emptied out. That it's still there, fully intact. But a dragon also once assured me it was her family that received the contract to burn Grandeur Abbey to the ground. The craziest story I've heard, though, came from a ghost, who claimed he was Luigi da Vinci, no less. The *original* da Vinci Idiot Genius. He told me it was his invention they used to float Grandeur Abbey to Grandeur's present location, Somewhere in the Southwest of America. But I never take much stock in what ghosts say. They're way too flimsy when it comes to the truth. But I digress.

A fair-haired boy stood up and announced he was Ethan Faraday and that he was nine years old, followed by Kayla Hawking, also nine. Both were born in Grandeur. Most are.

Kayla is another good example of the famous name thing. If, when you heard her name, you thought of the great British theoretical physicist, cosmologist, and author Stephen Hawking, then bully for you. But if you were thinking Kayla was Stephen's child, or grandchild, or niece, or something, there's where you'd be wrong. The Idiot Genius who landed Kayla's family in Grandeur was born a hundred years *before* Stephen Hawking. His name was Barwick Hawking, and he was actually the first person to send a monkey to the moon. He developed a special platform that canceled out Earth's gravity while magnifying the moon's. It worked great. He even figured out how to send stuff back from the moon, like freeze-dried monkeys. So what's the big deal, you ask? What's one monkeysicle in the big scheme of things? Well, the hitch was that his invention, if used by too many people all at once, would've destabilized Earth's tectonic plates, causing earthquakes and volcanic eruptions. The Black Fez (as near as I can tell, they've *always* been around) tried to get him to see the light, but being an Idiot Genius, he insisted that anyone clever enough to use his invention could be judicious. Wrong answer.

So into Grandeur he went, never to be seen Outside again. Normally, that would have been the end of it, because ideas like his are very, very rare. And the chances of someone inventing something like it twice were astronomical (so to speak). But these Hawkings are a determined bunch. Turned out not one, but *two* of old Barwick's descendants stumbled on the same thing! Everyone here has their fingers crossed that Stephen won't be the fourth Idiot Genius Hawking permanently brought to Grandeur, because Outside needs every Genius like him it can get.

The ten-year-olds went next. Ian Tesla, Riley Darwin, Christopher Newton, Nimet Simit, and Heathcliff Wudgepuddle. Then came the eleven-year-olds. Masa Mochi, Nicholas Franklin, Ji Taam, Zoe and Sarah Brontë, and the boy who dropped the spanner: Bertie Babbage (yes, as in Charles Babbage, the British inventor of the very first computer, even if he never got to build it). Fifty-some years ago, Bertie's grandparents left the Clockwerk Burg to open a soup shop in Greater Grandeur. Bertie's dad still runs it now.

On to the twelve-year-olds: Tanisha Varma, whose Idiot Genius hailed from India; Maximiliano Ramirez, whose Idiot Genius hailed from Honduras; and Ambrose Poupon, whose Idiot Genius hailed from Louisiana. Ambrose's family is Creole. If you're ever lucky enough to be invited to his parents' house for breakfast, lunch, or dinner, you say YES, thank you.

Next, the tall, dark-haired girl who'd been throwing herself shamelessly at Ravenlock stood up. "My name is Dashia Dragunov," she said. "I am thirteen years old." Dashia's Idiot Genius ancestor was from Russia, if you hadn't guessed.

"Callum Wellington Posh the third," announced a fair-skinned blond boy. "Also thirteen years old. I was born in Herefordshire, England, and was interred to this vile sphere approximately this exact same time last year."

I perked up at this news. Callum was the first kid I'd heard say he hadn't been born in Grandeur.

His sister was the second. "Ruby Allegra Posh," she said in a clear voice. "I'm one year senior to my brother and was also born in Herefordshire."

That left two: the obnoxious Ravenlock Sward and the lovely Samantha Steam. Samantha's parents had tired of the Steamwerks Burg's oppressive dress code and strictly controlled professions. And even though Steam was the most important name in all the Steamwerks Burg, Samantha's family came from a dead and withered branch, with none of the fame, trappings, or cavernous mansions that typically accompany such important names. Samantha was (and still is) furious that her parents chose to live in Greater Grandeur, as any place outside the burgs is called. You just had to look at her clothes, which weren't all that far removed from

Professor Farsical's—that dude who asked me to sign the Steam-werks petition. The only thing missing was the brass porthole in her skull. And it's a good bet she was saving up for one.

And with that, the class had spoken. Any guesses which ones will try and kill me?

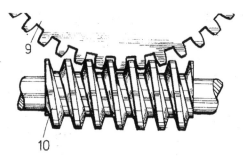

Professor Pedagogue
Takes a Nap

W ELL done." Professor Pedagogue clapped his metallic hands the way you do when you're not the least bit excited. "Now that we have that out of the way, on to lessons."

Ravenlock snorted. If Professor Pedagogue understood the emotion going through Ravenlock's mind, and I suspect he did, then he didn't show it.

"Have a seat, Willa," he continued. "Has anyone decided, since our last class, what trade he or she would like to apprentice to?"

Rufus Feynman raised his hand.

Professor Pedagogue sighed heavily. "Yes, Rufus, what would you—"

"I want to be an astronaut."

"No."

"A mathematician."

"No."

"A computer programmer, so I can make you smarter."

"Certainly not. May I offer you some suggestions?"

"Do you have to?" asked Rufus.

"In a word, Rufus, think thespian."

"You want me to be an actor?" asked Rufus.

"Ooh! Can I be a writer?" asked Zoe Brontë.

"Not if you want to be widely read," said Professor Pedagogue.

"A musician?" asked Ambrose.

"Not if you want to receive airplay. How about . . . a hamster groomer?" he said with forced enthusiasm.

"Can I be an architect?" asked CeeCee da Vinci.

"No, CeeCee, for the eight hundred eighty-seventh time, you may *not* be an architect."

"A sculptor?" she squealed, filled with the overabundance of hope that only an eight-year-old body can contain.

"Would you really have us give you a perfectly good slab of marble to ruin?" complained Professor Pedagogue. "Can you imagine how much practice you would need to become proficient? Don't you think sculpture is best left in the hands of a capable robot?"

CeeCee didn't answer.

"Let me give you some suggestions," continued the robot. "Think . . . grass mowing. Think . . . garbage collection. Think . . . window washing."

I raised my hand.

"Yes, Ms. Snap?"

"Wouldn't those tasks be better suited to robots?"

Professor Pedagogue's mouth dropped open, then creaked

closed. "Surely you jest. Why would anyone in her right mind want to waste the talents of a robot on menial labor? Only an Idiot would think up something like that. But then again, you are an Idiot. QED." QED is something Geniuses (and certain robots) love to say to Idiots. It basically means, "I'm right! Nyah, nyah, nyah-nyah-nyah!"

"He has a point," announced Bertie Babbage.

"You can't mean that!" I said, turning to face him.

"Oh, but I do! What right do we have to complain when a robot is better suited for the job? A robot can be an instant expert at anything it wants. Need a brilliant architect? *Fip!* Source downloads the necessary programs into its brain. Need a surgeon? An anti-gravity unit repair tech? A master chef? *Fip! Fip! Fip!* All it takes is a second and you've got one. Compare that to me. I'll be lucky to master more than half a dozen skills over my entire lifetime."

"Speak for yourself, you miserable Idiot," snarled Dashia Dragunov in her thick Russian accent.

"But I am."

Dashia glared at him. It always bothered her when Bertie made a good point. "Well, I, for one, don't see great art coming from the robots. They'll never be as creative as humans."

"Then I suggest you try opening your eyes!" said Bertie. "Take literature. Sure, I love Madeleine L'Engle, C.S. Lewis, and Jane Austen, I can't get enough of the Brontës or Tolkien"—Zoe and Sarah leaned over and gave each other a high five at the mention of the Brontë sisters, their Outside namesakes—"but have you ever read any of SCHEHERAZADE2000's stuff?" Dashia picked at her nails. "Well, have you?" Bertie pressed.

"Does it have vampires?" she asked. "Because I don't like zombies."

"Well, that's just it. Simply tell SCHEHERAZADE2000 some of your favorite authors and out pops another bestseller! It's a literary master. And it's not the only one. There's GRIMM900, WHEDON24—even the Clockwerks have produced a master with their DANTE500, thank you very much! And it's like that in every profession!"

"Are you saying, Bertie," sneered Ravenlock, "that the bots could easily run the famous Babbage's Bouillon, Bisque & Bean?"

Bertie pursed his lips, but he was well practiced in defending his father's soup shop. "I grant you, they might have a little trouble replicating the perfect purple hue of Grandma Babbage's borscht." The classroom laughed. "But yes, I think they could manage it."

Ravenlock smiled grudgingly. "You're probably right about the borscht, but tell me, doesn't your mother have her own secret little business on the side?"

"Yes. She runs a small architecture firm."

"And this firm competes with the bots, does it?"

"Actually, most of its contracts are small freelance jobs for the larger bot firms."

"Well, then," drawled Ravenlock, "maybe CeeCee could study architecture and work for your mother someday."

CeeCee beamed.

"But why would she hire CeeCee?" CeeCee made a face at Bertie. "No offense, CeeCee, but you'd sleep on the job half the day."

"Wait a minute!" I objected. "Humans have to sleep! It's what we do!"

"Yes. I understand that, but robots, most of 'em anyways, don't sleep for even a minute. Ah, but now I'm teasing you. My mom would never hire any bots. Can't stand 'em."

"Excuse me," I said, then asked a question I instantly regretted. "But why's her firm a secret?"

Ravenlock's eyes brightened. "Oh, yes! Shall I explain it to her? Or would you like to have that honor?"

Bertie's cheeks flushed. "First, Willa, you have to understand how hard it is for *Geniuses* to get work from the bots. Then, understand that Geniuses rarely hire Idiots. I mean, even some Idiots are loath to hire Idiots. So, if you're an *Idiot* running a business, your only chance of getting enough work from the bots is if you go through a shadow Genius company. For an exorbitant fee, I might add."

I should take a moment here to explain the difference between Geniuses in Grandeur and geniuses (note the small *g*) Outside. You see, Outside, 1 out of every 160 people has an IQ over 140 and is considered a bona fide genius. But only 1 out of 11,000 people have an IQ of 160, and just 1 in 3.5 million have an IQ of 180. By the time you get to 200, you're talking 1 in 4.8 *billion* people. That's right: There are only 1 or 2 people with an IQ of 200 or more on the whole planet—Outside.

Inside Grandeur, however, they play by a different set of rules. Here, you're not considered a Genius unless you have an IQ of 160, which in Grandeur works out, coincidentally, to 1 in 160 people. But since Grandeur started with a population made solely of Geniuses (Idiot family member abductions didn't start until 902 CE), that means about three out of four people you meet in Grandeur have IQs of at least 140. So, by Outside standards, three-quarters of the people in this classroom would be considered geniuses! Not me, of course. I'm nowhere close to being a Genius, capital G or otherwise.

One other thing you should probably know is that most Geniuses are born, not made. You can study all you want, but you're not going to raise your IQ more than 10 percent.

But don't let that discourage you. As most any Genius will tell you: IQ isn't the sole measure of one's intelligence. There are more variables than you might think, and your IQ measures fewer than half of them.

But back to the show. "Bertie!" shouted Professor Pedagogue. "Are you saying your mother runs an illegal—"

Click!

Professor Pedagogue's chin fell onto his chest. Ravenlock had sneaked behind him, pointed a small device at the robot's head, and apparently turned him off.

"Thanks, Ravenlock," said Bertie. "I always forget I shouldn't tell him that part."

"Not to worry, Bertie. He never seems to remember the last few minutes." Ravenlock looked at me. Suddenly, *I* was the center of attention. "We generally turn him off as soon as he arrives, but we thought you might like to see what you're up against when you're an Idiot in Grandeur. You see, only the Geniuses get proper schooling here. We Idiots are self-taught."

"It worked for Abraham Lincoln," I said.

Ravenlock smiled. "Ah, that's the spirit! Unfortunately, Grandeur has stacked the cards against you."

"What do you mean?"

"Your version of Grandeurpedia is calibrated for Idiot. It'll only feed you information it deems appropriate for your IQ."

"How fiendish!"

"Yes. Desperate times call for desperate measures. That's why we've resorted to countering with the most powerful weapon ever conceived by mankind. Put out your hand."

Weapon? I gulped. Ravenlock dropped something onto my palm.

I flipped it over. "This is a library card."

"Quite. Use it often. Use it well."

"Geniuses don't use libraries?"

"Not paper ones. Progress, you know. Now, any minute, this classroom is going to start filling up with Geniuses."

"But we just got here."

"Idiot school coincides with *their* lunch period," explained CeeCee. "So we never get more than about thirty minutes."

"Not that it matters," added Callum Posh. "Grandeur is positively stuffed with museums and science centers. They don't keep us out of those. At least, not yet."

I shoved my new library card into my pocket.

"We Idiots have to stick together," said Tanisha Varma. "Too many people see us simply as a necessary evil to keep the newly imported Idiot Geniuses happy, or at least complacent."

"That's awful!" I said. Instantly, I thought of my mother. She wouldn't ever think like that, would she? "People who think that way *must* be in the minority."

"True, but a powerful minority," said Maximiliano Ramirez. "There are even radical factions within the Idiot Genius community who would like to see us Idiots . . . eradicated."

"But if you talk to any old-timer worth his salt," said Ravenlock, "he'll tell you the reason we 'Idiots' were brought into Grandeur had nothing to do with keeping the newly imported Idiot Geniuses happy. No. He'll say we were imported to *save* Grandeur, to keep it from blowing apart at the seams."

I knew exactly what Ravenlock was talking about. Without my dad and me, Mom would never have lasted as long as she did Outside.

The noise of shoes on tile and muted conversations drifted in from the hallway. Ravenlock's eyes shot to the door.

"Places, everyone. I'm going to turn him back on."

Everyone took a seat. All except Ravenlock, who stood behind Professor Pedagogue while holding his small device close to the robot's head. *Click!* "On my count," said Ravenlock, taking his seat. "Three, two, one."

The class stood up as Professor Pedagogue's chin lifted from his chest.

"Thanks for the advice, Professor Pedagogue," said Rufus cheerfully.

"Any time," answered the confused-looking robot. "That's what they pay me for."

As we filed out, and the Geniuses filed in, one of the older Genius boys shouldered Ravenlock, hard. Then another. Then another. Ravenlock smiled and apologized each time, as if it had been his fault. He was a great actor, but he didn't fool me.

I sidled up to Nimet. "Hi. Where did you say you were originally from?"

"I didn't."

"Oh. So you were born . . . in Grandeur?"

"Nimet," said Ravenlock, striding past us, "is definitely from Outside. Northern Turkey, perhaps a province bordering the Black Sea."

I waited until we were outside and Ravenlock was nowhere to be seen. "How does he know these things?"

"Sihirbazı," Nimet whispered, her big green eyes filled with awe.

"Shiriwhozzie?"

"He's a wizard."

"Um, no. There's no such thing as magic. People like Ravenlock are just good at reading people and . . . have access to unconventional sources of information."

"Psst!" said the bush next to us.

Nimet didn't seem surprised.

"Psst!" the bush said again.

"It's Bertie Babbage," explained Nimet. "He's been hiding there ever since we came out."

The branches swayed and Bertie stepped out.

"You could see me in there?" His British accent was less sophisticated sounding than Ravenlock's.

Nimet nodded. "What do you want?"

"To talk to Willa . . . alone."

Nimet turned to leave, but I grabbed her hand and pulled her close.

"Anything you want to say to me you can say in front of Nimet. Nimet's my new best friend," I added quickly.

"But we just met—" protested Nimet, somehow managing to sound confused, hopeful, and regretful all at once.

"New! I said *new* best friend . . . emphasis on *new*. Get it?" I nodded like an Idiot.

Nimet gave me a resigned look. "You're going to get me into trouble, aren't you?"

"That depends. How fast can you run?"

"Like the wind."

"Then you shouldn't have anything to worry about."

"It's *you* that needs to worry, Willa," interrupted Bertie.

"What are you talking about, Bertie Babbage?" asked Nimet forcefully.

"Willa needs to come to my father's soup shop tomorrow, no later than four-thirty."

"Why?" I asked.

The way Bertie looked at me made a chill settle in the pit of my stomach. I'd seen his reaction back in the classroom. He'd heard my name before. But where? And why?

"The less I say the better."

"So you can't tell me why?" I asked.

Bertie cast his eyes downward. "I wouldn't ask if it wasn't important."

"Bertie!" scolded Nimet. "Tell Willa what it is you want or go away!"

Bertie opened his mouth, but nothing came out.

Nimet pulled me back a few steps. "Come on, Willa. Let's go."

"*Dracones finis!*" blurted Bertie.

It was something the Clockwerk Boy had said. "*It's my fate to decide?*"

Bertie nodded. "*You must sacrifice yourself to right the wrong.* They've already talked to you?"

"They? No. I heard it from a Clockwerk Boy."

Bertie seemed surprised. "A Clockwerk Boy?"

"Yeah, but how did *you* hear about it?"

"Would someone please tell me what is going on?" asked Nimet.

"Dragons," said Bertie. "The time-traveling kind. My dad does a lot of catering in the burgs, the Biowerks Burg in particular. One of our regular jobs is running the dragon kitchens during special events. You see, Dad came up with this spice mix he calls Old Thunder. The recipe is secret, but I'm pretty sure it's got some nitroglycerin in it because the kick you get—I mean, let's just say you don't want to get any of this stuff in your mouth. One time—"

"Bertie!"

"Okay, okay, so there's one of these special events tomorrow night. They're going to decide something big. And it has something to do with you, Willa. You *have* to be there—something about your timeline ending. You have to make a decision. It's *very* important. Lives are at stake. I can sneak you into the kitchens if you come to the soup shop tomorrow. After that it'll be too late."

"Time-traveling dragons? In Grandeur?" said Nimet. "Your gears are slipping, Bertie Babbage."

"Four-thirty," Bertie repeated.

"How long will it take?" I asked.

"I don't know."

"Well, what do I tell my parents?"

"I don't know."

I wanted to say no, but how else was I going to learn about my timeline? "Okay, we'll be there," I said.

"We who?" asked Nimet, twisting her hand out of mine.

"No way," said Bertie. "Just you, Willa."

I turned to Nimet. "Come on, Nimet. How often do you get a chance to serve dinner to dragons?"

Nimet gave me a look of horror.

"And Bertie," I said, "we'll need an excuse to tell our parents." I didn't like lying to my parents, but I had a feeling I'd never be able to explain this one. And if I could keep my timeline from ending, I was pretty sure they'd be all for it.

"There will be no *we*," protested Nimet.

Bertie looked pained. "Okay, I'll think of something."

"It better be good. I won't go without Nimet, either. Do you understand? Is your dad's soup shop in this thing?" I asked, pointing to my WatchitMapCallit.

"Yes. Babbage's Bouillon, Bisque & Bean. It's not far from here."

"And you'll be going without me," said Nimet, and she stamped her foot.

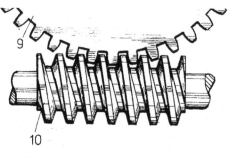

The *Jolly Rajah*

N IMET and I didn't speak again until I opened my apartment door.

"You want to come in?" I asked.

Nimet poked her nose in. "I have to check in with my parents first."

"Okay. Just come over after."

She nodded meekly.

Dad wasn't wearing his Outside clothes anymore. And from the looks of it, his new wardrobe had come out of the same time-machine closet as mine. The sweater he'd chosen was fine, and so was the white collared shirt underneath. But the pants, which ended just past his knees, made a showcase of the most outrageous argyle socks I'd ever seen. On his head squatted a golfer's cap.

"What happened to those pants?" I asked.

My dad glanced admiringly at them. "I believe these are what you call plus fours. All the rage, dear. Shall we go out for some lunch?"

"Not with you dressed like that."

"Hey, it was this or a suit!"

I grimaced.

Dad made his WatchitMapCallit appear. "Well, let's see. Nearby restaurants . . . oh, here's one: the Slug and Lettuce."

I made a face.

"No?"

"Do you see my face?"

"All right, point taken. Um, how about . . . Jellied Eels and Squid Lips? No? I'm shocked. And it's just down the block from us. Okay, okay, here's another—the Jolly Rajah Man-o'-War o' Pancakes. Breakfast, Lunch, and Dinner. Open 24 Hours. Its logo has a very happy-looking elephant wearing an eye patch and flipping pancakes."

Man-o'-war, I thought. Being a Cambridge girl, I knew all about those. In fact, when I was eight, Dad took me for an overnight on the USS *Constitution*, an eighteenth-century wooden-hulled, three-masted heavy frigate moored in Boston Harbor. She's the oldest fully commissioned ship in the US Navy. We dressed in period clothes and used only the items the sailors of the day had, which meant no electric lights or modern plumbing. Because I was so young, they made me a powder monkey. My job was to run sacks of gunpowder from the magazine to the gun crew during battle. We slept in hammocks and ate authentic hard tack (minus the authentic worms).

"How close is it?"

"A couple streets over, on Baba Kharak Singh Marg. I think marg means passage or street. It's in something called the Biowerks Burg. What do you think that means?"

"I have no idea," I fibbed, as my stomach grumbled. "Let's

go find out."

Dad poked and prodded his WatchitMapCallit. "I can't remember . . . how did I . . . where's the map thingy?"

I tried not to sigh—it's part of my let's-not-make-Dad-feel-any-stupider-than-he-needs-to-around-technology program, which I instituted shortly after I realized how hard he works to make me not feel stupid around tools. I don't think he wants me to be a plumber, or even work a trade, but he *does* want me to know the basics about hammers, wrenches, power tools, even acetylene torches. And he's pretty tricky at making it fun, too. For example, almost every weekend, he'll bring something new home, and we'll go out in the garage, don our protective welding helmets and gloves, and play the *Will it burn or will it melt?* game. That's how he taught me to solder metal pipes and stuff together. It's not a bad skill to have knocked out by age eleven.

"Got your back, Dad. Pull up Grandeurpedia, type in *Jolly Rajah*, then tap the little icon that looks like a dancing map."

"Ah! I see. So that little guy's a dancing map, huh? I thought he was a demented waffle."

"Can I ask a friend along?"

"Someone you met at school?"

I nodded.

Dad smiled at me. "How about you! Sure, bring your friend."

Nimet was waiting outside our door. I think she was trying to work up the nerve to knock. I made introductions, told her where we were going, and asked if she wanted to join us. Her face lit up when she learned which restaurant we'd picked.

I was a little surprised by the lack of markers as we crossed the boundary into the Biowerks Burg. No gates, no walls, no dotted glowing lines down the middle of the street (like there were on the WatchitMapCallit), nothing but a strange symbol on the street signs.

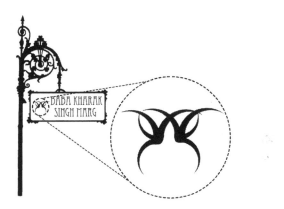

Within a block, though, everything changed. The architecture went from brick to stone. Large mosaics were everywhere, tucked into arches and recessed walls. Food vendors crowded every corner, and the people on the street seemed friendly. Many of them wore colorful, loose-hanging robes, and almost all of them had some sort of small animal companion. I say *some sort of* because I had a hard time identifying what I was seeing. Some looked like they'd started out as monkeys or cats, some like lizards or birds, but all of them had a look of added intelligence that I wasn't used to seeing in the eyes of pets back home.

Unfamiliar smells wafted through the air, too, as if behind every corner lurked a hidden spice market. Even the shop names were different. For example, while still in Greater Grandeur, we passed shops like Finch's Shoe and Boot, Where Every Shoe Fits;

the Slug and Lettuce, whose menu in the window didn't seem nearly as frightening as the name; and Dorothy Parker's, a teen fashion store that promised lots of "Sassy Colonial Style."

But once we entered the Biowerks Burg, we ran into Darzee's Bestiary, We Make Clothes for Every Body; Chamgadar's Ocular Replacement, For When You *Really* Need that Second Pair of Eyes; Ferdinand's Electrophoresis, Your DNA Separation Experts Since 1428. (Ferdinand's had a sign in the window touting that they only used Fair Trade organic seaweed for their agarose gels.) See what I mean?

Even Nimet was different here. She smiled more, running a little ahead of us and pressing her nose to the shop windows. When I tried to follow her through the shifting crowds, she would vanish and reappear at will. More than once, I thought I heard her laughing.

Stopping to catch my breath, I turned around to see how far back my dad was, and found myself eyeball to eyeballs with a basket full of furry faces.

"Out of the way, monkey-brain," one of them squealed.

The woman carrying the basket was about ten feet tall, eyes all glazed over. She wasn't slowing down.

"You make a better door than a window!" screamed another furry face in a high-pitched, catlike whine.

I felt a sudden tug at my elbow, pulling me out of the way. It was Nimet.

"Thanks! I thought she was going to run me over. What's her problem?"

"She's a shopping golem. Not a lot of brainpower, but great for fetching things. She didn't mean you any harm, but it isn't wise to step in front of one."

"And the furry heads in the basket?"

"Ferricats, and freshly brewed by the sound of them."

"How's that?"

"Half ferret, half cat. The baristas brew them."

I continued to stare like an Idiot, waiting for her to say something that made any sense.

Seeing my face, she said, "Baristas blend DNA, making completely new 'brewed' creatures. Don't ask me how. They're very secretive."

"I talked to a dog today who said he had vocal implants."

"That's different. Lots of animals get vocal implants."

"Cats?"

"Mammals, avians, reptiles—"

"Animals . . . act different here. They seem smarter than they do . . ."

"Outside." Nimet nodding knowingly. "That's because none of the animals in Grandeur observe the Great Pact of Silence."

"They have a pact?"

The Jolly Rajah Man-o'-War o' Pancakes was easy to spot, even from a distance. Its entrance looked like a giant elephant's head, with the ears acting as doors. Inside, it looked like you were walking onto a wharf in a sheltered cove, and tied up to it was a full-sized wooden man-o'-war. I'm talking one big wooden boat. The words *Jolly Rajah* were painted in big red letters on the bow.

At first, Dad and I just stood there, stunned. Dad looked down. I looked up.

"Where's the restaurant?" asked Dad.

"Um, there's a deck up there, with masts, and rigging, and cannons," I said.

"It's . . . floating . . . in real water," said Dad disbelievingly. The smell of the sea reminded me of summer on Cape Cod. I could see fish in the water. The illusion was powerful and complete.

We gawked at each other like Idiots.

"How big is this place?" I asked Nimet.

"Who cares?" she shouted, grabbing my hand and pulling me across a gangway. "All aboard that's going aboard!"

We entered between decks. New smells greeted us here: aging timber, spent gunpowder, maple syrup, pancakes. Everything was oversized, like the carpenters had used plans a quarter size too big. Rows of giant cannons protruded through open gunports. Great oil lamps swayed from the ceiling, and customers packed the tables and booths. And just like in the logo, the waiters were dressed like pygmy elephants walking upright on two legs. I say pygmy, but they were still about eight feet tall.

"It all seems so real," said my dad. "Would you get a load of the costumes? It must be hot as a furnace inside one of those suits!"

"Empty booth!" yelled Nimet, and we hustled our way over and slid into a table tucked between two forty-two-pounders (that's man-o'-war talk for *really* big cannons).

We hadn't been sitting for more than a minute when we caught sight of a waiter coming our way. Every time one of his ears skimmed the ceiling, it set forty or more golden earrings jangling. He was wearing a big puffy pirate shirt, tight around his enormous belly and open around his neck. An elephant-sized black patch was fastened across one eye. His hat would've covered our entire table, and his billowy orange pants swished with each thudding step. Part of me wanted to know more about the eye patch. But you have to be careful with eye patches. You never know when one could be real. And asking is tricky. I mean, if it's real, and the owner takes it upon himself to prove it, you might get more than you wanted to see. Yep, some curiosities are better left unsatisfied.

As he thudded closer, one extraordinary fact became clearer and clearer.

"Willa," said my dad, his voice rising a full octave. "Willa, I don't think he's wearing a costu—" His face froze, lips puckered. I suppose the walk there should have prepared us a little.

"You're an elephant!" I said, incredibly more loudly than I'd intended.

The waiter stopped short, his face turning crimson. He gripped the business end of a boarding axe tucked in his belt and the entire gun deck went silent. Nimet slapped her hands over her face. Somewhere a mug smashed, a fork clattered.

"And ye're a stinkin' ape!" he trumpeted.

Tears welled up in my eyes, like I was some kind of baby or something. I *hate* it when that happens. I felt terrible. I hadn't meant to be rude. But I was *so* hungry, and the thought of not getting to eat only made it worse.

"I'm so sorry!" I blurted. "I didn't mean anything by it. I—"

The elephant's good eye opened wide. "Didn't mean anything by it!" he roared in disbelief.

"It's our first day in Grandeur," my dad squeaked, still using the mousy version of his voice.

"Your first tide! Ha! Well, why didn't ye say so!" His face softened and thick wrinkles formed around the corners of his eyes. When he laughed, his enormous belly threatened to pop his shirt seams. "Then I forgive ye, o' course. But in the future, you should know that I and my kind are *elefantkin*." He smiled broadly and tweaked the gold ball that tipped his shorter tusk. "Me name's Jajanana Toosk, but you can call me Jaja."

"Are those menus?" I asked meekly. Jaja's pirate talk had a strong Indian accent, giving it a sound like nothing I'd ever heard.

"Oof! Pardon me manners, aye indeed." Jaja did a double take at the sight of Nimet. "Shiver me timbers! Why, it's Nimet Simit. Never seen you here without your Mum or Da."

At the mention of her parents, Nimet became anxious. "Yes, that's true, but . . . today . . . my friend Willa—"

"Matey! You don't say!" Jaja looked at me with approval.

I couldn't take it anymore. I seized one of the menus and yanked it free of Jaja's grasp.

"Pardon me, Jaja, but I'm starving!"

Alarmed, Jaja bent at the knees. "Starvin', you say!"

"I haven't eaten anything since breakfast, and that was—"

"Why, blow me down! Why didn't you say so first thing?" Jaja bent his head back and let out a trumpeting blast. "All hands! Starvin' patron on the starboard gun deck, midships."

From all directions, even above and below, came a deep singing, punctuated by a rhythm of heavy footsteps.

What shall we do with a hungry patron,
What shall we do with a hungry patron,
What shall we do with a hungry patron,
Early in the mornin'.

Elefantkin stomp-danced into the room, appearing from hatches and doorways, all bearing platters laden with pancakes, bacon, sausages, and fruit. Their singing filled the room.

Hooray our cup she rises,
Hooray our cup she rises,
Hooray our cup she rises,
Hot cocoa in the mornin'.

Plates flew in every direction. I was surprised to see how very human the elefantkin's hands were, and the table quickly filled until every single square inch was covered with some type of breakfast food or a heavy tankard. Their singing reached thunderous proportions.

"Excuse me, please," I said.

Fill her plate with a pile of pancakes,
Fill her plate with a pile of pancakes,
Fill her plate with a pile of pancakes,
Early in the mornin'.

"Excuse me, please," I said a little louder. "Are these sausages and bacon vegetarian?"

The singing stopped.

"Vegetarian?" roared Jaja.

And as fast as the plates appeared, they all vanished. All except a small, lonely fruit plate and three dainty forks. Wearing a dark frown, Jaja eyed me suspiciously with his one good eye. I looked at Nimet, but she seemed just as surprised as we were.

"Kidding!" yelled Jaja.

And just like that, all the waiters burst back into hearty song.

Pour on the syrup and slather the butter,
Pour on the syrup and slather the butter,
Pour on the syrup and slather the butter,
Early in the mornin'.

The plates, platters, and tankards, enough food for a party of twenty, were back in the blink of an eye. And as the waiters filed out of the room, the last one handed Jaja a big platter with a sizable selection of everything. Jaja roared with laughter as the singing faded back into other parts of the ship.

Eat 'em up slowly and keep 'em comin',
Eat 'em up slowly and keep 'em comin',
Eat 'em up slowly and keep 'em comin',
Early in the mornin'.

"Tuck in, me hearties! No one starves on the *Jolly Rajah*. At least, not while I still draw breath. And while thar be aplenty o' places in the Biowerks Burg that sell animal flesh, this be not one o' them. No animals died to make this feast. Although we do serve eggs. Any man-o'-war worth its salt keeps a few hens below deck." And with that, Jaja took up the spatula from his platter and neatly deposited a single fried egg on the only corner of my plate that was threatening to look empty. "Missed a spot thar," he said. "Eat up! Eat up!" Jaja grew visibly happier with every bite we took.

"With all due respect," said my dad while chowing down on a vegetarian sausage, "we'll never be able to eat all of this."

Jaja replaced the sausage my dad had just devoured with one exactly like it from his platter. "Bah! Eat up! Eat up! And don't forget to save room for dessert!"

"Dessert!" I said, my mouth full of the most delicious pancakes I'd ever tasted. "Oh, these are heavenly," I moaned.

Jaja's eyes lit up appreciatively. There was no one happier than Jaja when he was serving food.

"Speakin' o' rooms. Where be you hangin' your hammocks? I only ask on account of in Grandeur, everything is billed directly to yer cabin. And before you start to worry, the *Jolly Rajah* uses one set price, very reasonable and all you can stuff in yer gob."

"We're in Whitehaven Mansions," said Dad.

"Oooh, a lovely berth, and not very far. I hope to be seein' ye here often. I get many patrons from Whitehaven Mansions. What deck ye on?"

My dad set his fork down suddenly. "Where *are* my manners! I haven't introduced myself. I'm Jack Snap, Willa's dad."

"It be me great pleasure to meet ye."

"We're in 56B," I added.

"Ye don't say," remarked Jaja, a distant look in his eye. He repeated the room number softly two or three times. "Ye don't say."

"The robot who showed us the place said there hadn't been anyone staying there since—"

"1926," finished Jaja. Dad lifted his eyebrows. "I never forget a patron," explained Jaja. "A guest Genius, she was. Brought in special to solve a great mystery. In the end, tho', no one thought much o' her solution. A good sign that—ye know the greater good is bein' served when all parties ain't satisfied. Aye. Well, I'm sure Grandeur knows what she's doin'. All misdeeds deserve a reckonin', I suppose." Dad and I exchanged a glance. This was the first time we'd heard Grandeur referred to as a woman, but not our last (and not always as a woman either, but sometimes as "old man"). "Never forget a patron." Jaja's eyes lingered on me. "A firecracker, she was. Relentless, when she had a job to do. May I inquire as to who the Idiot Genius in yer family be?" he asked sensitively.

"That would be my mom, Dr. Audrey Snap."

"Audrey. Aye. Lovely name. And I suppose ye'll be startin' Idiot school soon."

"We've just come from there," I said, nodding to Nimet.

Jaja beamed at Nimet. "Ah, a very fine family, the Simits. Ye'll find yer deck at Whitehaven filthy with fine Idiots. There's Ethan Faraday, always playin' with the electricity, that one. And Rufus Feynman, no shortage of energy there. Of course, right across yer passageway is Heathcliff Wudgepuddle. I'd keep an eye on him. Clever little devil. And then thar's the Brontë twins, Zoe and Sarah. To tell the true, they're a bit depressin' to be around for too long. But ye probably already met 'em at Idiot school, eh?"

Jaja replaced the stack of pancakes I'd just eaten. As I slathered them with butter, the friendly elefantkin used his trunk to retrieve a syrup pitcher dangling from his longer tusk and poured away. We were a concert of eating perfection. Later, after dessert, Nimet requested three wheelbarrows to get us back onto dry land.

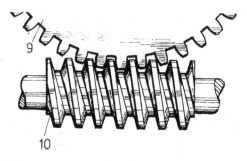

Beyond Spotless

WALKING home I kept my eyes peeled, glancing through every open window and door for more of the baristas' brewed creatures. I saw someone walking a hermit crab the size of a basketball, a foxlike cashier wearing a hat and vest, and a small winged dragon perched in a cage, preening its bright green feathers. All I kept thinking was that if Grandeur's other burgs were even half as exciting as this one, then I wanted to visit them all.

"Do brewed creatures live outside the Biowerks Burg?" I asked Nimet.

"Some. All brewed creatures outside the burgs require special papers. If they're smart enough to live on their own, I hear it gets expensive."

I steered us farther away from my dad, which wasn't hard. He tends to be one of those slow walkers you always lose track of in malls or grocery stores.

"Where do you think the dragon kitchens are?"

Nimet looked worried. "Before today, I never thought the time-traveling dragons were real."

"But we just passed the cutest little dragon in a shop window!"

"Those are pets, Willa. The time-traveling dragons in the stories are . . . quite another thing."

"Are they . . . you know, gnashing teeth, long claws, fire-breathing, wings—*rrraaaaawwwr!*—dragons?"

Nimet nodded, then pulled me away from a tall-eared creature drifting our way. "If you have any sense, Willa, you will not go to the dragon kitchens with Bertie Babbage tomorrow. Wherever they are, it'll be deep within the burg. It won't be like here, out on the fringe, where shop owners rely on the people living in Greater Grandeur for business. The deeper you venture in, well, things can get strange, even by burg standards."

I tapped my WatchitMapCallit and pulled up Grandeurpedia.

"You won't find anything about the dragons in there," said Nimet.

I sighed. "I thought Grandeurpedia was supposed to have *everything* in it."

Nimet pursed her lips. "It doesn't."

"What else is missing?"

"Oh, lots, especially things having to do with the Institute of Intellect. Can I ask you a question?"

"Always, Nimet."

"What was it like . . . meeting the Black Fez?"

I gave her a quizzical look. Had Ravenlock erred about her being from Turkey? I tried to remember what Nimet had said when she'd introduced herself in class, but I couldn't.

"I was too young to remember," Nimet explained, as though reading my mind.

"Well, for me, it was . . . completely unexpected—I'd never

been in a . . . a time bubble before. We don't have stuff like that Outside. But I guess it's commonplace here."

"It's not. People here are not encouraged to play with time."

I wondered what that meant for Professor Farsical and his time-eddy detector. Was he up to something illegal? "Hold on, don't the Black Fez police Grandeur?"

"No. We have the soothies for that."

Sooth, rhymes with *truth*. Tuppence had warned me about them. "Oooh, tell me about soothies."

"I saw some once in the Steamwerks Burg. They like to travel in groups of three. There's very little crime in Greater Grandeur. So that's good. Unless . . ."

"Unless what?"

Nimet glanced around, checking to see if anyone was within earshot. "Unless they think you might be an . . . Evil Genius." She whispered the last two words.

"That's a new one! Evil—"

"Shhh! Not so loud!"

I lowered my voice. "I can't even say their name?"

"It's bad luck."

"But I don't believe in luck, good *or* bad. Luck is like the tooth fairy, or Santa Claus."

A tremor gripped Nimet's entire body. The purple fez atop her head jiggled like a volcano about to explode. "Saint Nicholas was a real person! He lived in what is now Turkey. And he would still be there if the Italians hadn't stolen his bones!"

"The Italians stole his bones?" I said incredulously.

"Yes! They put some in the city of Bari and some in Venice."

"How do they know the bones were from the same guy?"

"Do you want to talk about the soothies or Santa Claus?"

"Um . . . soothies. Let's get back to them."

"All right, then. So if they think you're a . . . you know . . . they'll *sift* you."

There was that word again. "Newton's apple! What does that mean?"

"They use a sifting rod. It looks like a fat pen with a light at one end. When they think you're hiding information, they press the tip to your forehead, and it catalogues and analyzes every thought and memory in your brain."

"That's the creepiest thing I've ever heard that's actually real. Have you seen anyone get sifted?"

"I've read it in books and seen it in movies."

"Doesn't count. Do you *know* anyone who's been sifted?"

Nimet shook her head. "But I can tell you what happens."

I wanted to know, and I didn't want to know. "Okay . . . what happens?"

"First, it's incredibly painful. Then your memories stay scrambled for days afterward. You see, your brain is naturally a jumble, so the ordering actually mixes everything up. And if they sift you repeatedly . . . the damage becomes permanent. Oh, and it leaves a burn mark right in the middle of your forehead."

"Have you seen the mark? I mean, in person?"

"I'm not sure."

"How's that?"

"I've seen people with the word *sifted* tattooed around a mark on their foreheads. But I guess the mark itself could be a tattoo. I just don't know."

"Why would anyone do that?"

"They think it's funny, or cool. Some people are just crazy."

"This sounds like an urban legend. Maybe this 'sifting' stuff is to make people think twice about becoming Evil Geniuses."

"People don't choose to become Evil Geniuses, Willa. They're born that way."

It was a chilling idea, that people had no say in what they were. Part of me wanted to scream out and say she was wrong, that people can always change, but the more I thought about it, the more I worried she might be right.

As we emerged into Greater Grandeur, the clouds had thinned enough that I could just barely see a corner of that thing covered with propellers poking through. It glowed orange fire with the sun nearing the edge of the dome.

"What *is* that thing?" I asked Nimet.

"That's the Windwerks Burg. It floats from burg to burg, never staying in one place too long. Sometimes, it goes way up into the dome, and you won't see it for weeks until it comes back down. It arrived at the Biowerks Burg day before yesterday."

"Does it ever land?"

"I don't think it was designed to."

A shiny thing the size of my fist whizzed down the street.

"Hey, and what are those? They're *everywhere!*"

"That was a bippy bot. They come in all sizes. Most people call the smaller ones bippies, and the larger ones parcels. If you think this is bad, wait until the holidays. The gift bots alone will *amaze* you. My favorites are the bippies, like the one that just zipped past us. I use mine all the time—"

"You own a bippy?" I said, suddenly wanting one of my own. "Are they expensive?"

Nimet looked at me like she thought I might be kidding. "Well, yeah. But you already own one. They come with the apartments. Didn't anyone tell you?"

Maybe I should have listened to Mr. Nuts and Bolts' tour a little better.

"I must have missed that part. Can you show me?"

"Sure."

Back in the lobby at Whitehaven Mansions, I spotted Heathcliff's father, Dr. Wudgepuddle, at the front desk. I pointed him out to Dad and mentioned Mom and I had bumped into him earlier.

Dad flicked his fingers toward the elevator. "You two girls run along. I'll introduce myself to our new neighbor."

The elevator ride consisted of silence. Not two steps out of the Biowerks Burg, Nimet had reverted to her old self.

As we approached my apartment, the door across the hall whipped open, and there stood Heathcliff Wudgepuddle. He was only a year younger, but he was about half a foot shorter than me. At the sight of us, he pushed his oversized glasses higher up his nose and tried to smooth down his short, mousy hair. It didn't take. The smug look on his face would've almost made you think he'd been waiting for us to show up.

"Ladies," he drawled. "Wanna play?" Who calls ten- and eleven-year-olds *ladies*? "You don't have to pretend. I saw you two staring at me all through class."

Nimet's eyes widened.

"Heathcliff," I said, "you sit *behind* us."

He brushed that off with a wave of his hand. "Whatever."

"We would not play with you if you were the last boy in Grandeur," said Nimet, a bit more harshly than I thought necessary.

Was this the kind of thing Tuppence was talking about? Heathcliff was odd, even creepy-odd, but a great evil? No. Then I remembered what Jaja had said: *I'd keep an eye on him.*

"Trust me," I told Nimet, grabbing her hand. "Heathcliff, let's go."

"Really?" he squeaked. Then, in a deeper voice, "I mean, now you're talking."

I fought down the urge to vomit.

"I cannot go into a boy's apartment," Nimet whispered behind me.

I squeezed Nimet's hand tighter and dragged her into the Wudgepuddles' living room. The apartment was laid out differently than ours, kind of in reverse, and with a few rooms out of place. It was very disorienting.

"I guess your dad will be up soon. He won't mind us being in here, will he?"

"My dad?" All the color drained out of Heathcliff's face. "What's *he* doing back?" There was a sound at the door. I heard our fathers' muffled voices. "Quick, my room!"

"I cannot go into a boy's bedroom," whispered Nimet from behind me. I braced myself to haul Nimet against her will, but to tell the truth, she didn't put up much of a fight.

The apartment door opened and banged shut.

"Why are we hiding?" I hissed.

"No reason."

"Your room is much too neat," observed Nimet.

And she was right. Heathcliff's room was beyond spotless. It was immaculate. I felt like I was dirtying up the place just by leaving my shoe imprints in the carpet. I thought of my room in

Cambridge, my dad's workspace in the garage, my mom's old laboratory. Organized messes all. Mom kept a sign on her desk that read *A clean desk is a sure sign of a diseased mind.*

Another disturbing thing: Heathcliff's room was brain-themed. Artwork, models, even the screen saver on his computer all had to do with brains.

"Got brain on the brain?" I said, trying to smile and not sound like I was making fun of him.

His face lit up. "Isn't the brain fascinating? A lot of people see the brain in halves, left brain, right brain. But it's so much more! The frontal lobe, for example, is in charge of personality and emotions. Whereas the parietal lobe handles things like touch and visual perception."

I felt my eyes glazing over. Unfortunately, he was just getting wound up.

"The occipital lobe interprets color, light, and movement. The temporal lobe's job is understanding language, memory, hearing. But what's *really* cool is how small the part is that makes you *you.*"

Say what you like, Heathcliff was one seriously intense ten-year-old boy.

"In fact," he continued, "if you could extract *just* that part and transplant it into someone else's brain, you'd have room to spare. If you wanted to, you could fit a dozen people's 'experiences' into a single brain."

Now that *was* cool. "Wait, you mean like multiple personalities?"

"Not necessarily. More like the specific memories that govern the way you think."

"I see." Actually, I didn't. But I thought I saw a chance to change the subject, so I took it. "So . . . your dad works with the BrainRents?"

"Yeah, he works in the Lab." He said it in a bragging way. I shrugged, like it meant nothing to me, which it practically did. "He's in charge of the whole NPU department."

NPU, Neuro Processing Unit. Mr. Nuts and Bolts had mentioned it this morning. Something about the way the BrainRents tapped into your unused brain cells and used them like a computer chip.

I looked at Nimet to see if she was taking this in and if it meant anything to her. But now that Nimet was in a forbidden land, she'd changed, like part of her was trying out being bad. "I have never been in a boy's room before," she wondered aloud.

Something told me I needed to get her out of here, but I had a few more questions. "What does your mom do?" I asked Heathcliff.

"She worked with my dad."

"Worked? What does she do now?"

"She's been . . . put on something top secret. I can't talk about it." He was hiding something.

I moved in closer, into his personal space. "So Heathcliff, what's the *real* reason we're hiding from your dad?"

He licked his lips. "The thing is . . . he's been acting weird lately, like he's turning into someone else. He'll go into the bathroom for hours. I'll bet you he's there right now."

"What does someone do in the bathroom for hours?" I asked, both wanting and not wanting to know the answer.

"I can't figure it out," he admitted.

Nimet was now sitting on Heathcliff's bed, running her hands over the bedspread and grinning like an idiot. "I'm on a *boy's* bed."

"Aaaand it's time for us to go," I said, jumping up and pulling Nimet behind me. "See ya, Heathcliff." And out the door we went, tiptoeing down the hall. Whatever had possessed me to bring Nimet along? A craven hamster had better instincts for espionage! We'd made it halfway through the living room when the bathroom door opened and Dr. Wudgepuddle walked out.

"What are you two doing in here?" he asked.

"I invited them," Heathcliff said nervously. "We were playing in my room."

Dr. Wudgepuddle gave Heathcliff a foul look. "Oh, really."

"Is that the bathroom?" I asked.

Heathcliff's dad shot me a heart-chilling look.

"Yes, but—"

"Oh, good, 'cause we really have to go." We dashed in, closing and locking the door.

"What are we doing in here?" hissed Nimet.

I know what you're thinking. Why not just run out of the apartment? I really didn't know myself. It just *felt* like the right thing to do.

It looked like our bathroom across the hall, only with different wallpaper. "Help me look around."

I pulled on the mirror. Nothing. I turned the sinks on and off.

"Why would someone spend hours in a bathroom?"

"Willa," Nimet hissed, pointing down at our feet.

Puddles of water covered the floor. "So he's a messy hand-washer. What about it?"

Nimet opened the cabinet beneath the sink. "Tesla's coil!"

Inside was more water, a locked box, and the strangest arrangement of plumbing pipes I'd ever seen. I pulled out my notepad and started drawing them.

"What are you doing? We need to get out of here," urged Nimet. "The longer we stay—"

"I want to show my dad what these pipes look like."

"So take a picture with your WatchitMapCallit!"

"You can do that?"

Nimet pushed me aside, tapped on her wrist, and snapped a picture. "I'll send it to you. Now let's get out of here."

"Wait." I flushed the toilet and ran the water again. "Okay, now we can go."

Dr. Wudgepuddle was waiting for us, his arms folded across his chest, a scowl creasing his face. Heathcliff had shrunk back into the shadows.

"We'll just be leaving now. Bye, Heathcliff!"

I didn't look back.

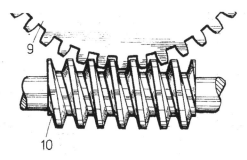

A Deadly Secret

O OH! Pretty! Your furniture is beautiful!" said Nimet as she took in our living room.

"Doesn't your place look like this?"

Nimet silently shook her head.

"It's Art Deco, 1920s, English," I said, parroting my mother. "Let's go to my room. You can meet the Magnificent Lady Grayson and tell me about the flying bippy bots. And there's something else I want to show you."

I opened my bedroom door, and Grayson—all crazy eyed—shot out screaming, "N-e-v-e-r-l-e-a-v-e!"

"Um, that was the Magnificent Lady Grayson," I said. "I guess you'll meet her later."

Nimet stepped into my room gingerly, like she was sneaking past the ropes of a museum exhibit.

"Everything all right?" I asked.

"So it's true, what Jaja says. Nothing has changed here since 1926."

"Some things are *kind* of new. I mean, I'm pretty sure all the clothes are new because it's like they've all been perfectly tailored just for us. And the food in the fridge and pantry isn't stale or spoiled, but the brands look like they're from . . . 1926, I guess."

"This building was built in 1926. Jaja says a small army of bots built it in less than a week. Things like that happen in Grandeur."

"What do you mean?"

"A whole building will appear practically overnight."

"That can't be true." I opened my closet door. "You want to try on my clothes? I saw some flapper dresses in the back."

Nimet smiled uncertainly. "Can we?"

"Oh, yes we can!"

We dove in, hauling out armloads of garments and throwing them on the bed. I even opened all the bureau drawers. We tried on everything. And I have to say, when you have red hair and striking green eyes, it turns out you can totally get away with wearing a purple fez with just about anything.

While we were dressed in fancy evening wear, Nimet crossed to the window, opened a small glass door, and retrieved a metallic ball nestled in the curve of the window ledge. She held it up for me to see. It was adorable.

"Here's your bippy. You open it like so." She turned a knob and a small hatch opened. "This one can carry about a quarter pound. Not very useful for packages, but plenty good for notes or small items. Just tell it where you want it to go, or who you want it sent to. It'll do its best to deliver it."

"A bit like an owl," I observed.

"An owl?" asked Nimet, staring at me blankly.

"Not a reader, eh?"

"Actually, I study for hours every night."

"Who are some of your favorite authors?"

"You won't have heard of them. They've all been dead for centuries—" She trailed off, looking embarrassed.

"So if I said the word Oz, you'd say . . ."

"Those were books?"

Whenever a person utters those words, somewhere a library or bookstore falls right down dead.

"Don't worry. I'll—I'll get you a copy."

"You'd better not. You're going to get me into enough trouble as it is."

I lost it. "I will get you a copy, and you will read it, and you will love it, or we can't be friends!"

Nimet stared at me like a startled puffer fish.

"I'm sorry, Nimet. I didn't mean to yell. It's just . . ."

Nimet closed up the bippy with a loud *snap!* Thankful for the distraction, I pointed to it and asked, "Do you think this one still works?"

Nimet turned it over and over like she was inspecting an apple. "Not much to go wrong, really. They use very little energy, and this one's been charging in its cradle all this time." She let go of the bippy, and it hung in the air like a balloon with just enough helium to keep it airborne.

"How do they work?" I asked.

"This type interacts with Grandeur's sphere using gravity pulleys." I shook my head and tried to look clueless. It was easy. "Okay, imagine three invisible tethers running from the bippy to the sphere that can be lengthened or shortened as necessary. All the bippy does is send the coordinates to the sphere. The sphere does all the work."

"Is that how the MiniDirigies work?"

"No, they use a completely different technology."

"It's like magic." *Not that I believe in magic.*

Nimet nodded her head. "Yes. Not understanding how something works can add an air of mystery."

"Now let me show *you* something." I fetched the Clockwerk Boy's memory book from its hiding place. Nimet gasped when she saw it.

"Is that . . ." She leafed through the first few pages. "This is a memory book! Did you get this from the Clockwerk Boy you were talking about with Bertie Babbage?"

"Yes. What kind of symbols are those?"

"Pictograph binary, generated with a mainspring-mechanical rotor cipher to boot. Uncrackable. Unless you've got the key."

"Yeah, I was afraid you might say something like that."

"But if you had the Clockwerk's internal codes, I bet Bertie Babbage and CeeCee could reverse-engineer a matching mainspring-mechanical rotor cipher to decode it."

"Yeah, whatever you said. The thing is, I don't know how to find the Clockwerk who gave me this."

"Wait a minute! Is this from the same Clockwerk that ran down on a MiniDirigy this morning?"

"You heard about that?"

"A Clockwerk running down in Greater Grandeur is big news."

"And why's that?"

"Well, a Clockwerk *knows* when its mainspring is winding down. It would be like one of us forgetting to eat for a week until we fell into a coma. The report said he was a very old model. Maybe his gears are missing a few teeth."

Nimet flipped back to the beginning of the book. "Have you read the message?"

"There's a message?"

"Yes, in English. Listen."

Dear Ms. Snap:

    I must speak with you at your earliest convenience. I'm in the employ of the Blasted Dragon. On Sundays you can find me in the billiards hall there. I will not

*remember you, or anything about you,
until I read this memory book. Simply
place it before my eyes. You are the only
one I can trust to do the right thing.
Much depends upon your actions. Your
timeline is running out.*

Nimet closed the book and handed it back to me. I returned it to its hiding place under the sweaters.

"Not exactly cheery," said Nimet. "What are you going to do?"

"Go to the Blasted Dragon, I suspect. Have you heard of it?"

"It's an inn, located in the heart of the Biowerks Burg. I've only seen it in pictures—very unusual architecture. It's *not* a safe place."

"I was afraid you might say something like that. Want to come with me?"

"No!"

Sometimes, you have to know when to go all in. And I knew in my heart this was one of those times.

"I have a secret, Nimet."

Nimet groaned. "I'm very bad with secrets."

"Hear me out." I then told Nimet everything that had happened on the MiniDirigy: the Clockwerk Boy, Tuppence, the cane, everything.

"*You must sacrifice yourself to right the wrong,*" Nimet repeated. "First the Clockwerk Boy, then Bertie Babbage."

"Do you think the dragon kitchens are in the Blasted Dragon?"

"It's a good bet. But you should not go. Not by yourself. And definitely not with Bertie Babbage."

"I don't see as I have a choice. All paths lead back to the Blasted Dragon. You heard what the Clockwerk Boy said! My timeline's in danger!"

"I can't believe you met a mettle man. I have lived here nearly all my life and never even seen one. And you—on your first day!" Nimet pressed a button on the Clockwerk cane and it grew to its full size. "This is quality work, Willa. I've never seen craftsmanship this good. Not even in museums."

"He said he thought I'd need it more than him."

"Sounds ominous." Nimet shrank the cane down and handed it to me.

"Come with me to the Blasted Dragon," I begged.

"No, Willa."

We sat in silence for a long time.

"I have a secret, too," said Nimet.

"Ooh! I love secrets!"

"Mine is a terrible secret."

"Those are the best kind. I'm good at figuring them out, too. So you might as well get it over with and tell me all about it now."

Nimet's face filled with horror.

"Nimet, what's wrong?"

"Promise me you won't try and find out!"

"Why not?"

"Because . . . if you knew . . . I'd have to kill you."

"What?!" At first, I thought Nimet must be kidding around, but the look of pure terror on her face changed my mind. "I see." I gulped. "Okay, new plan. You keep that one to yourself, and we don't ever talk about this again."

"I wish it were that easy."

"What's the trouble?"

"The trouble is . . . *I'm* very bad at *keeping* secrets."

"Nimet, I gotta tell ya. That's one doozy of a combo. Is this why you don't have any friends? Because if you told one of them your secret you'd have to kill them? Or have you been—" I couldn't finish the thought.

Nimet began to cry. "No, Willa, I haven't killed anyone, if that's what you're thinking. *You* were my very first friend!"

The Magnificent Lady Grayson, hearing Nimet's distress, pushed open the door I thought was locked, jumped into Nimet's lap, and purred violently while showing her famed silky white underbelly.

"Am, Nimet. I *am* your very first friend. Now listen to me. We'll work around this. We're going to stay friends. I promise."

"But what if I talk in my sleep?"

"Sleepovers are off limits!"

"What if it slips out in little pieces, and you slowly put it all together?"

"Not gonna happen," I said with all the conviction I could muster, even though, deep down, I felt none of it. What can I say? I *love* secrets. Sooner or later I was going to figure it out.

"But you said you loved secrets. And that you are good at figuring them out!"

"Idle boasting," I lied. "I, um, was just trying to—trying to—impress you? Nimet, is there any possibility you're blowing this out of proportion? I mean, you're ten. How could you have a secret so important you'd have to kill me?"

Grayson looked up at me and mouthed, *Say what?*

"It's a *family* secret," said Nimet in a whisper before her eyes grew wide and she slapped both hands over her mouth.

I leapt onto the bed, covered my ears, and chanted, "La, la, la—not listening—la, la, la."

After Nimet went home, I decided the best thing was to push Nimet's family secret as far out of my mind as possible. So I sat on my bed with Grayson, and we ran some of the tutorials on our WatchitMapCallits until dinner. It was amazing all the things it could do. In camouflage-mode, it was nearly invisible. In ranger danger-mode it could warn you about something, like *Incoming falcon—10 o'clock high!* Which can come in handy if your nemesis has stolen a Norse god's feather cloak, transformed himself into a falcon, and become intent on shutting down the World Mill, grinding to a halt the change of seasons and possibly time itself. Not that . . . you should worry about things like that happening. Um . . . it can also translate gerbil . . . and neutralize most liquid poisons by breaking down their chemical compositions using laser beams. *Pew! Pew!* Imagine that!

"So what are you going to do about the Blasted Dragon?" asked Grayson.

"Hold on. Were you eavesdropping at my door?"

"I'm a cat. I don't have to loiter by closed doors to eavesdrop." Grayson pointed to her ears. "Have you noticed how big these things are? I can hear a squirrel flip the safety off a Smith & Blazooski mini stun cannon at nine hundred pounces, downwind."

A few days ago I would've doubted that. "How long's a pounce?"

"Old World or New?"

CHAPTER ELEVEN

"New?"

"Ninety-six paws." I stared at her like an Idiot. "Eight feet."

Something told me Old World versus New was a rabbit hole I didn't want to dive down right now.

"Do you think Nimet's dangerous?"

"I don't think she's going to kill me, if that's what you mean. I think she's just a little confused."

"I would go with you to the Blasted Dragon."

"No. I'm not taking you into a burg until I have a better idea of how things work around here."

Grayson growled in disgust and showed me her tail.

"Attractive."

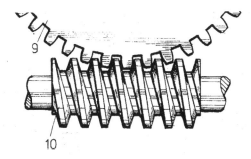

The House of Gear

A ROUND six o'clock, Mom conference called us on our WatchitMapCallits to say she was headed home with Chinese carryout. I wasn't sure I'd be able to eat another thing, but once she arrived, it smelled so good I couldn't say no.

While Dad opened the steaming food containers, I laid out plates, chopsticks, napkins, and glasses. In the living room, Mom regaled us with stories about her amazing new laboratory and the things she would be able to do there. During the few moments we caught her chewing, we sandwiched in snippets of our foray into the Biowerks Burg and our lunch at the Jolly Rajah Man-o'-War o' Pancakes. We'd just gotten to the part about the fruit plate when the wall screen in the living room lit up and began ringing. Bright blue words flashed: *Incoming call for Jack Snap.*

Dad wasn't sure what to do. Neither was I. My mom said, "Just say hello to it, dear."

"Hello?" said Dad.

Suddenly, a scruffy-looking man appeared. He sat behind a cluttered desk in the middle of a very messy shop. Half-opened boxes with metal pipes and faucet fixtures littered the room. Part of one wall was covered with computer tablets.

"Mr.—" He glanced down at a tablet in his hand. "Snap, is it?"

"Yes. How can I help you?"

"Oh, I can see you're eating. Should I call back at another time?"

"No, this is fine."

"Good. Well, my name is Angus Witkowski and I'm the dispatcher for Quick as That Plumbing. I've been alerted that you're available for jobs. Is that correct?"

"Yes."

"Well, I wouldn't normally have called you at this hour for your first job, but I'm short at the moment, and I've got an emergency at a very important customer's house."

"I'd like to help, but I don't have my tools. We just arrived in Grandeur this morning."

"Not a problem! I can have a TeenyWeeny at your place in no time flat. Nothing's far in Grandeur." Angus smiled hopefully.

Dad's eyebrows shot up. "A TeenyWeeny?"

"Oh, right. First day and all. A TeenyWeeny MiniDirigy, fully stocked with pipe, tools, and torches. I've worked with plumbers fresh from Outside before. You'll do fine. There's no code to worry about on this one. Gear Hall is as old as Grandeur itself. The only problem's going to be the size of the place. I hate to send you out all alone. Even havin' a runner for the TeenyWeeny would help. You got anyone you could take along?"

Dad looked over to Mom, and she smiled. "Your first job."

I plugged *Gear Hall* into Grandeurpedia.

The sprawling estates of the family Widder-chine, located in the heart of the Clockwerk Burg, include Gear Hall, Mainspring Manor, and the Machinery. In addition to being Grandeur's finest example of a Clockwerk manor house, Mainspring Manor contains the largest Clockwerk museum located anywhere. The second-largest Clockwerk museum is located, not surprisingly, at Gear Hall.

I raised my hand. "Ooh! Ooh! I'll be your wrench monkey!"

Dad turned back to Angus. "Looks like I'm your man."

"Great! I'll have the TeenyWeeny in front of"—he glanced at the tablet again—"Whitehaven Mansions in a jiffy. Nice digs." And then the screen went dark. But before it went completely black, something strange happened. At least, I think it happened. You see, as the image of Angus got darker and darker, I could've sworn he morphed into Tuppence, the mettle man I'd met on the MiniDirigy that morning. I even thought she winked at me.

"Did you see that?" I asked.

Mom and Dad looked up from their plates. "See what?"

"Oh, nothing."

The TeenyWeeny was a teeny-weenier version of a Mini-Dirigy, about the same size as Dad's old van. Like its larger cousin, it had a long cigar-shaped thing on top, which extended over each bumper by a good three feet. Dad reached up and rapped his knuckles on the cigar-shaped thing. It sounded hollow.

"So this is what replaces tires?" he said, looking at me.

"Doesn't seem very likely, does it?"

"During the Age of Sail, when John Ericsson invented the marine screw propeller and piloted his ship, the *Robert F. Stockton,* around the river Thames, the local watermen renamed it the *Flying Devil.*"

I made the sign of the cross. "'Tis a DevilDirigy, I say!"

Dad always laughs at my jokes. Either that, or he likes my Scottish accent.

Opening the rear door, we inspected the tools. It was the same stuff he carried around in his van back home. Plumbing technology, apparently, is eternal.

The front seat wasn't very different either, only there were no controls for the driver. The instant we buckled our seat belts, the TeenyWeeny came to life and lifted into the cool night air. On the dash, a big map showed where we were.

From the air, the Biowerks Burg looked eerie—something about the color of the lights. Farther out, I could see more odd patches. Other burgs, I guessed. Some were darker. Some were brighter. The largest lay under a thick blanket of smog or steam.

"Dad, Mom was an only child, right?"

"That's right."

"And her parents died when she was young?"

"Right again."

"And you met her at some boat festival?"

Dad smiled. "It was a couple months before the festival. I was out for a run and just about to cross the Mass. Ave. Bridge when, suddenly, there was your mother, paddling along the shoreline with a bunch of other people in a long wooden boat."

"But you only noticed Mom."

"Well, she does stand out in a crowd. So I followed the boat back to the MIT boathouse. Turned out she was part of a team raising money for Broken Whiskers Pet Hospital. I signed on that day. One thing led to another."

"And she grew up there? Her whole life, I mean?"

"No. She grew up across the river, in Boston." Dad thought for a moment. "That's funny. I can't remember the neighborhood. She'll tell you, though. If you really want to know. Why do you ask?"

I hesitated. "Dad . . . did you ever get the feeling that Mom was from someplace else?"

Dad turned and gave me a very serious look. "Every day, Willa, every day."

The TeenyWeeny began descending—straight into a dark burg filled with trees. I checked the map.

"The Clockwerk Burg."

"Angus wasn't kidding! Nothing's far in Grandeur."

Then, together, we said, "Whoa!"

From the center of the burg, looming like a brick castle, was a vast industrial site. Towering brick turrets rose out of a glowing haze.

"That's the Machinery," I said, checking the map. "And those mansions on either side must be the rival houses Widderchine: Mainspring Manor and Gear Hall."

"Rival?"

"According to Grandeurpedia, they've been feuding for centuries."

"Did it say why?"

"Nope."

The upper stories of both houses soared above the tree canopy. Lanterns flickered on every balcony.

"'Mainspring Manor is a classic Clockwerk manor house,'" I read from my WatchitMapCallit. "'Moved brick by brick from Grandeur Abbey, Somewhere Northeast of London.' It says here they use no technology newer than fifth century. Wow! That was a really long time ago."

"Grandeur was in England?"

"Grandeur *Abbey* was in England. They dropped the *Abbey* part when they moved everything here in . . . hold on . . . 1375 CE."

"Willa, I'm getting the feeling that even back then, they were ahead of everybody else."

"Yeah, I guess so."

The TeenyWeeny banked in the direction of Gear Hall, toward a walled-in courtyard that looked like it was tailor-made for dirigy landings.

"Look!" I said. "Someone's down there."

Standing by a gate was a young boy holding a light. The Teeny-Weeny set down silently, and the map went dark. Dad grabbed a tool belt from behind the seats, and we hopped out.

But it wasn't until the boy was right next to us that I noticed he wasn't a normal boy. He was a Clockwerk Boy, but smaller and newer looking than the one I'd seen this morning. The light from his torch flickered like a flame, but the whirr of a slowly unwinding spring gave away the trick.

"Can I help you with your bags, sir?" he piped.

Dad loaded him up, then handed a few things to me.

"Do you have a name?" Dad asked.

"You may call me Glym Jack, if it pleases you. I'll be your linkboy tonight."

I dove into Grandeurpedia and entered *linkboy*.

link·boy \lĭngk′boi′\ *noun*

a boy who carried a flaming torch to light the way for pedestrians at night. In the language of thieves, or *thieves cant*, they were called Glym Jacks or mooncursers, the latter because their services weren't needed on moonlit nights. First known use of *linkboy* 1652.

"Glym Jack . . . way cool," I said under my breath.

"Why, thank you, miss," he said in his flutey voice. "Are you the plumbers?"

Considering the tools we were carrying and the TeenyWeeny with *Quick as That Plumbing* plastered on the side, I guess it's safe to say there are Clockwerk Idiots, too.

Glym Jack guided us into the manor through dimly lit corridors and past shadowy rooms. This part of the house was drab and smelly.

"Do you hear that?" asked my dad.

There was a low grinding sound, coming seemingly from everywhere and nowhere.

"I do. I can feel it in the floor, too."

I stopped and pressed my palm against the wall. Sure enough, the entire house was faintly rumbling. I was just starting to wish I hadn't asked to come along when Glym Jack opened a door and we entered a room that would have been right at home in Buckingham Palace, only maybe three hundred years ago. A butler, dressed in tailcoat and white gloves, was there to take over.

"Right this way, sir," he said, nodding. "The door we came

through blended with the wall so well that, once closed, it vanished from view. The bad smells faded, replaced by those of furniture polish, candle wax, and high-quality machine oil.

"What's that sound?" I asked the butler.

He paused to listen. "Sound? What sound?"

If it had been the sun hanging over us in the middle of a desert, it wouldn't have been more noticeable. Dad and I exchanged worried looks.

Then, laughing at himself, the butler said, "Oh, you mean *that* sound! Those are the winding stations. Once you've been here long enough, you stop noticing the noise. The stations are posted throughout the house and grounds." He stepped over to what looked like a bank of old wooden phone booths, the kind you might find in the lobby of an ancient hotel, and opened a door. We peeked inside. Except for a gear-toothed nub sticking out from the back of the wall, and a lever toward the front, it was completely empty. He gave the lever a push, and the gear nub began to turn.

"Clockwerks use these to keep themselves properly wound," he explained. "The winding stations at Gear Hall run every minute of every hour of every day."

He shut the door and guided us through a grand foyer, saying something about being discreet and not going anywhere we weren't supposed to, blah, blah, blah, whatever. I'm not sure what else because my face was plastered to a glass display case. Inside of it was a BrainBox. A brass plaque on the outside read:

Torsicus Widderchine's BrainBox
fabricated by Thiphania Widderchine
(circa 1216)

There were more brass plaques inside, displaying computing power, rpm, stuff like that. But before I could take it all in, Dad came hustling back and ushered me up a wide staircase. If they had any elevators, they didn't want *us* using them.

The sink in question was on the sixth floor in a tiny hall bathroom. Dad didn't have to look for more than a few seconds before he asked to see the basement. Seven floors down, it smelled like an entire grocery store of eggs had gone bad.

"Looks like you have a much bigger problem down here," Dad told the butler. He offered me his handkerchief, but I'd already buried my nose in the crook of my elbow.

The butler was immediately defensive. "I can assure you it was not like this earlier today."

Dad shone a small flashlight onto a pipe with a big hole in it. "Looks like someone's been pouring some strong stuff down your pipes. It's been pooling in this bend here and finally eaten its way through. I can patch this up tonight, but you should have your main pipes inspected as soon as you can. Before I seal it up, though, I'd like to drag some chain down here from that bathroom upstairs."

I don't understand most of Dad's plumbing talk, but I'd heard him talk about dragging chains through the pipes of really old houses to break up rust deposits. Lucky for me, I got stationed upstairs. My job was to make sure the chains came off the spool and made it down the drain without getting tangled. After that, all I had to do was wait around until he'd patched the big pipe in the basement.

Did I mention how bad I am at sitting around doing nothing? Besides, Tuppence had obviously set this up. She wanted me here for a reason.

I crept down a dim hallway, listening briefly at each door I passed. This part of the mansion was either vacant or filled with early-to-bed types. I'd listened at about ten doors when I heard some voices echoing in what must have been a cavernous room down the hall. I padded along as quietly as I could, stopping beside a door left slightly ajar.

"What's taking so long this time?" demanded a Clockwerk-sounding voice.

"Every person's brain is different, Wyrmgear. Some are easier to crack than others. You know that!" a man replied. "Rest assured. I'll have it soon enough."

I recognized the voice. It was Dr. Quimby Wudgepuddle, Heathcliff's dad! I was certain of it.

"What's wrong with the old-fashioned way?" said a third voice that sounded like a woman. "Every human has its price."

"The best way is to pluck it out of her brain without her ever suspecting," said Wudgepuddle. "Don't you worry your gears, I'll get it one way or the other. I always have, haven't I? Just a few more days! Now, about this Clockwerk. Have you found it?"

After a long pause, the woman said, "Tell him, Wyrmgear."

"We're still looking into it. But we think, by your description, that it was a free Clockwerk hired for the party that night."

"It was asking a lot of questions," said Wudgepuddle. "It was snooping. If it talks, we'll all be sent to Delusion before the day is out!"

"Need I remind you Clockwerks are not sent to Delusion, Doctor?" said the woman slowly. "Clockwerks are . . . dismantled."

"Either way, I insist you destroy that BrainBox!"

A low rumble shook the house. "Have you lost your mind?" roared the woman. "A properly working BrainBox is a precious thing! And if this one is as old as you describe, doubly so. Besides, his memory has surely reset by now. There's nothing to fear. Whatever it once knew is gone."

"Did you hear an older Clockwerk wound down in a Mini-Dirigy today? Have you looked into it?"

"It may be big news when a Clockwerk winds down in Greater Grandeur, but I can assure you it's more common than you know. And *old* can mean anything. Is fifty years old to you? Because it isn't to me," said Wyrmgear.

"Fine," grumbled Wudgepuddle. "I'll look into it myself."

"That won't be necessary," the woman assured him. "Wyrmgear will look into it. He'll leave no gear unturned. Isn't that so, Wyrmgear?"

Wyrmgear made a gear-gnashing sound.

"How does a Clockwerk infiltrate your household in the first place? Don't you have enough Clockwerks of your own?"

"We only employ Clockwerks of integrity at Gear Hall," sniffed Wyrmgear. "A free Clockwerk of high standing doesn't have to explain itself to anyone."

"I don't like this. How do you even know it was free?"

"We don't," conceded the woman. "The official registry was destroyed in the Great Fire of 1926."

"My point exactly," said Wudgepuddle.

I angled my head, trying to see what else was in the room. It was a library, that much was clear, with cast-iron stairs and railings, and levels of books going down, down, down, as far as I could see.

"What about—" continued Wudgepuddle, "I read something once about Clockwerk memories . . . lingering in the metal of their gears."

Wyrmgear laughed. "Within the metal itself? Preposterous! Here's what I will do. When I find this mysterious Clockwerk, I will have its BrainBox removed and placed into one of our vaults. Time means less to me than to you. Would a hundred years suffice?"

"That would be *very* satisfactory," said Wudgepuddle, sounding much relieved. "We can't afford any missteps when the stakes are this high."

"About that," said the woman. "A laboratory of unlimited size that could be hidden in the wink of an eye? I could make Gear Hall great again with something like that. Are you certain your intelligence is correct?"

"Has my intelligence ever been wrong before?" huffed Wudgepuddle.

"But can we really trust it?" asked Wyrmgear. "I mean, after all, a device that can hold vast amounts of real estate in something the size of a handbag?"

I gasped.

"What was that?" asked Wudgepuddle.

"Follow me!" said Wyrmgear, and I heard footsteps pounding up the steps.

I tried to run back to the bathroom, thinking I'd just play dumb, but I must have gotten turned around in the crazy maze they call Gear Hall. I was paused at a corner that looked suspiciously familiar when I heard Wyrmgear's voice moving in my direction. Two quick turns later and I found myself trapped in a dead end with four closed doors. The first was locked. So was the second. I lunged for the third doorknob just as it retreated, causing me to stumble and fall forward. That's when I saw it, through the widening crack: an eye staring back at me.

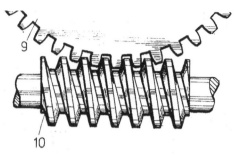

The Eye in the Door

A THIN white hand grabbed my wrist and pulled me into the room. The door slammed shut. It's a miracle I didn't scream bloody murder. As my eyes adjusted to the candlelight, I spun around looking for the hand's owner. I saw blueprints, lots of them. I saw shelves, a bed, bins, all covered or filled with every manner of spring, spindle, and gear imaginable. But the thing that really grabbed my attention was the gigantic kinetic sculpture taking up easily a third of the room.

Suddenly, a girl a little taller than me stepped into view. Black hair framed her pale face. She was dressed like a goth girl—all black lace and velvet—only with a clockpunk twist.

She gulped. That's when I realized she was as startled as I was, maybe even more so.

"Hello," she said, then quickly looked away, as if doubting whether or not *hello* was the right thing to say.

"Hi," I said. "Thanks. I'm here with my dad—um, we're here to fix your sink? But I kind of got lost, and then someone started chasing me, and . . . and . . ." And I ran out of things to say.

A hopeful spark glowed in her sad eyes. "I'm Tiffany," she said. "Tiffany Widderchine. I live here. This is my room. Do you like it? I'm allowed to decorate it myself . . . within reason, I mean. Not *my* reason, of course." Anger flared across her brow, and her voice changed. "We can't have that, can we. Because as everyone knows: too much free will can be a dangerous—"

"I'm Willa," I said, fighting back the urge to make a run for it. "I'm . . . the plumber's helper."

Tiffany's eyes filled with pity. "Oh. I see. You're an Idiot. Tell me, what's it like to have an Idiot for a father?" She didn't say it the least bit meanly, so I tried my best not to take it that way.

"What makes you think my dad's an Idiot?"

"Well, he's a plumber," said Tiffany, as if that was all the explanation needed.

"Are you saying there aren't any Genius plumbers?"

"Oh, I'm sure there are, somewhere, just not in Grandeur." Tiffany's eyes suddenly grew large. "You're from Outside!"

She circled me slowly, staring like I was some kind of mad squirrel, strapped into the cockpit of a stolen 400-ton Robo-Troll, uprooting trees in Central Park, seconds away from simultaneously breaking the Mid-Atlantic Faerie Treaty of 1764 and waking the most dangerous band of excommunicated two-headed giants ever imprisoned in the New World. . . .

Um, not that anything like that happens a few months from now, mind you. It's a total hypothetical. In the meantime, though, don't go digging around aimlessly in Central Park, okay?

"Yes," I said. "We arrived this morning. But getting back to my dad. I'm not saying he's a Genius or anything—far from it—but if he was, just for the sake of argument, then wouldn't he be a Genius plumber?"

"Well, technically," she began. "I mean, I understand what you're trying to say. But if that were the case, then your dad wouldn't be a plumber so much as he'd be an *ex*-plumber."

"I see," I said.

"No, you don't," corrected Tiffany.

"You got me there," I admitted. This conversation was going nowhere. "So what's this thing?" I asked, pointing to the huge kinetic sculpture in the room. Maybe you know kinetic from science class? It means moving—in this case, a slow-motion ballet of turning spindles and gears.

Tiffany's eyes danced. "Oh, that? It's nothing, really. Just a small detail of a larger project I'm working on. I like to build working models before they're shrunk down. It helps me see things I might otherwise miss."

It was large, all right, and crammed with gears and springs and rods. A heavy brass framework held it all together. "It must weigh a thousand pounds," I said.

Tiffany nodded. "Closer to fifteen hundred, I think."

"Does it run on electricity?"

"No. This machine runs off a standard #9 mainspring," said Tiffany.

"That's gotta be some spring!"

"It is. But you wouldn't know about the mainsprings we have in Grandeur. They still haven't been invented, Outside."

That kind of thing—inventions developing in Grandeur that aren't duplicated Outside—happens more often than you might think. You see, some ideas are inevitable, but most dangle from a tenuous thread attached to a single person's thought. It's mind-boggling, really, to contemplate how many new inventions have been lost to the distraction of a telephone call, to not being jotted down, or even to a fiendish cat who doesn't want your mother dragged off to a hidden city located Somewhere in the Southwest of America. And once an idea is lost, there's no guarantee that anyone else will *ever* think it again—EVER. So next time you have a really great idea, make sure you write it down!

"Every Clockwerk mainspring in Grandeur is based directly on the one invented by Mermadak Widderchine," continued Tiffany. "They're thousands of times more powerful than anything ever attempted Outside and can be made quite small, too."

"He ended up in Grandeur because he made a spring?" I asked.

"No. It was his mother who got him trapped in Grandeur."

"I can relate."

"You mentioned electricity. Well, Clockwerks require a lot of winding, more than can be done by hand. In the old world, we used waterwheels. But Grandeur has no rivers. So we rely on the Dieselwerks and Steamwerks Burgs to keep the winding stations turning. Almost all the burgs, to some degree or another, have their little cheats. But we all do our best to keep them underground or out of sight."

She sat down on the floor and pulled a lever, setting off a chain reaction of increased activity in her . . . project. "Watch this." A kind of life pulsed through the machine, some areas speeding up, others slowing down. It reminded me of the Rube Goldberg machines my science teacher, Mrs. Gabo, assigned my class to design. Only this one was real.

I sat down beside Tiffany.

"You built this all by yourself?" I asked.

She stared intently into the maelstrom of brass activity. "Yes."

"What does it . . . do?"

Tiffany tilted her head ever so slightly and looked at me through the corners of her eyes. "It's thinking," she whispered, and the odd smile that lingered on her face made a shiver go down my spine. "But just a little bit. Can you tell what?"

I looked into the sea of spinning gears, hoping for clues. "Are you saying this is a Clockwerk person's mind?"

"Sort of. It's a tiny part of a BrainBox—a module to be precise. But it's not *made* to look like one. I've disguised it. So *they* won't notice. This project is an experiment to improve vision processing."

"Oh, yeah," I said, nodding as if I understood. But she saw right through me—Geniuses are good at that, and I should have known better.

Tiffany sighed. "It's nothing to be ashamed of."

"What?"

"You know. Being an Idiot."

"I'm not the least bit ashamed," I said. And I meant it.

"Of course you're not," said Tiffany. But the way she said it sounded more like, "Of course you are." As if that wasn't bad enough, I could hear traces of my mother's voice in her tone.

"Do you disguise *all* your projects?" I asked, trying to get back to the machine.

"Only for the last few years."

I thought back to the Clockwerk Boy's huge eyes. How did he recognize people without electronic cameras and powerful computers? Suddenly, I was very interested in vision processing, even though I knew I wouldn't understand it. I took the bait.

"So," I began, trying not to sound too interested, "how *do* Clockwerks see?"

Tiffany studied me warily, as if trying to judge how serious I was. "Do you know how a DLP projector works?"

"A what?"

"A Digital Light Processing projector," she said slowly, like I was an Idiot. "DLP. They use them to project movies onto theater screens. You've been to a movie theater, right?"

"Yes, of course. Don't be silly! Everyone's been to a movie theater!"

Tiffany's face froze, and that sadness behind her eyes shut me right up.

"Not everyone has time, you know," she said testily. "Some people have things to do, equations to solve, Clockwerks to build."

"Right," I said softly. "How stupid of me. Maybe we could catch a matinee some afternoon."

That caught her off guard.

"You mean . . . at the same time?"

"Yes, sitting in adjacent seats, eating popcorn out of the same tub."

She hesitated, started to say something, then stopped. "So, haven't you ever wondered how it works?" she asked finally.

"How what works?"

"The DLP projector that makes the movie!"

"Oh, no, never. Give me some popcorn, maybe a box of Junior

Mints, and my brain is yours for three hours or less."

Tiffany laughed. "It's really very simple. Imagine a laser shining bright white light onto a mirror. The light bounces off the mirror, goes through a lens, and lands on the big screen."

"How do you know about lasers?" I interrupted.

"Just because I don't use a technology doesn't mean I don't know about it. Now, back to the big light shining on a mirror. Are you imagining it? Feel free to close your eyes if it helps."

I closed my eyes. "Okay, but movies aren't all white. Some parts are in color, or black." Tiffany said nothing. "So what about those parts?" More silence. I cracked an eyelid. "Hey, I thought you said you were going to tell me."

"Oh, I'm sorry," she said in mock surprise. "Are you saying you're interested in how a DLP projector works?"

I sooo wanted to say no. But I couldn't *now*. "All right. I suppose I deserved that. Hit me with it."

"Well," began Tiffany, "imagine the mirror is really composed of millions of little tiny mirrors, each one of which can be angled off independently to one side. In fact, imagine they can be angled away and back thousands of times in the span of a single second, and by doing so, fool your eye into thinking it's seeing any one of a million shades of gray."

I opened my eyes. "You lie!"

Tiffany gave me a troubled look. "No. Why would I lie? I'm telling you how a DLP—"

"Right! My bad. Continue."

Tiffany furrowed her brow at me, looking puzzled and more than a little vexed. "All right. So imagine all the mirrors were pointing away at once. The movie theater would then go completely—"

"Black!" I shouted. Tiffany clapped. "But what about the color part?" I asked.

"Easy. But the next part is a little technical."

"Pile it on. My mother's an Idiot Genius."

Tiffany's glee evaporated, her mind careening off to some unpleasant place. "Someday . . . you must tell me what that's like."

I nodded, but from the look I was getting I was thinking that day would probably be never.

"Color?" I prompted, cautiously.

"What?" she said.

"The DLP projector?"

"Oh, of course. Now who's the Idiot, right?" I smiled. "Well, you see, the human eye can detect a flash as short as a 300th of a second, but movies are delivered at a much slower rate, traditionally flashing a new image every 24th of a second. Nothing is really moving, you know. It's the brain that puts all those still images together so that it *looks* like everything's in motion." That much I knew. "Now, a 24th of a second may not sound like much to *you*, but to a machine it's an age. A machine can do an awful lot of things during a 24th of a second."

"But how does it make color?" I asked again.

"I'm getting to that," said Tiffany patiently. "After the light bounces off the mirror, but before it's left the projector and gone to the screen, it passes through a high-speed spinning disk filled with different wedges of color, one wedge being clear, of course."

"Of course," I said. "Otherwise you couldn't have white."

"Precisely! The tiny mirrors are the key. Even though the color disc is spinning crazy fast, the little mirrors are faster. Way faster. And they can hit any color on that disc they want. A little blue here, a little green there. And remember, those little mirrors can twitch away so fast that they can make any shade of that color they want to."

"You lie!"

Tiffany's eye twitched. "Stop . . . saying that."

"I'm sorry," I said. "It's just that you sound like you're making this up off the top of your head."

"I promise you I'm not."

"Okay, but how does this relate to how a Clockwerk person sees? Clockwerk people don't have lasers shooting out of their eyes."

"Exactly true! But you've nearly got it, don't you see?"

I thought. Hard. "Nope."

"Reverse it! The big movie screen is the world. Light from the sun or a lamp bounces off the world, through the lens, and onto the millions of tiny mirrors that then project onto a very, very tiny array of metal that reacts differently depending on what hits it. The metal triggers different gears depending on the different type of light—and presto! A three-dimensional matrix of the world is formed."

"Einstein's hair! I see it! But wouldn't recording all those bits of light need *tons* of memory? I thought Clockwerks didn't have much in the way of storage."

"That's true, a Clockwerk's eyes *do* generate a lot of information, but the Clockwerk doesn't have to save all of it to see where it's going or remember where it's been. And when it *does* decide to save something, it only needs to take a little snapshot. Think about it. We're not all that different. Nobody remembers EVERY-

THING they see."

"You haven't met my mom."

Tiffany grimaced. "Mothers . . . where would we be without them?"

"I wouldn't be here, I can tell you that."

"Oh, Willa, and just so you know: Here in the Clockwerk Burg, it's considered extremely rude to say things like *Clockwerk people*, when referring to sentient Clockwerks. Sentience isn't confined to two arms, two legs, and a head. Here it comes in all shapes and sizes. Personally, I believe the final decision on what is and what is not sentient should be left to the Clockwerks. Do you agree?"

I got the weird feeling my answer to this question would make or break any chance of friendship I would have with this odd girl. It was a difficult moment. Tiffany had obviously given this subject a great deal of thought. But this was the first time I'd thought about it. The only thing I knew for certain was that I didn't want to start our friendship based on a lie. Fortunately, without thought or hesitation, my heart knew exactly what to say.

"Wholeheartedly," I said.

The look on her face told me she would need more than words from me, but that it was a good start.

"One more thing," she said. "You might want to lose that 'Einstein's hair' thing. You're not going to win over any Geniuses using that one."

"What's wrong with Einstein's hair?"

"Well . . . he was an . . . an Idiot, you know."

"HE WAS NOT! Einstein was a genius! One of the very best!"

Tiffany looked at me like I was a puppy who needed its head

patted. "Outside, Willa, Outside. But not in Grandeur. You see, Einstein's IQ was only 159."

"IT WAS NOT! His IQ was 160. I've heard my mother say it a gazillion times. And in Grandeur that *still* makes him a Genius!"

Tiffany shook her head sadly. "A common rounding error, Willa, among Idiots, at least. We don't *round* things here in Grandeur. That's how he escaped the notice of the Black Fez. But to call him one of the best? He's directly responsible for the creation of the atom bomb! What could be more Idiotic than that?"

It was as if the ground beneath my feet had begun to shake.

"If you'd thought up the atomic bomb," she continued, "would you have told anyone else? Well, would you have?"

"I—I—"

"Exactly. If anything, he was an Idiot Idiot."

That was going too far. Einstein was a Genius, with a capital G. I was about to go all $E = MC^2$ when suddenly the door burst open and a tall Clockwerk stepped through the doorway. His eyes swept the room, landing on me.

"Who are you?" he demanded, and I recognized Wyrmgear, the Clockwerk I'd overheard in the library. "How did you get in here?"

Tiffany leapt to her feet and shot between us. "What happened to knocking, GrandClock?" she snapped. "You're supposed to knock before you come into my room. It's one of the *rules*."

GrandClock, she called him. Like Grandfather? Was it common in the Clockwerk Burg to have sentient Clockwerks in one's family tree? It was a question that would have to wait.

Wyrmgear sprang back, but he couldn't take his big eyes off me. "You," he said, pointing. "Out!"

"She's the plumber's helper," said Tiffany. "I found her . . . wandering the hall. And I invited her to my room. Now it's *you* who need to leave." Wyrmgear hesitated. "I'm allowed to have friends now." A terrible chill infused Tiffany's voice. "Mother said so."

Wyrmgear danced backward mechanically, like a puppet on strings.

"We'll talk about this later," he told Tiffany. "Carry on." And he swiftly closed the door.

"What was that about?"

"They're afraid I'm too much like Thiphania."

Thiphania. I'd *just* seen that name. "Thiphania . . . Widderchine? The one who made the BrainBox in the glass case downstairs?" Tiffany nodded, looking a little sick about it. "But what's wrong with that? She was brilliant, right?"

"They've been keeping me under lock and key ever since I designed my first BrainBox. Frankly, I'm getting tired of it. But they can't stop me forever. I inherit this place when I turn fifteen. After that, I can do whatever I want."

"Inherit? So your mother's . . ."

"Dead." Tiffany turned away.

Now I was confused. Hadn't Tiffany just said something about her mother to Wyrmgear? I wanted to ask, but I'd just met the girl.

"I'm so sorry."

"It's all right," she said.

But it clearly wasn't. I could tell she didn't want to talk about it, so I changed the subject. "Why are they keeping such a close eye on you? Was something wrong with your BrainBox?"

Tiffany stared into her machine's whirring gears. "Absolutely *nothing* was wrong with my BrainBox."

"Nothing?"

"Well, maybe one small thing."

"And what was that?"

"First, you have to understand that people our age aren't allowed to make modern BrainBoxes. But I couldn't do what I wanted with an antique, so mine was completely modern—compact, sentient, decades of long-term memory."

"How old were you?"

"Eight."

"Eight! Eight years old?"

"Yes. But I'm thirteen now. I know what I'm doing."

"So . . . did you not build it right?"

"The fabrication was perfect. The Machinery doesn't make mistakes. And it wasn't the body. Back then, I had access to all manner of Clockwerks. Finding the body was easy. I just snatched one that wasn't being used for much."

"Not a sentient one, I hope?"

"No! Of course not! What do you think I am, a monster?" Then she let out a laugh that would've creeped out Frankenstein.

I shook my head no, but I was really thinking, *um, maybe?*

"The Clockwerk I took was in charge of grooming my mother's cat. Getting the BrainBox fabricated was easy. I just snuck into the Machinery one night and slipped my plans into the master inbox."

"No one caught on?"

"Clockwerks in the Machinery aren't designed to question. Besides, in my plans, I made it look like the BrainBox was for a new line of babysitting teddy bears. I called mine the Nanny

Bear."

"Brilliant! I would have loved having a teddy bear take care of me!"

"I know, right?"

"So . . . what happened?"

Tiffany started to pace, a strained lilt creeping into her voice. "Well . . . I didn't follow *all* the rules . . . not by half."

"So?"

Tiffany got a far-off look in her eyes. "He didn't mean to do it."

"Nanny Bear?"

Tiffany held out her hand for inspection. Her ring finger was missing its top two joints. "It was an accident. A simple misinterpretation of how to properly punish—"

"NANNY BEAR CUT OFF YOUR FINGER?" The bottom dropped out of my stomach.

Tiffany pulled back her hand. "Not all of it. Just a little. It's not like I can't use it anymore. Anyway, Wyrmgear wouldn't listen to reason." Tiffany's voice rose in agitation. "Nanny Bear just needed some simple modifications. I knew exactly what I'd done wrong! I could've fixed him. I know I could've! But Wyrmgear wouldn't listen. No! The fool removed my BrainBox . . . and destroyed it! Now they won't leave me alone for five minutes with anything more complicated than a music box—for fear I might snatch one again. I'm so tired of antique BrainBoxes."

Tiffany got a gleam in her eye, one I recognized immediately.

"You'll be fifteen soon," I offered.

"So I should just waste the next two years of my life? I don't think so! But don't worry. I'll figure something out. I always do.

The key is to keep your mind and eyes open. Opportunities are thick on the ground, Willa. You only have to recognize them. You never know when you might learn something important—or who you might learn it from."

I couldn't believe what I was hearing. My mother says those very same words. And then it dawned on me: Tiffany may have been only thirteen, but she was already a full-blown Idiot Genius.

"Gotta go," I said, running to the door and heaving it open.

"Already?" asked Tiffany, sounding like she might cry.

"I'm sure my dad's looking for me." At least, I hoped he was. "It was nice meeting you."

I ran all the way to the basement. He wasn't there. Neither was any of his gear. I told myself Dad would never leave me behind . . . not willingly, anyway. My heart began pounding in my chest. Maybe I missed him somehow on the way down. Gear Hall was huge. He may have used a different set of stairs. I flew up the main staircase. Rounding a banister, I ran headlong into him.

"Whoa! Where are you going so fast? And where have you been?"

"I was looking for you!"

"Yeah, right," he said doubtfully. "I tried to reach you on the WatchitMapCallit, but I couldn't get it to work. And then some angry robot yelled at me to get off the job. You know anything about that?"

"He wasn't a robot, Dad, he was a Clockwerk." My voice started to crack, the way it does when I know I'm going to let him down. "I'm so sorry, Dad. It's my fault. I met a girl and we hung out in her room. I didn't know it would cause any trouble."

"Don't worry about it." He handed me a bag of tools. "The job is finished. The bill's in the mail, or whatever they have here. But let's not waste any time showing ourselves out."

Glym Jack could barely keep up with us. Dad threw his gear in the back, slamming the door. And once we were in the confines of the TeenyWeeny's cab, I remembered why I didn't want to be a plumber.

"You smell awful!"

"Comes with the job, pumpkin."

I hung my head out the window and debated telling Dad about Wudgepuddle's plan to pick Mom's brain for the inner workings of the pac-a-purse. But if Wudgepuddle figured out Dad was the plumber called to Gear Hall? That would point back to *me* being the one who overheard Wudgepuddle talking to Wyrmgear. That was the last thing I needed. Besides, I couldn't really imagine Mom using her BrainRent. She wouldn't like the idea of something taxing her brain's resources, and what did she need with dolleurs?

After landing, we put the borrowed tools back where they belonged. Dad's all about leaving things right for the next guy. Which is definitely nice, but I was sooo tired.

I staggered to my room, shut the door, and flopped on the bed. How could so many crazy things happen in one day? I felt like I could sleep for a week.

"Willa!" said Grayson, leaping onto my back and giving me a shake. "Don't go to sleep!"

"Too late," I mumbled. "I'm already asleep. Can't you tell? I'm dreaming you're on my back, and that you can talk, and that we aren't back in Cambridge, in *my* room, right across the street from Squirrel Brand Park."

CHAPTER THIRTEEN

"But Willa, we have to talk. I can't stay cooped up in this place. . . ."

But it was too late. I was down for the count.

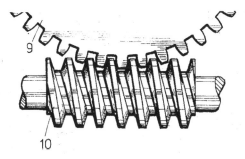

The Tantalizing Ticket

I WOKE slowly, the memory of my crazy dreams still burning brightly in my head: mad laughter, encryption codes, my mother's face, the pac-a-purse, and streams of ones and zeros filling up the empty corners of my brain. I felt like a pickpocket had spent the entire night rummaging through my memories. Now that my eyes were open, my mind felt even slower, like a slug climbing an icicle.

I willed myself upright and zigzagged to the mirror. The person looking back at me was a wreck. She was unwashed. She'd slept in her clothes. But the most frightful part was the dead hedgehog smooshed onto one side of her head. Hold the Watchit-MapCallit, that was no dead hedgehog—that was her hair. And her mouth—my mouth—was as dry as a dust pit on Mars.

Suddenly, Grayson and I were nose to nose. She was yowling, but everything sounded muffled and far away. Then I felt a painful tug on my ear.

"Willa!" She waved the BrainRent in front of my face. "You've got to stop wearing this thing!"

My mind cleared. I snatched the BrainRent from her furry paw. "Why?"

She gave me a smack on the side of my head.

"Ow! What was that for?"

"Do you remember the robot who brought us here?" she asked.

"Of course! How could I forget?"

"Remember when your dad asked what the little glowing pips on the BrainRents meant?"

"Yeah, he told Dad they weren't important."

"The whole time you were asleep, all ten of the pips were glowing! And when you got up, all ten were still glowing!"

"I don't see you taking yours off!" I snapped a little too defensively.

"The pips on mine have never gone above three, and I don't wear mine at night!"

I put the BrainRent back on my ear. "How many are glowing now?"

Grayson inspected the device. "Three."

"Okay, so maybe I'll just wear it during the day."

"Better not at all."

"I can't do that. I'm saving up for something. I gotta earn as many dolleurs as I can."

Grayson frowned, sending her whiskers in odd directions. "I don't like that Nimet Simit."

"You sure didn't mind curling up in her lap and getting your belly scritched."

"That was *before* she said she'd have to kill you!"

"I have to admit, that was a little weird."

"A little!"

A knock sounded at my door.

"Yes?"

"Almost time for Idiot school," said my dad's voice. "And if you want any leftovers from the *Jolly Rajah*, you'd better hurry."

I arrived at Idiot school a few minutes late, which matters more when your whole school day only lasts thirty minutes. Ravenlock Sward was waiting for me in the hall. When I tried to walk past him, he blocked my way.

"You never answered my question."

"What question?" I asked, avoiding his eyes.

He spoke slowly and deliberately. "What did that Clockwerk Boy want with *you*?"

I couldn't shake the feeling that I didn't want Ravenlock involved. "I was with my parents on the upper deck," I lied. "I didn't even see the Clockwerk Boy."

I tried to squeeze past him into the classroom, but he put his hand on my arm. It wasn't a violent motion, but it took me by surprise.

"Hey! Hands off!"

"You're a bad liar. You have a tell."

His eyes bored into mine. "I do *not* have a tell! And even if I did, you haven't known me long enough to know what it is. Which it isn't!"

"Don't lie to me, Willa. This is more important than you know."

I wanted to tell him I wasn't a liar, but having just been caught in a lie kind of ruined that.

"Your parents went to the upper deck with an Ibid," he continued, "but you remained below. The Clockwerk Boy came to see *you*. He even gave you something. But the most amazing thing happened after he wound down." Ravenlock lowered his voice. "When you talked to a mettle man."

He couldn't possibly know all these things just by looking at me. And I would have remembered if he'd been there.

"You're scaring me. Let me go to class."

"There's *nothing* for you to learn in there, and *everything* to learn out here." He gripped the doorknob so tightly his knuckles glowed white. A vein throbbed on his forehead. "There's an evil coming to Grandeur, Willa Snap."

"That's what Tuppence said," I whispered. Oh, good. Now I'd verbally acknowledged my lie. A knot formed in my throat. Tears would be next, and that's something you can never show a bully.

"A *great* evil," he continued. "And you're a fool if you don't tell me what you know."

"I don't trust you!" I said, and the first horrible tear fell hotly down my cheek. It wasn't going to be the last.

Ravenlock's attention shifted to the doorknob. It was turning against his will. He bore down on it, but still it turned. The door creaked open a crack, and a sneaker pushed through. Ravenlock let go, and the door swung wide. There stood Nimet Simit. First she looked at me, then at Ravenlock.

"You should be ashamed of yourself," she spat at him.

Ravenlock made a growling noise. Taking advantage of the distraction, Nimet pulled me into the classroom and closed and locked the door.

"Are you all right? Did he hurt you?"

"Just my pride," I said. "Thanks."

Nimet gave me an odd look. "For what?"

"Coming to my rescue."

Nimet smiled. "I wouldn't leave my worst enemy alone with that villain."

"Should we leave him out there? I know he deserves it, but won't he get in trouble?"

"That lock won't slow him down for long. Come, let's take our seats."

As we passed Bertie, he stopped twirling his spanner and gave me a questioning look.

Four-thirty, I mouthed. He collapsed into his chair, looking relieved.

Nimet was right. It took Ravenlock less than a minute to open the door.

"Today," began Professor Pedagogue, "we will talk about the exciting and rewarding occupation of sorting glass, aluminum, and plastic bottles for recycling."

The class groaned as one.

After class, Bertie was waiting out on the sidewalk.

"What have you got for us?" I asked him.

Bertie produced a blue envelope from his jacket pocket. "Show your parents this."

I flipped it over in my hands. It was sealed. "What is it?"

"A ticket to tonight's Mermaid Lakeside Theatre production."

"Suphanallah!" cried Nimet.

I didn't need a translation from the Turkish to know that Nimet was floored. I, on the other hand, couldn't imagine what the fuss was about. "A play?"

"It's Shakespeare's *Much Ado About Nothing*."

"Shakespeare? I don't know, Bertie."

"You don't understand, Willa," said Bertie. "Think period costumes, original dialogue, all performed . . . by cats." Nimet made a squeaky fangirl noise. "Not an easy ticket to get."

"How did *you* get one?" asked Nimet.

"A gift from a cat bat mitzvah party we catered. The strange thing is, Dad doesn't even like plays."

I tapped the envelope in my hand. "Cats . . . performing Shakespeare . . . you know, Bertie, that's so crazy they just might go for it. But where's the second ticket?"

"Willa," Bertie protested, "sneaking *you* into the dragon kitchens is one thing: *you* have to go."

"I won't go without Nimet. Haven't I made that clear?"

Nimet shook her head in disbelief. "Hello? Don't I have a say in the matter?"

Bertie pulled out a second blue envelope and dangled it front of Nimet.

Nimet followed its every move. "I—I—I mean, it's not like we get to see the show. We'll be laboring in the dragon kitchens, right?"

"I don't know why I'm telling you this . . ." Bertie grimaced.

"Spit it out," I told him.

Bertie sighed. "You can redeem the tickets for a show next week."

Nimet's hands began to tremble. "All my life I have wanted to see a Mermaid Lakeside Theatre production. Did you know the great Grimalkin is performing as the Modern Major General in Gilbert and Sullivan's *Pirates of Penzance* this fall?"

"No," I said.

"No, of course not. Why would you?" Nimet reached for the envelope, only to pull her hand back at the last minute. "I read every review."

Bertie nodded knowingly. "I've seen you worshiping the playbills. Nimet, they're front row seats."

She made a whimpering sound. "I'm going to regret this, aren't I?"

I said *no* as Bertie said *yes*.

"Oh, all right. Count me in." Nimet removed her purple fez and tucked the envelope carefully within. "Tanrı yardımcımız olsun." Bertie and I exchanged glances. "It means: heaven help us."

CHAPTER FIFTEEN

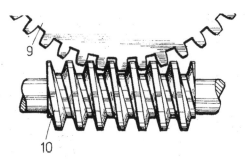

The Blasted Dragon

FOOLING my parents was the easy part. The hard part was telling the lie. I know I'd lied to Ravenlock, but that was because bullies don't deserve the truth. My parents were another matter. I kept telling myself it was because my timeline depended on it—that they would have done the same in my place. But the worst part was what I was doing to Nimet. She'd obviously lived a sheltered life. Now I was teaching *her* how to lie.

Babbage's Bouillon, Bisque & Bean was located at the foot of a MiniDirigy platform. Its street-facing accordion doors were folded into the building's corners, allowing tables and chairs to spill out onto the sidewalks. Nearly every seat was taken. Bowed heads slurped great bowls of steaming soup.

Bertie, wearing an apron and polishing a bowl with a soft cloth, waved us over. But it was slow going. Customers kept asking him for things: bread, water, another napkin. Everyone seemed to know his name. I grabbed a pitcher of water and shoved a stack of napkins at Nimet. Finally, Bertie was able to slip out.

"Follow me," he said, and we slowly made our way to the

soup kitchen.

He led us past a veritable wall of tureens filled with bouillons, bisques, broths, soups, stews, and chowders.

"Is it always this busy?" I asked, eyeing the corn chowder hungrily.

"No. This is an early rush from Theatre Row."

We halted by an open door. Inside, a taller, beefier version of Bertie rummaged through a desk drawer. He was bespectacled and wore a white chef's uniform.

"Papa, here are the two helpers I told you about. Willa, Nimet, this is my papa."

Mr. Babbage looked us up and down. "Right, then. Do you swear by them?"

Bertie gave each of us a thoughtful look, his eyes lingering on Nimet. "Yes."

"Very well." Mr. Babbage placed four slips of paper and two pens before us. "This is a standard waiver, and this is a standard oath stating you won't say anything about what you see in the . . . you-know-what kitchens. You sign here."

"You mean the dra—"

"Yes, those," interrupted Mr. Babbage.

I picked up the pen and signed both forms. Nimet, however, picked hers up and began reading out loud.

"*While working under dragon employ, I hereby sign over all rights to contest loss of life or limb, including, but not limited to, the accidental misplacement of my body via temporal vortexes, cracks, shifts . . .*"

Nimet looked at me like I was insane.

I pointed my finger at the big X at the bottom of the paper.

"You sign right there," I said softly.

"But—*accidental misplacement of my body via temporal vortexes?*"

"Standard dragon contract," explained Mr. Babbage. "Had to sign one myself. I've never seen them send anyone anywhere. If you ask me, it's just something they say to add mystique."

I handed Nimet the pen. "*Right* . . . there."

Nimet gave me a dirty look before signing both pieces of paper.

"Very good," announced Mr. Babbage after examining our signatures. "Bertie, there's a Clockwerk cab waiting for you in the alley. When you get there, give Morgan this." Mr. Babbage handed Bertie an envelope. "Make sure she reads it. Oh, and Bertie . . . best if you go through the front door, eh?" he said with an odd little grin.

Bertie's face grew a shade paler. "Yes, Papa."

The cab looked out of place in a back alleyway in Greater Grandeur. All shiny metal, glass, and whirring gears, it reminded me of a giant jeweled beetle, only with tall spindly wheels instead of legs.

A Clockwerk coachman sitting on top tipped his metal hat. "Good day, young master. Where to?"

"The Blasted Dragon, please," Bertie answered.

The carriage doors opened up like the petals of a flower, a narrow set of stairs protruding like a long crooked tongue.

The inside was elegant, with polished wood and cushioned seats. Two silver vases filled with white flowers hung on the walls. A light breeze filtered through the windows. It was like stepping into a fairytale—only one *without* magic.

"The Blasted Dragon," said Nimet miserably. "I can't believe you talked me into this!"

Bertie shifted nervously in his seat, glancing at Nimet. "Neither can I."

"Finished?" I asked them. Grudgingly, they both nodded. "Bertie, is this place really as dangerous as it sounds?"

"It's a right dodgy place. That's for sure. But we're service, not patrons."

"And that makes a difference?"

"A bit. It means we have the protection of the house. So, if anything bad happened to us, the owners would be displeased . . . theoretically, anyway."

"Theoretically," repeated Nimet.

Bertie nodded. "The most important thing is to project confidence. Brewed creatures can smell fear a burg away."

Nimet gave me a furtive look. "Did you bring . . . the book?"

I shook my head. "He's only around on Sundays."

"What book?" asked Bertie.

"Remember the Clockwerk Boy I told you about?" I asked Bertie.

"You mean the one that told you about *Dracones finis*?"

"Exactly. After he told me my timeline was in danger, he gave me a memory book. But he wound down before he could say more. The point is, he said I could find him in the billiard hall at the Blasted Dragon."

"He must work on the time machine. Clockwerk shifts end Sunday mornings. Some of them hang around and play pool. They're wicked good shots."

"People play them for dolleurs?" said Nimet incredulously. "They'd never win."

"The Clockwerks give tremendous odds, and sometimes they *do* lose, though it might be on purpose, to keep people betting. If you happen to see him, though, give us a shout. We might be able to arrange a meeting somewhere safer."

"Just about any place would be safer," said Nimet. "How does a gearhead like you know so much about time machines, Bertie Babbage?"

Bertie looked at us like he couldn't decide how much he wanted to tell. After a time, he said, "I don't *just* work in their kitchens. You see, the inn sits on the entrance to a series of natural caverns. That's where the dragons live, underneath the inn. That's where they build the time machines, too."

"They have more than one?" I asked.

"No. The dragons either dismantle or destroy the current machine if the soothies get too close. Which is no small feat. These time machines are gigantic, hundreds of feet tall, but surprisingly low-tech. The key seems to be spinning around huge concentric iron rings—they have to be iron, and the angles of rotation and speed need to be incredibly precise. The dragons employ a slew of Clockwerks and chimp twists to climb into the machinery and make adjustments and repairs between test runs. The dragons prefer Clockwerks because their memories roll over, and they can't repeat what they don't remember. They'd use all Clockwerks if they could get enough of them."

"What's a chimp twist?" I asked.

He managed a bashful grin. "Me. Or any kid handy with a spanner."

"But your memory doesn't roll over," I said.

"True. But who's going to believe me? I'm just a kid."

"Hold on, there's something I still don't understand," I said.

"Join the club," said Bertie.

"Where did the dragons come from? I mean, how come nobody knows anything about them?"

"But you do know about them. They're in stories all throughout history. Every culture in the world has dragon stories."

"But if those stories were real, why isn't there any evidence of them in the fossil record? Surely some of their bones would have been discovered by now."

"Oh, well, that's easy. Don't you see?"

Nimet and I exchanged glances. "Talk to us like we're Idiots."

"They're time travelers."

"Still not getting it," I said.

"The dragons aren't *from* our past. They only visit it."

"They're from our future?" asked Nimet.

"That's one possibility. Personally, I think they're from another planet," said Bertie.

"What, Martian dragons?" I asked. "You can't be serious."

"Why not?" asked Bertie. "You don't believe we're the only life in the universe, do you?"

"No. That would be stupid."

"Or the most advanced?"

"That would be equally stupid."

"Well, all right, then."

I couldn't argue with his logic.

"So they really have a working time machine," said Nimet.

"They seem to think so," said Bertie.

"They don't know?" I asked.

"They've never actually sent anything through time with it. At least, not this one. If they did try and use it, the soothies would shut them down for sure. They don't like the dragons mucking about with time. But the dragons get edgy if they don't have a working machine on hand. You know, in case of temporal emergencies and all. And as long as they only do tests, the soothies leave them alone. Either that or they can't detect the tests."

"The soothies aren't the only ones keeping an eye on the dragons," I said.

"What do you mean?" asked Bertie.

"Have you ever heard of a Professor Farsical?"

Bertie shook his head.

"He visited our apartment yesterday. He said he was petitioning to have Greater Grandeur and all its burgs turned into a Steamwerks society, but I think he was there to see me. He said the dragons were planning to send something, or someone, through time, and he said he could detect reverse time-eddies coming from me."

Bertie winced. "That's not good."

"What's a reverse time-eddy?" asked Nimet.

"Okay," said Bertie. "See, time is more fluid than you might think. We perceive it running in only one direction at a constant speed, like a ship sailing under a steady breeze. But it doesn't have to be that way. And when some*thing* or some*one* is yanked from its timeline, it creates a disturbance, sending ripples in all directions. The ripples going backward—"

"Are reverse time-eddies," I said.

Bertie knit his eyebrows. "Never heard about anyone detecting them, though."

The rotten-egg smell of brimstone drifted through the window. Nimet held her nose and made a face. The road had narrowed, and the buildings we passed were covered in soot.

"We're getting close. Any more questions?"

"Where will you be working?" asked Nimet.

"Don't worry. We'll be together the whole time."

We emerged into a hazy courtyard. The Blasted Dragon's stone exterior looked like two immense dragons curving around face to face, their outstretched wings forming a high-pitched roof. A row of scorched steps between their smoking snouts appeared to be the only way in or out. A rumbling shook the cab.

"What's that?" asked Nimet nervously.

Bertie glanced uneasily at the top of the steps.

"Wait for it," he said grimly.

A few seconds later, the dragons' mouths erupted in a fiery red blaze, completely engulfing each other's heads.

Nimet let out a little shriek.

I turned to Bertie. "That's fake, right?"

"Yeah . . . never really had the nerve to check that out."

The Clockwerk cab let us out at the foot of the steps, then wheeled away. We stood side by side by side, staring up at the twin smoking jaws.

"This place tends to attract a rather odd crowd," said Bertie.

Nimet gulped. "Can't imagine why."

"Best if you let me do all the talking."

"Roger that," I said.

"Oh, and whatever you do, don't accept any gifts—especially eggs or live young."

Horrified, Nimet and I mouthed the words *live young* to each other.

The ground began to rumble again.

I grabbed my new friends' hands.

"On three?" I asked.

"Better make it one," said Bertie.

"One!" yelled Nimet, and we bolted up the vibrating stairs and dashed in, screaming our heads off the entire time.

The instant we crossed the threshold, the opening behind us was consumed by fire. The searing heat drove us blindly forward into the dark inn. As my eyes adjusted, the first thing I noticed was that everyone was staring at us. The second thing was that the brewed people in the room outnumbered the, uh, old-fashioned people. I saw mixes of cat, armadillo, bird, and many things I couldn't identify. In the back, a booth of boisterous elefantkin were engrossed in a heated game of poker, swigging from tall bottles and swearing salty oaths.

"Come on," said Bertie, as he unsuccessfully tried to pry his hand loose from mine.

The crowd lost interest in us as we crossed to the bar, and our ears filled with the sounds of their different languages.

Bertie hailed the barkeep. "Morgan."

"Hired help through the service entrance, young Mr. Babbage," she said. "You know the rules."

Bertie drew the letter from his pocket. "This is for you."

She eyed it for a moment before clomping over and taking a closer look. Morgan was a brewed horse-like creature, though she stood upright. She wore a tattered green dress over her shiny black coat, its low back showing off her well groomed mane. A single broken horn stuck out of the middle of her forehead.

Morgan plucked the letter from Bertie's hand. Her hands, like those of the other brewed creatures I'd seen, looked surprisingly human, although when she balled her fists tight, they looked very much like hooves. Morgan turned her mane to us as she opened the letter.

After a time, she turned back around, fumbling with the envelope. "Tell your father he's a good man. Tell him—" Morgan stopped fumbling and withdrew from the envelope a second letter. It was written on a thinner paper stock. When unfolded, it was just translucent enough for me to make out a flowing, almost feminine, script.

"What's this?" she asked, glancing at Bertie with a suspicious eye.

"Don't rightly know."

Morgan glared at each of us. When she got to me she snorted loudly. Alarm? Anger? A sudden need to sneeze? I couldn't tell.

"What was it you wanted me to tell him?" asked Bertie timidly.

"Get out of my bar!" she brayed, crumpling the letters.

We heeded her advice, racing into the belly of the Blasted Dragon as fast as our feet would carry us.

"What was that about?" I asked when we were out of earshot.

"I have no idea. She's rarely in a good mood, but she's never yelled at me before."

We entered an elevator and went down for ages. A blast of warm air greeted us when the doors finally opened. Nimet and I stuck our heads out and looked both ways. The passageway was human sized and well lit.

"This isn't a cavern," said Nimet.

Bertie strode past us. "It will be."

Sure enough, the corridor changed as we progressed. The tile floor continued, but soon it was snaking around rock formations and black chasms. When I saw my first damsel, I let out a little cry.

"What is it?" yelled Nimet.

I pointed.

"Oh, I should have warned you," said Bertie. "Don't worry about that. It's just a statue. Squire carves them."

"There are more?" I asked.

"The caverns are littered with them, all screaming for help."

I caught Nimet's eye. "Sounds like this Squire guy's got some serious white knight issues."

"Oh, he's got white knight issues all right," said Bertie. "Just not like you're thinking. And he's not a guy. He's a . . . kind of dragon. They call him a worm. He's really small compared to the others. He says he can't become a real dragon until he's eaten his first king or something. I don't really understand it."

We spotted another three damsels before we ran across the first knight being devoured by a dragon. There was something tragically comic about the damsels. It wasn't just me.

"Is it wrong to laugh?" said Nimet, placing a hand over her mouth.

Bertie came back and gazed at the statues. A damsel stood tied to a stake. Above her, a knight dangled from the crushing jaws of a fierce dragon. "Yeah . . . if you think this is bad, wait until you hear his jokes. All right, now, best get to it." Bertie pointed to a big set of doors. "The kitchens are through there. But before we can get started, we need to suit up."

Bertie guided us to a room where the walls had been carved flat and smooth. Rummaging through some lockers, he pulled out several white chef's jackets.

"Yeah, this'll do," he said, holding one up to my shoulders. "Give it a go."

The fabric was so thick and stiff, my shoulders drooped under the jacket's weight. I had a sudden vision of being turned into blackened toast.

"Are we going to get . . . breathed on?" I asked.

Bertie handed a pair of pants to Nimet. "Hope not. But these are to shield us from kitchen steam."

Once suited up, he plunked a metal helmet onto my head. The grill covered my entire face.

"Um . . ." I kept waiting for something else to come out of my mouth, but nothing did.

"To protect your eyes from the flying shrimp. Spiny little devils."

"Shrimp?" Nimet squeaked. She touched the thick grill covering her face. "They have wings?"

"No, but they have this way of flicking their tails that makes them fly around like rogue popcorn kernels."

I adjusted to the grill pretty fast, but the walking was difficult. I felt like Frankenstein's monster in a chef's suit. Bertie pressed a button, and a wall slid away, revealing a long row of wicked-looking skeleton armor. Only the bones were on the outside and made of metal.

Bertie walked behind one and stepped into it. "Close up one section at a time. I suggest you start at your feet and go up."

"Bertie . . . just how big are these shrimp?" I asked.

"Oh, this isn't for protection. It's an exo-suit."

"Then what is it for?" asked Nimet, fumbling with a latch at her leg.

"So we can lift heavy stuff, like pots and pans."

Bertie reached his arms into the suit, and it hummed to life. He twisted his upper body, and the rear of the suit swung shut and latched into place. It was a practiced movement, one he'd done a million times. He clomped over to help us. Once activated, my suit felt like a second skin.

"All we need now are our herding rods and a couple of extra battery packs, and we'll be ready for business."

"Why do I get the feeling I don't want to know what a herding rod is?" Nimet asked me.

Bertie plugged four battery packs into a belt around my waist, handed me a three-foot rod, and plugged its cable into a port on my forearm.

"You activate it by squeezing the grip here." Bolts of electricity arced from the rod to one of the metal lockers, scorching its paint off.

"Watch where you point that thing," Bertie advised.

Nimet held her rod at arm's length. "And these are for shrimp?"

"Ornery little buggers. Hard to blame them, really. If you were going to steam me and feed me to dragons, I'd put up a fight, too."

Bertie thudded out of the room. Nimet and I glanced at each other.

"And here you thought I was going to get you into trouble," I chided her.

Nimet rolled her eyes.

The kitchen was cavernous, built by and for creatures much larger than ourselves before being retrofitted with makeshift ramps and stairs. Steam hissed from dark corners. The smell of ocean brine and salty spices—Old Bay, if I wasn't mistaken—assaulted my nostrils.

"Come on!" yelled Bertie. "Let's go!"

Nimet and I thundered down to a platform of metal grates. I could see machinery but not the floor, far below. At one end of the platform, Bertie stood next to a heavy iron gate. We clanked over as fast as we could, which was pretty fast.

"Nimet," said Bertie, "you stand here, behind this shield. To open and close the gate, pull this lever. The instant the gate opens, the shrimp will stampede through—"

I laughed. I couldn't help myself.

Bertie turned to look at me. "Yes, Willa?"

179

"Well—it's just—you know . . . the image of shrimp—stampeding!" I made little crawling motions with my newly enhanced fingers.

Bertie didn't laugh. "Right. Now, Nimet, make sure you don't leave the gate open for longer than fifteen seconds. You got it? Fifteen seconds."

Nimet nodded nervously.

"Willa, you're with me."

We thudded partway back across the platform. Bertie grabbed a pair of tongs off a post and used them to pull up and drag away a big circular hatch in the floor. A white blanket of steam rose from the hole and engulfed us. I couldn't see five feet in front of me.

"Our job, Willa, is to herd the shrimp down this hole without falling in ourselves."

I peered down the hole. It hissed up at me.

"That's the steamer, huh?"

"Correct. Now, rods at the ready?"

I gave my herding rod a squeeze. Electricity danced down its length. "Ready as I'll ever be."

"Any time, Nimet," Bertie yelled into the steam. "Remember, fifteen seconds."

Gears whined. Metal scraped against metal. Seawater sluiced down the platform, followed by a clicking, rumbling sound. Then a high-pitched shriek filled the air, and Nimet streaked out of the steam bank, leapt over the trapdoor, and flashed between us.

"That's not good," I said.

"Nimet!" screamed Bertie.

A shrimp the size of a large dog flew out of the steam and hit me full in the chest. My feet came out from under me and after a moment of weightlessness, I landed hard on my back. Brine bubbled out of the shrimp's mandibles and all over my face. *Bleck!* Its antennae slapped the decking like bullwhips.

"Bertie! Help!"

"Your suit! Use the power of your suit!"

"Oh, right!"

I pushed myself up onto my elbows and tossed the shrimp down the hatchway to its doom. That was easy. As I got to my feet, however, a dozen more came rumbling out of the steam. I activated my herding rod and put it to use—*ZAP! ZAP! ZAP!* I tossed and kicked the stunned shrimp down the hole. I was getting the hang of this. The next time a shrimp flew out of the steam toward me, I ducked.

Then came the second wave. No problem.

Followed by a third. Problem.

My herding rod started taking a longer time between *ZAPS!* A shrimp smacked me from behind, knocking me dangerously close to the hatchway. I backed off as yet another wave rolled in. A flying crustacean took me down on my back again. It must have weighed forty pounds. As if sensing my vulnerability, more piled on. The exo-suit wasn't built to protect me from this kind of thing. I was struggling for air.

"Willa!" screamed Bertie, sounding like he was a world away. "I'm not gonna make it! You have to get to the gate!"

I opened my mouth and all the air in my lungs rushed out in one gasp. The weight of the shrimp was crushing me. The world started going dark around the edges, and the horrible sound of the shrimps' clicking and clacking faded.

The next thing I knew, I was sucking in a blast of cool air.

Then a jolt of electricity ripped through my exo-suit, followed by another jolt, and another. With each shot of electricity, my body stiffened, then relaxed. This was not how I expected my first catering job to go. Finally, the weight on my chest lessened. My vision cleared. Through the haze I saw herding rods—lots of herding rods—twirling and discharging. But I couldn't make out any of the people rescuing me. As soon as possible, I wrenched myself into a sitting position and gripped my own rod tightly.

"I'm okay," I yelled. "Go help my friend. He's closer to the gate!"

The herding rods danced away. *ZAP!-ZAP!-ZAP!-ZAP!-ZAP!-ZAP!*

I kicked the remaining shrimp off my legs and got to my feet. The exo-suit shuddered. A light on the back of my glove flashed the word "BATTERY" in red. My suit's joints stiffened. I took one last step and teetered on the edge of the open hatchway. Backward, forward, backward, forward. The flashing red light on my glove winked out.

"Goodbye," I said.

A moment later, the words "EMERG/AUX POWER" flashed amber and I was back in business. I leapt over the open steamer in one bound and ran toward the *ZAPPING!* sounds. Suddenly, I was waist deep in ornery shrimp. This time, I used my rod sparingly, kicking and tossing whenever I could.

Just ahead, I heard Bertie yell, "I'm okay, I'm okay! Get to the gate!"

I struggled to Bertie's side. He was *not* "okay." He was buried in shrimp. I couldn't haul them off fast enough. We were being overrun.

CA-CHUNG! CA-CHUNG! CA-CHUNG!

One of our rescuers had reached the gate. We were saved. I doubled my efforts and cleared Bertie's chest and arms. He sat up. "I'm gonna kill Nimet," he coughed, spitting out a mouthful of brine.

I pulled my friend to his feet. He was on auxiliary batteries, too. We hobbled through the steam toward a lone hunched figure panting like a dog. Her helmet was missing, and her hair—sticking out in every direction—stood out like a flaming torch. She'd strapped a dozen battery packs to her waist and clutched four herding rods in each hand. A feral gleam blazed in her eyes.

"Nimet," said Bertie, awed.

Startled by our approach, Nimet raised her herding rods, electricity arcing from their tips.

Bertie crouched. "Stand down! Stand down, soldier!"

"It's all right, Nimet," I added cautiously. "It's just me and Bertie."

At first, she stared at us like she didn't know who we were. Then, slowly, she lowered her weapons and dropped them to the floor. "Sorry about that," she said, tilting her head toward the gate. "Eyestalks," she added, as if that explained everything.

We rushed in and gave her a hug. "Wow, Nimet! That was amazing!"

A distant, unearthly roar interrupted our revelry.

"Dragons," breathed Nimet.

"Hungry dragons," confirmed Bertie. "Come on, the three of us should have enough juice to round up the stragglers." Bertie stalked off into the steam. ZAP! "And we'll need a fresh round of battery packs," he yelled. "Last thing you want is to fall into a dragon's mouth when you're filling it. He sure won't thank you for that."

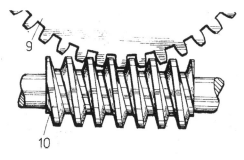

The Dragons' Dilemma

B ERTIE picked up a giant pitchfork and started shoveling the steaming-hot shrimp ten to a wheelbarrow.

"There will be three dragons at tonight's table."

"They sit at a table?" asked Nimet.

"More like a stone mound with a flat top. Willa, you'll be feeding Vapherra—she's green and prone to moody outbursts. If you see smoke coming out of her nostrils, that could mean she's about to blow, so keep an eye out for that. Nimet, you feed Meerax. She's the one who travels through time in her mind. Now, I've heard some crazy rumors about how if people stare too long into her eyes, they start experiencing past lives, so—you know—heads up."

"What color . . . is she?" said Nimet, her voice strained.

"She's a dark, dusty purple, but if she starts to glow, give her some breathing room." Even through her face grill, I could tell that Nimet was less than pleased with what I'd gotten her into. "Me, I'll take Wynoc. He's . . . really big and old and stuff."

"Sooo . . . what are Wynoc's issues?" I asked.

Bertie glanced at the floor. "I don't know if you'd call it an issue, but his breath does smell an awful lot like what you'd get if a thousand-year-old sulfur mine threw up all over you."

At the entrance to the caverns, we strapped on belts slung with hammers and chisels. I hefted one of the hammers. It must have weighed thirty pounds, but the exo-suit made it feel as light as a toothpick.

"Bertie, please don't tell me we have to shell the shrimp," said Nimet.

"No. Dragons like things that crunch."

"Like foolish knights?" I offered.

Bertie brandished his chisel. "These are for when a dragon gets something stuck in its teeth." Nimet made a face. "Don't worry about hitting a tooth—they're as hard as diamonds." Bertie laughed. He was having a good time. "Ready to feed some dragons?"

We wheeled our shrimp onto a network of catwalks and pushed them through a forest of stalactites.

"Is that all there is to it?"

"Yeah, it's easy. Just park your wheelbarrow next to your dragon's head and wait for it to open its gob."

"And we fork in the shrimp?" asked Nimet.

"Exactly."

Nimet made a mousy noise that would've done my dad proud.

The exo-suits made the trek effortless. As we got closer, we could hear the dragons talking.

"Why do they have English accents?" I asked.

Bertie shushed me. "No more talking!" he hissed.

The caverns were vast. You could've flown a hot air balloon

in ours, so long as you didn't fly too close to the ceiling. In an adjacent cavern, I spotted the time machine. Its central tower must have been two hundred feet tall. The outer rings encircling it stretched even farther. Giant iron balls bulged along its long arms, making it look like some kind of crazy amusement park ride that weighed millions of pounds. A long, low bridge ran between the two caverns, connecting the time machine to the dragons' mound. A lone Clockwerk hurried down its length.

We arrived at nearly the same time, us from above, and the Clockwerk from below. When it reached the mound, it walked right across a dragon-sized schematic and held its clipboard high. Wynoc raised a magnifying loupe to his eye and, after a careful examination, pronounced the time machine operational.

The catwalks curved, split, and doubled back on themselves. The three of us each went down a different path, but we ended up quite close to one another. We'd have to run around the long way, though, if any of us got into trouble.

"I'm a little confused, Meerax," said Vapherra. "Tell me again *exactly* why we haven't contacted the girl?"

Meerax stretched and opened her eyes. "Because to do so would mean veering from the only path I've seen that can save us."

"I don't understand. You always say the future is limitless."

"Yes, but as you approach the end of a timeline—as your time gets short—so do your possibilities."

"So the closer we get to *Dracones finis* . . ."

"The more certain it becomes. But there is one thread. It is tenuous, to be sure, but it exists."

"Are there no threads that might save us where we contact the girl?"

"None that I have seen. Of course, my understanding is incomplete, a patchwork quilt of moments. Interpreting them is not always easy. But I've held nothing back. You know what I know."

"She must go of her own choosing," said Wynoc.

"Yes," hissed Meerax.

"We must not tell her whom she is to save," said Wynoc.

"Yes," hissed Meerax.

"Her body will not come back alive," said Vapherra.

"Yesss."

Bertie's shrimp fork clattered on the catwalk. He lifted the grill on his helmet and mouthed "Don't go." But all I could hear were the Clockwerk Boy's words: *You must sacrifice yourself to right the wrong.*

Vapherra turned an eye to me and opened her huge jaws. I heaved in half my load before she began chewing.

"If only . . . we could tell her . . . that she's to save—"

"Not another word, Vapherra! I beg of you."

Wynoc opened his jaws, and Bertie began heaping shrimp into his gaping maw.

Smoke billowed from Vapherra's nostrils. "This makes no sense! How can she decide if she doesn't even know what we want to ask her?"

"Ah!" said Meerax. "But that is where you're uninformed. Willa Snap already knows what we want to ask her. She knows everything."

Bertie flung his shrimp—fork and all—into Wynoc's mouth.

Nimet glared at me.

I tossed the last shrimp out of my bucket and headed for the kitchen, Bertie hot on my heels.

Back at the steamer, Bertie spun me around. "Why didn't you tell me the dragons had already contacted you!" he yelled.

I handed Bertie another shrimp fork. "Try and hold on to this one, will ya? And they didn't contact me! Nimet's dragon is lying."

Bertie furiously forked shrimp into his wheelbarrow. "Dragons loathe deceit. To *them*, the truth still means something."

He wheeled off. I followed.

"Bertie! I swear! I don't know a thing. They never contacted me! It's got to be a lie!"

Bertie ground to a halt. "MEERAX . . . ISN'T . . . LYING."

"But—"

"No buts! Listen, I took a big risk bringing you here. I thought I could trust you. I thought . . ."

"What? What did you think?" I felt myself blush. Why was I blushing? How embarrassing. And now I was blushing because I was blushing.

"I thought . . . we could be friends. I should have known something was up when I heard you arguing with Ravenlock out in the hall. For all I know, you could be an Evil Genius! I'm such an Idiot!"

"We *are* friends, you Idiot." It came out ten times louder than I meant.

Bertie looked at me coolly. "I don't know what your game is, but please keep me and my family out of it!"

I dropped the handles of my barrow and planted myself in front of him. "Bertie! You can trust me. I'm *not* lying." He wrenched his barrow backwards and veered around me just as Nimet wheeled in.

"What am I going to do, Nimet? Bertie thinks I'm a liar." A knot started forming in my throat. "Some stupid idea about dragons always telling the truth."

"Hold on. Are you saying the dragons never contacted you?"

"Oh, no. Not you, too? I swear, Nimet. I don't know what Meerax's talking about. You *have* to believe me."

Nimet studied my face. "I believe you, Willa Snap. Now tell me, do you have any idea who they want you to save?"

"No idea. But Vapherra thinks if I did, then I'd go. So maybe I should go."

"Bad idea!"

"And why's that?"

"BECAUSE IF YOU GO, YOU DIE!"

"Right. Forgot about that."

"You have to get back out there. We need to know what they're saying. Don't worry, I'll be right behind you."

I blinked away a tear, steered my load of whacking great ginormous shrimp onto the catwalk, and ran as fast as my exo-suit would go.

"This is absurd!" declared Vapherra, a note of hysteria creeping into her voice.

"You know as well as I do, Vapherra, that the time continuum thrives on the absurd," Meerax scoffed.

"I know, Meerax, I know," said Vapherra. "But our window to send her is closing."

"She knows everything she needs to know," Meerax assured her.

"How?" wailed Vapherra. "How does she know?"

I plunked down my wheelbarrow of shrimp.

Yes, I thought, *how do I know?*

"Because she's standing right beside you," said Meerax, "listening to our every word. Isn't that right, Ms. Snap?"

Wynoc made a rumbling sound that terrified me until I realized it was laughter.

Vapherra looked at Wynoc disdainfully. "You knew?"

"Only just now," said Wynoc. "It's the one way Meerax's future thread made any sense." All eyes turned to me. I briefly considered running away. "So what say you, Ms. Snap? Will you help us?"

"I, uh—"

"You must not fear us, my dear," said Vapherra. "We will honor your decision."

"I, uh—"

The dragons leaned toward me. Even the Clockwork was staring at me. He was an old Clockwerk. A familiar-looking—hold on. It was the Clockwerk Boy!

"I won't go," I blurted.

Vapherra nodded acceptingly. "Very well. It is done."

A commotion erupted at the base of the time machine. Clockwerks and chimp twists ran pell-mell in all directions. A dragon who'd been working with them took to the air. With two beats of its wings, it flew to the mound.

"What news?" asked Wynoc.

"Soothies!" panted the dragon. "They're coming."

"Collapse the cavern."

"But Wynoc, without the time machine—"

"Do you wish to be sifted?"

"Of course not, but—"

"Then help me clear the cavern of our workers." Wynoc turned to Vapherra. "See these three to safety, then see to yourself. Meerax, warn the others."

"Four!" I said, stepping forward and pointing to the Clockwerk Boy standing on the schematic. "There are four of us here."

With the greatest of care, Wynoc picked up the Clockwerk Boy and placed him on a catwalk.

"Run, my little Clockwerk," commanded Wynoc, and the Clockwerk Boy set off.

"Nimet!" I screamed. "That's him! That's the Clockwerk Boy!"

"On it!" screamed Nimet, and she charged after him.

"Willa!" shouted Bertie. "The exo-suits won't work outside the caverns. Nimet will never make it out of the elevator!"

"Go after her!" I hollered.

A few wing beats later, it was just me and Vapherra. She burned the time machine schematics to dust with one blow of her fiery breath.

"What are you waiting for, Ms. Snap?"

"I'm sorry I didn't go," I said.

"Don't be. Time travel is a messy business. Fixing one thing always requires breaking something else."

She was trying to tell me something. I could feel it. Is there some kind of rule that dragons have to be cryptic?

"Vapherra, who was I supposed to save?"

"Meerax was very clear. If we are to have any chance to survive as a race, we can't tell you."

"But isn't it too late now?"

"I do not believe in fate. Where there is life, there is always hope."

"Can't you tell me *anything*?"

"Perhaps . . . there is one thing."

"What?"

"Meerax said that . . . to save this person . . . you would have gladly given your life."

"And you wait to tell me this now!"

"Would it have made a difference?"

I thought about it. Did I really want to die at eleven? And what if the dragons were wrong? What if they sent me through time and I died for nothing?

"Probably not," I said honestly. "Are you going to be okay? What about the soothies?"

Vapherra looked at the time machine. "We've done nothing wrong," she said, but she sounded nervous.

The catwalk trembled. A giant boulder had smashed into one of the time machine's arms, breaking it in half and starting a chain reaction of imbalances. The central tower leaned heavily to one side.

"Run!"

I pounded down the swaying catwalk. Bertie waved me into the locker room. "Hurry!" He was pale as a ghost. "What took you so long?"

"I was hardly a minute."

"We have to get you out of that suit!" Bertie's and Nimet's exo-suits stood to either side of me, emptied like burst cocoons.

"And Nimet—"

"She's following the Clockwerk Boy. Now turn around so I

can undo this thing. We have to get above ground!"

I wriggled my hands out of the exo-suit's gloves, and it immediately began powering down. "Could the soothies really sift a dragon? Wouldn't their brains be too big or different or something?"

"Soothies have access to a lot of crazy tech. I imagine they could sift anything they wanted."

"Ever seen someone get sifted?"

Bertie tensed. "It's not something you want to see twice." The room shook. A chunk of ceiling broke loose and landed next to me with a thud. "Time to go."

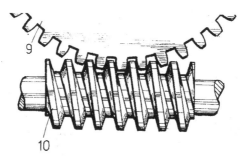

Flight of the Clockwerk Boy

T HE elevator's lights flickered, and the floor bounced like a trampoline with every rumble from the collapsing caverns. Bertie must have jabbed the button for our floor a hundred times before the doors finally opened. We raced through the inn's kitchens. I'll leave the location of the rear service door to your imagination.

All the shops outside were closed up tight. Besides us, the only people in the courtyard were stragglers stumbling away from the Blasted Dragon.

"It's so quiet," I said.

I knew Bertie was agitated. Anyone could have seen that. What I didn't know was how scared I should have been by the sight of his trembling hands.

"Soothies," he said under his breath.

I made to tap my WatchitMapCallit, and Bertie's hand shot out like a striking snake.

"Not unless we have to," he said. "Nimet said she'd call us a cab."

We looked around. There was no cab.

"I don't want to wait out here in the open, though," said Bertie. "Come on!" We ran beside the darkened shops to the edges of the courtyard.

"What do soothies look like?"

"They dress all in white and usually come in threes." Bertie ducked down behind a post and whipped his head around. "Why, did you see one?"

"Who dresses all in white?" I complained.

"Willa! Did you see one or not?"

"No, I didn't."

Just then our Clockwerk cab entered the courtyard and pulled up to the Blasted Dragon's front steps.

"We need to get in that cab," said Bertie.

"That means backtracking."

"I know, but if they come out and find the cab—"

"They'd trace it back to Nimet."

"Precisely."

The run to the cab couldn't have lasted more than a minute, but it felt like ten. As we waited for the carriage door to open, the dragon heads at the top of the steps made a *pock!* sound.

"That's the sound it made right before we ran through!"

Bertie tensed. "Don't look back! Don't let them see your face!"

The cab doors finally opened. We flew up the steps and threw ourselves flat on the floor. Bertie yelled out an intersection to the coachman. As the doors shut, we heard the *foom!* of the dragon's fiery breath. I tilted my head just so and peeped out the window. Racing down the stairs were two men and a woman dressed in white. Even the lenses of their sunglasses were white. All of them were focused on the cab. I plastered myself flat. We didn't speak or move again until the carriage was a block away.

"Well," said Bertie, "now we know how your Clockwerk Boy got his information. He overheard the dragons talking about you. That must be how he found you, too. Meerax must have mentioned your arrival time."

"Yeah, already put that one together."

"Willa?"

"Yes?"

"I'm sorry I didn't believe you when you said you didn't know what the dragons were talking about."

I sat up. Finally I had something to feel relieved about. "But you believe me now?"

Bertie raised his eyes above the level of the window sill. "Yes. Meerax believes in the augury unconditionally, so she figured the only way it could be right was if you were standing there listening."

"Yes!"

Within a block or two, the streets were crowded with people going about their daily business. Bertie opened the window and shouted a different destination to the Clockwerk coachman.

"You gave him false directions?"

"I didn't want the soothies knowing where we were really going. Now we just have to figure how to contact Nimet."

"Is all this secrecy really necessary?"

"You can't be too careful where soothies are concerned." Bertie's face lit up. "I know. Roary Cats!"

I gave him a blank stare.

"Roary Cats, you know! It's a WatchitMapCallit game. You start out as a lost band of kittens, abandoned in the Festering Forest by the Princess Talebearer. We've all been playing it in Idiot school since—oh, forever! Don't you have Roary Cats Outside?"

"No, but it sounds brilliant. And Nimet plays?"

"Kind of. She's awful at it. Can't figure out how to level up her kitten."

"A-a-a-n-n-d . . . this helps us how?"

"Oh, right. Well, when we play games, our WatchitMapCallits communicate with each other peer-to-peer." I stared blankly. "They talk directly to each other, no Grandeurnet. The point is we can use the talk feature within the game and everything we say will be private, or more private. I mean, someone could still try and snoop, but it wouldn't be easy on account of Ambrose Poupon upping our encryption every few months. He's a whiz at coding. Still, we should be careful what we say. There's only one problem."

"What's that?"

"She'd have to be smart enough to figure out it's me trying to communicate with her."

"Nimet's smarter than you think."

"Willa. I've known Nimet since she was six. She has serious social issues. She's said more to me today than in the last—"

Bertie's WatchitMapCallit made a little roaring sound. He stared at it like an Idiot.

"What was that?" I asked.

"Someone's trying to contact me through Roary Cats."

"Gosh, I wonder who it could be?"

Bertie tapped his WatchitMapCallit. The screen showed an image of a sleek, ferocious cat named Dandelion Slayer.

"Is that you?"

"Hush."

The image shrank to a tiny box, revealing an angry-looking fluff-ball of a kitten wearing a purple fez and batting at a flock of taunting butterflies.

"Her name is Pouncy?" I whispered in Bertie's ear.

"Shh! And don't mention the butterflies," whispered Bertie.

"I wouldn't dare."

The peeved kitten stopped swatting and stared out at us. "Where are you?" it asked in a frightened kitten's version of Nimet's voice.

"More importantly, where are you?" said . . . Dandelion Slayer.

"Do you remember the field trip we took to see Quill & Spieler?"

"The magicians that made Ravenlock vanish into thin air? I will *never* forget that."

The kitten nodded. "Yes! How did they do it? One second Ravenlock was standing right in front of us . . . and then . . ."

"I remember. Samantha fainted dead away." Bertie craned his head out the window and looked up into the sky. "I think I know where he's going."

"And you would be right," said Nimet. "I shadowed him to this place. I don't think he noticed me."

CHAPTER SEVENTEEN

"We'll be there in another minute. Hold tight." Bertie tapped the screen and the WatchitMapCallit vanished.

"Shadowed him?" I said. "Who does she think she is, a spy?"

"Willa, when we get there, I'm going to drop you off. I need to get back to the soup shop and tell my dad what's going on. In the meantime, don't talk about the soothies on your WatchitMapCallits. Only in person or through bippies."

"Got it."

We found Nimet in a stand of trees bordering the entrance to a park.

"Tomorrow—Idiot school," called Bertie as the Clockwerk cab rolled away.

Inside the park, I could see shoppers weaving through tents, sampling wares. Quite a few were dressed in aviator gear—goggles, leather flight jackets, long scarves, and the like.

"So where is he?" I asked, looking around. "Where's the Clockwerk Boy?"

"How good are your climbing skills?"

I glanced up. "He's in a tree?"

"No, silly." Nimet took my hand, led me away from the tree we were standing under, and tilted her face skyward.

I couldn't believe my eyes. For blocks and blocks around, the Windwerks Burg blotted out the sky. Hundreds of taut black lines ran from its platforms, about fifty yards above, to anchorages all over the park.

"Look at the size of those birds!" I shouted.

"They're not birds, Willa."

I looked more closely, following the path of a winged figure coming in for a landing. It was a woman! Ending with a flourish of powerful wing beats, she landed not ten feet from us. As she unbent her knees, the wings folded up and disappeared into her leather flight jacket.

"Do we get to fly up there!"

"Hardly."

"Why not?"

"Windwerks wings are incredibly expensive! Two pairs would cost a small fortune."

We made our way past the shoppers. The tents housed a little of everything: tailor shops, food vendors, handmade toys. Leather helmets and aviator goggles appeared to be big sellers. I ran to a table where a girl no older than me was mending a pair of the wings. She'd opened the leather jacket's seams, exposing the complex metal mechanisms inside. There was a maker's mark over the mainspring cover: House da Vinci, just like my Clockwerk cane.

Nimet appeared at my side and led me to a quieter part of the park where, in a clump of trees, a rope ladder hung. "The gusts higher up can come out of nowhere. So keep at least one good handhold at all times," she advised.

I gave Nimet a sideward glance. "Visit the Windwerks Burg often?"

"Once or twice," she said innocently.

The long climb up the rope ladder was only the beginning. Next came a series of metal ladders and platforms, some large, some only ten feet across. It felt weird that none of them had safety railings, though rope holds and metal rings were abundant.

"What keeps this place in the air?"

"I think they use the same technology as the dirigies, only on a larger scale. The propellers are just for positioning when untethered and electricity generation when secured."

Nimet paused to look down at the ground for about the tenth time.

"I thought you said it helps if you don't look down."

"It does," she said distractedly, while staring intently at the ground.

A sudden thought made my stomach go queasy. "Do you see a soothie?"

"No. No! Nothing like that."

Pausing on one platform, I slid my arm through a ringbolt to secure myself and kneaded the sore muscles in my forearms. "So where are all the people?"

"Most of the housing is topside. They prefer cloud and sky."

The trees in the park below were starting to look fake; the people, like ants.

"How much higher, do you think?"

"See that little platform on the corner? That's where I saw him go."

"You saw that from the park? Do you keep a telescope hidden under that fez?"

"How would I fit a telescope under my fez, Willa Snap?" she asked, pushing her purple fez a little tighter over her flaming red hair.

Nimet wasn't kidding about the sudden gusts of wind. What with the propellers, exposed ladders, and odd layout of the various decks and buildings, it was a veritable whirlwind of invisible currents and eddies. I felt like a pinwheel.

The final ladder leading up to the Clockwerk Boy's place cut right through the middle of the platform. There was no door, and it felt impolite to appear without knocking.

"Hello, anyone home?" I shouted over the wind.

I heard metal footsteps, and the Clockwerk Boy's big glass eyes came into view.

"Just me," he said in his flutey voice. "May I be of service?"

"Hi, my name's Willa Snap. I'd like to talk to you for a minute. Is it all right if my friend Nimet Simit and I come up?"

"Why, certainly. Please do."

The Clockwerk Boy's "home" was a platform with one wall and three open sides. It was strangely bare of the things I associated with living quarters, and a cold, steady wind whipped through the place. There was no kitchen, no refrigerator, no stove, no bed, no chairs, no rugs. The few things that did look normal felt out of place: several paintings, a mirror, a glass-fronted bookcase. The biggest thing in the room was an elaborate workbench littered with gears and metalworking tools.

"I don't get many guests," he said. "Sorry for the mess."

"It's lovely," said Nimet, blowing into her hands for warmth. "Did a friend paint you those?"

The Clockwerk Boy turned his head to look at the artwork. "I have no memory of them. But it's quite possible they hold some significance to my past."

Nimet made a face like that was one of the saddest things she'd ever heard.

"Where are my manners?" asked the Clockwerk Boy. "You must be chilled in this environment! I wouldn't be surprised if I kept a kettle around here . . . somewhere." The Clockwerk Boy set a small tin on his worktable and began rummaging through a cupboard.

"That's very thoughtful of you," I said. "But I'm really here because you asked me to find you."

"Did I? How intriguing. I'm afraid I don't recall your face. Do we know each other?"

"You really don't remember anything about me?"

He straightened up and took a long look at me, a tea bag dangling from one hand.

"Ms. Snap," he said.

"Yes!"

"The dragons . . ."

"That's right!"

"They . . . spoke about you tonight!"

I forced myself to take a deep breath. "He only remembers me from tonight," I murmured to Nimet.

"He's a Clockwerk, Willa," Nimet reminded me. "What did you expect?"

I crossed the room to the bookcase and started snooping. His books were all in the snug little boxes my mom called slipcases. *Elefantkin Can Remember*, *They Came to Grandeur*, *Five Little Dragons*, *The Mystery of the Blue MiniDirigy*. The last one on the shelf was *Peril at Gear Hall*, and next to it sat an empty slipcase.

"We met yesterday morning," I told the Clockwerk Boy. "A little after nine, I think."

He filled the kettle and set it on a gas burner that looked like it was made for a completely different task.

As he thought, I could hear the gears in his BrainBox whirring. "That would explain it. My memory reset yesterday at precisely nine twelve and thirty-two seconds."

"The thing is, you gave me a book."

"Did I? How very odd. I don't remember ever buying a—" He turned slowly to where I stood.

"You gave me a *memory* book."

"Do you still have it? Did you bring it here? How did I come to give it to you? Did I give you any instructions? Did I . . . did I give you something else, as well?"

"Yes, I have the book, but not on me. You gave it to me on a MiniDirigy. You asked me to find you and show it to you, and yes,"—I ran my fingers over the Clockwerk cane in my pocket—"and yes, you gave me something else."

The Clockwerk Boy handed us steaming cups, and we warmed our hands as the tea steeped. "I don't understand. Why haven't you followed my directions? Are you being followed? Are we in danger?"

"No, no, nothing like that. I didn't know where you lived. It was only by a stroke of good luck that I found you."

"If you don't mind my asking, what did we talk about yesterday?"

"You knew me by name. You told me I must sacrifice myself to 'right the wrong.' You said the dragons' fate was mine to decide and that my timeline was in danger. That's why I came to the Blasted Dragon today. And you gave me your Clockwerk cane. You said I'd need it."

"Sounds serious. I wonder how I learned your name."

"You don't remember any of it?"

"No. However, if you brought me the memory book, it's possible I could tell you what motivated me so. But know this: I would not run myself down for anything less than mortal danger. It's the way all Clockwerks are geared."

"I don't understand."

"Allow me to explain. While my programming gives me a certain amount of free *will*, there are many restrictions on my freedom. A Clockwerk is not allowed to do whatever it pleases."

"How terrible," I said.

"On the contrary, I find it comforting. For example, one function of my primary coding is to protect myself and others from harm. For example, *I* am not capable of willfully walking off this platform and falling to my death, whereas *you* have no such restriction. *I* cannot willfully take the life of another. *You* can."

"Okay, now you're terrifying me."

"Oh, dear. It was not my intention to—"

"It's fine. But what would have made you come find me?"

"It's a curious matter. I wish I knew more. For example, if I had information to give you, and knew your name, why didn't I meet you at your apartment?"

"You were in a terrible rush, and you were winding down. I understand you have no control over your memory resetting, but why didn't you pause to wind yourself up properly?"

"Indeed, why not?" The Clockwerk Boy thought this over. "It does take time for a proper winding. And while winding, I am . . . vulnerable. Perhaps yours wasn't the only timeline in danger."

"You mean, maybe yours was too?"

"It's a possibility. And of course, let us not forget the dragons. All their lives were in danger."

I gulped down my tea. It felt warm and restorative. "Well, I've passed over my chance for time travel. Maybe the information in your memory book isn't important anymore."

"It's a sound hypothesis. And yet, I feel a thoroughness is in order here."

That sounded good to me. "It's getting kind of late. Can I bring you the memory book tomorrow?"

The Clockwerk Boy consulted a calendar on the wall. "It says here my contract with the dragons was scheduled to end this afternoon. It appears that, for the moment, my time is my own."

"Great. I'll be by first thing."

"I look forward to it, Willa Snap."

"That reminds me, I don't know *your* name."

The Clockwerk Boy tilted his head. "Hmm. I don't recall ever needing a name."

Nimet made a sad *aw* sound, like she was viewing a basket of wet kittens.

"You've got to be kidding! How do people get your attention?"

"'Hey, you Clockwerk over there,' serves well enough, I suppose."

Now it was my turn to make a little *aw* sound.

"I guess we'll be going, then," I said.

"It was a pleasure meeting you both."

I wasn't looking forward to the climb back down. My muscles were trembling as it was, but I didn't want to complain in front of Nimet—especially since she seemed completely unfazed by all this climbing. So down we went. Ladder after ladder, through platform after platform.

"Thanks for getting me here, Nimet."

"It was nothing. I just followed him."

"You were amazing back in the dragon kitchens, too. How did you learn to jump around like that?"

"I use the stairs a lot. Really, it's nothing."

"It was a lot more than nothing! It was like you were a trained ninja assassin." Then a really funny idea lit up in my brain. "Hey, is that your terrible secret? That you and your family are trained ninja assassins?"

I felt a pinprick on my neck, like a bee sting. I looked up just in time to see Nimet lower a short black tube from her lips.

"Hey, what's with the blow gun?"

An intense *whoosh* of ill swept through my organs. My head went dizzy. My fingers slipped free of the ladder. Suddenly, I was falling downward, or the ladder was falling upward. Then it stopped all at once, like I'd landed on my back, but I didn't feel any pain. My ears filled with static.

Above me, Nimet let go of the ladder and flew through the air, like . . . like . . . a ninja. Next thing I knew, her face was right in front of mine. She was checking my eyes or something.

"Nimet," I heard myself croak. "Why the . . . tears?"

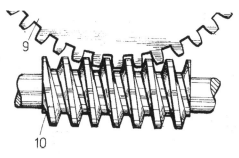

Nimet's Secret

MY name is Nimet Simit, and it is my sad duty to inform you that I will be finishing what is left of this now most unfortunate story. I would ask your forgiveness, but how does one forgive the unforgivable? I don't even know why I'm wasting your time. It doesn't matter now. Nothing matters. I have killed my first and very best friend.

Okay, killed is a tad premature. First, I have to get her safely back to my parents' apartment. Only then can I deliver the death blow with the blessed knife of our secret assassination guild and ascend to my proper role as a ninja assassin. Won't my parents be proud.

It will be a short-lived pride, however, as I have no intention of following in their footsteps. I have known this for a long time, and I wish I could put an end to this farce now, but my training has done its job too well. I cannot, and will not, disgrace my family's generations of honor. However, after I kill Willa, I will take my own life with the same knife. Let my parents sort *that* out.

An infinitesimal tremor in the decking brought me back to the present. I swiftly detached my belt buckle and, using its mirrored back, peered over the edge. Unfortunately, the platforms below blocked my view. I placed an ear to the ladder rungs, closed my eyes, and listened. The vibrations were faint but unmistakable. Someone was ascending from below. A man, wearing a ring on his left, non-dominant hand.

My ninja instincts kicked into high gear. I shed and reversed my clothing, including my fez, rendering me black as a shadow. Peeling off the outer skins of my shoes exposed the notch at the big toe—handy for gripping walls and ropes. A quick cataloguing of Willa's pockets yielded one working-order Clockwerk cane, fully charged, and a note pad wrapped in leather. I took the cane.

1st lesson in transporting a body:
make it look less like a body

I bagged her to the neck and placed a hood over her head.

2nd lesson:
keep your own arms and legs free

I bound her wrists and looped her arms around my neck. She couldn't have weighed more than eighty pounds, which was good, since the dummy my mother made me practice with weighed a solid one thirty-five.

My next course of action required some creative thinking. Obviously, using this ladder was no longer an option. The last thing I needed to tangle with was an unknown assailant. And who was it, anyway? A soothie who'd been lurking in the Blasted Dragon?

More puzzling: who was its target? Me, Willa, the Clockwerk Boy? As tantalizing as these questions were, I knew they would have to go unanswered.

I held the cane over my head and pressed a combination of buttons on its handle. Propeller blades popped out and clicked into place. As I stepped off the edge, the whirling blades lifted us into the air. The cane responded to my commands almost magically with each shift of my wrist. We circled the ladder until we were out of the climber's field of vision, then I cut the power and we dropped like a stone. At the last moment, I brought the blades to full throttle, deftly placing us in the topmost branches of a tall tree.

Securing the cane, I pulled a small telescope from my fez and trained it on the lone figure above. It was definitely a man, but he climbed like a woman. Very odd, but really of no concern to me.

Getting Willa's body back to my parents' apartment unseen in broad daylight was challenging, but not beyond my abilities. The Clockwerk cane came in quite handy, lifting us from rooftop to rooftop until we dropped down the ventilator shaft leading to the secret door behind the painting in our living room.

All I needed now was a little luck . . . on my unluckiest day.

I transferred Willa's arms from my neck to a hook in the shaft and entered the apartment alone.

"Mom?"

My voice sounded foreign to me.

Nothing.

"Dad?"

Still nothing.

My first bit of luck. Figures.

I retrieved the ceremonial knife from the mantelpiece, where my parents had proudly displayed it since my birth, and turned over the blade in my hands. An elongated *M* was etched on either side. Another mystery that would remain unsolved.

As I opened the painting to the ventilator shaft, I'm ashamed to say part of me wanted to find an empty hook. But the poison flowing through Willa's veins was far too powerful for anything like that to happen. Willa felt heavy now, like my heart and soul.

As I laid her limp form on the hearth and cut away the silk bag, the protective veneer from all my years of hard training cracked. I didn't even realize I was sobbing until I traced the source of the wetness falling on my knife blade.

Willa groaned. Her eyes were closed, but I thought she sensed me there.

"I'm so sorry, Willa," I said, raising the knife high above my head. "Nice knowing you, bestie."

I plunged the knife toward Willa's heart. . . .

And then, a lot of things happened at once.

My dad appeared out of nowhere, screaming, "Whoa! Whoa!" and waving his arms. My mom—she must have been behind me—picked up the big silver platter on the end table and flicked it like a Frisbee. I was so distracted by my dad I didn't even see the platter until my knife blade pinned it to Willa's chest.

My dad's eyes were huge. "What are you doing?"

I couldn't tell if he was shocked, relieved, or angry, but I'd been holding in a lot, ever since Willa had guessed my family's secret, so . . . I guess I kind of lost it.

"What does it look like I'm doing?" I screamed. "I'm killing my best friend! So you and Mom can be happy, and I can ascend to our family's stupid profession!"

"You—you have a best friend?" asked Dad. "Eylem, did you hear that? Our daughter has a best friend."

They embraced, beaming at me, just like the first time I broke a choke hold.

"Nimet," my mother gushed, "is it really true? You have a best friend?"

"Since yesterday," I said sourly.

They sighed happily. "And you were going to kill her—for us?" she asked.

I nodded.

Mom did the little dance she usually reserves for special occasions, like the first time I scaled our building during a rainstorm using only my bare hands.

"Do you know what this means?" she asked.

My shoulders slumped. "That you both have a very disturbed idea of what constitutes positive reinforcement?"

"No!" laughed my dad. "You've ascended! You're in! You're one of us! "

"How does that make you feel?" asked Mom, smiling. "Pretty good, huh? Huh?"

I looked down at Willa's comatose body. "Yippee," I said softly, trying to hold back the tears.

"And now that you belong to the oldest guild of assassins—" my dad started to say.

"Well, maybe not the oldest," my mom interrupted.

"Right. But certainly the most secretive," added Dad.

"Or at least *one* of the most secretive—"

"Who cares?" I screamed, and the sobbing began in earnest.

"Look, Bora. She weeps with joy!"

Dad placed his hands on his hips and furrowed his brow. "You know, Eylem, I'm not so sure those are happy tears."

"Oh, of course they are! Bora, don't you think I can tell when my own—" Mom tilted her head. "Wait . . . you're not happy, little Nim-Nim?"

Mom's not exactly the sharpest throwing spike in the weapons cabinet. Don't get me wrong, there's no one I'd rather have by my side in an uneven sword fight, but how could she understand so little about my pain?

"HOW COULD I POSSIBLY BE HAPPY? I'M ABOUT TO KILL MY BEST FRIEND!"

My dad nodded. "Ohhh, right. That. Eylem, it's time we told her."

"Told me what?" I sniffed.

"You don't have to kill your friend," explained my mother.

"Even assassins are allowed to have besties," explained Dad. "You simply can't ever let her find out what we do."

"But she already knooooooooooows," I wailed.

My dad fidgeted with a shuriken—that's a throwing weapon shaped like a huge, insanely sharp, metal snowflake. He fidgets when he's embarrassed. "Yeah, that won't . . . be a problem."

They were making less sense by the minute. "But we're assassins!"

"Well spotted," said Dad softly.

"And assassins *kill* people!"

Mom and Dad exchanged a nervous glance.

"You've trained me my whole life," I continued, "so I could join a guild so secretive *you* don't know its name! And now you're saying I don't have to kill Willa, even though she knows what we are? What kind of sick joke is this?"

"Oh, it's no joke, Nim-Nim," said Dad. "We're assassins, all right."

Mom knelt down and looked me in the eye. "We're *memory* assassins!"

The ramifications dawned on me slowly, and then all at once. And just like that, my parents were the coolest people on Earth again. I jumped into the air, throwing the knife point-first into the ceiling. I spun around, my arms outstretched, laughing and laughing and laughing. I had never been so happy. This even beat mastering kayakujutsu—that's the art of gunpowder, firearms, explosives, things like that.

"Willa won't remember what we are?" I asked.

"Not a chance," assured Mom.

"Only what we want her to," added Dad.

"But won't she wonder how she got here?"

Dad blew this off with a wave of his hand. "No problem. We'll plant a few details in her memory and return her to her apartment. It'll be fun!"

Then I had a terrible thought. "What if she . . . re-remembers?"

A shadow passed over Mom's face. "Don't worry, she won't."

"But what if she does?"

My dad stared at the floor, repeatedly popping out and retracting the steel spikes in his shoes. "You better tell her, Eylem," he finally said.

"Can't we wait until she's older?"

"Tell me what?"

"No more secrets," said Dad.

"I suppose you're right. Here's the thing, Nim-Nim.

Rarely—very rarely—a memory doesn't die the way it should. And we can only alter a specific memory so many times . . . so . . . if she does re-remember . . ."

I looked at Willa. "Or figures it out again!"

My dad shook his head. "No-no. *That* we can fix. New memories are easy. It's the re-remembering that's the problem."

"What if she figures it out . . . and doesn't tell me?"

Mom placed an arm around my shoulder. "Nim-Nim, when you're a memory assassin, having friends is a great responsibility. You will have to be clever and vigilant."

Willa coughed. Mom touched a hand to her face and announced, "She's coming out of it. Time for your first lesson, Nim-Nim."

"One more question. If we have the ability to assassinate memories, why are we trapped in Grandeur? I mean, how did the Black Fez ever manage to take the two of you in?"

Mom produced an iron tiger claw from her hair and began cleaning her nails with it.

"Mom?"

"The—the Black Fez aren't immune," she mumbled.

My dad started lightly puffing a tune on his blow gun tube. "Blackout," from the Broadway show *In the Heights,* if I wasn't mistaken. (My parents are massive Lin-Manuel Miranda fans.)

"If they aren't immune . . . what are we doing here?"

Dad stopped mid-note, almost said something, then went back to his tune.

"One day, when you were just three years old," Mom began, "we were on a mission to assassinate some very dangerous memories that had leapt from a book that never should have been written, let alone read. But we weren't the only ones on a mission that day. The Black Fez caught us . . . in the act."

I shook my head. "Oh, no! No-no-no."

"Naturally, our guild has been tracking the whereabouts of a certain fabled secret city and its Order of the Black Fez for centuries," she continued.

"This isn't happening. You're not saying this."

"It just seemed too good to be true. I mean, what a lucky break."

"You're saying we came here ON PURPOSE!"

"Grandeur has a lot to offer, Nim-Nim," she said defensively

"LIKE WHAT?"

"The baklava with walnuts and pistachios at Firin's Bakery," my dad said earnestly.

My mother nodded fervently. "The aşure pudding at Mustafa's Cafe 1364. Pure ambrosia!"

My mouth began to water. "You mean the . . . the yummy one . . . with the pomegranate seeds?" Our stomachs growled in unison. "Wait, this is crazy! Are you saying we're trapped here because of baked goods?"

"The truth is, Nim-Nim," said my mother, "we like it here. Grandeur has quite the thriving Turkish community. We've made friends."

I couldn't believe what I was hearing. "We're talking about our freedom!"

"Salep dondurma," said my dad. (You would call it ice cream, but this stuff *never* drips off the cone.) I felt a little dizzy.

"Lokma," said my mother. (Think sweet little crunchy doughnut balls coated with sugar syrup. It's like having heaven in your mouth.)

I stood my ground. Then my mother dropped the big one.

"Wouldn't you be sad if there weren't talking squirrels?"

"What are you saying?"

"Outside hasn't developed vocal implants for animals."

"No . . . no talking elefantkin?"

"No elefantkin at all, I'm afraid. Remember, brewed creatures are another technology foreign to Outside."

I blinked. "Okay, I'm good with it. Let's pretend this conversation never happened."

"What conversation?" said my dad.

Obviously, I can't divulge the techniques of memory assassination. Suffice it to say that my first lesson was very . . . interesting. I'd hoped to get more practice when we tried to slip Willa back into her bedroom unnoticed, but Willa's father was so deeply asleep it was like he'd been drugged. And her mother was nowhere to be found, despite the late hour. But that mystery can wait. What's important here is that this isn't my story to finish after all. It's Willa's. And in case you're wondering how I slipped this chapter into Willa's manuscript without her knowing, it's because I added it myself while en route to the publisher. That's right! I can step Outside, I can step inside. Outside, inside, Outside, inside. How, you ask? Because I'm Nimet Simit: ninja memory assassin extraordinaire!

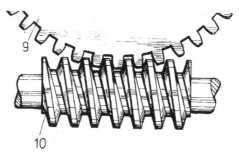

Grimalkin's Curiosity Shop

T HAT night I dreamt a mad, furry woman in a gray maid's uniform was chasing me through aisles of spinning gears and pulsing springs. She wielded an enormous feather duster in each hand, and every time I glanced over my shoulder to see if she was still there, she'd smack me in the face. *Woppetta, woppetta, woppetta!* When I woke, Grayson was sitting on my chest batting me with the pads of her paws. She was wearing her kitty-sized BrainRent, and the little speaker on it was blaring: "Wake! Up! Wake! Up! Wake! Up! Wake! Up! Whaaaa!—"

I pushed her off my chest and onto something crinkly. Sitting upright, I noticed my entire room was covered in discarded papers. I smoothed one flat. It was filled with diagrams, numbers, equations—all drawn in a rather shaky hand or, more likely, paw.

"What's all this?"

Grayson pounced on me, taking me by surprise and pinning me to the bed. Her eyes were wild and her fur unkempt.

CHAPTER NINETEEN

"Must get out!" she said in a panicky voice. "I'm *not* a house cat! If I stay indoors, I'll LOSE MY MIND! Do you hear me? I'LL GO MAD!"

"*Go* mad? Already missed the boat on that one, don't you think?" I pushed her off my chest and scooped up a handful of the papers. "This looks like . . . a cat-sized dirigy? A balcony-mounted airship docking station? Hey, this looks like our balcony!" Grayson, who was now standing on her back legs, paws clutched to her chest, nodded like a simpleton. "Grayson, you'll never escape Grandeur in a KittyDirigy of any make or size."

"KittyDirigy!" she said nervously. "Ha! I like that! Can I use that? Never mind. That's not my plan!"

Grayson bounded to the desk and speared her latest designs. She shoved a pawful of papers in my face. Her claws were stained black with ink.

"Parks!" she yattered. "Grandeur is full of wooded parks! Ponds! Fish to watch! Birds to chase! TREES TO CLIMB!" Her gestures were growing more expressive. I sensed a buildup to something big. "Kittens to save! Dogs to put in their places!"—wait for it—"SQUIRRELS TO EAT!"

There we go. I held up a hand. "Okay, okay, I get it. But how much will all this cost?"

As she counted on her claws, her eyes ticked back and forth like one of those silly cat clocks where the tail is the pendulum.

"Eight thousand two hundred nine dolleurs and twenty-nine cents!"

"And how many dolleurs have you earned with your Brain-Rent so far?" I asked.

"Six!"

I made a quick computation. "Great. So, adjusting for inflation, you'll have it installed in a little less than four years time. And that's only if you keep wearing the BrainRent, which you already said you don't want to wear!"

Grayson stiffened, her whiskers drooped, and she fell flat on her back.

"Oh, Grayson," I said, scritching her exposed tummy. "You've got too much squirrel on the brain."

"I heard that," she said. In a twitch, she was up again, pressing her cold nose against mine. "I've got . . . an *angle.*"

"What are you meowing on about now?"

She paradropped off the bed and rooted through the mess on the floor like a prize pig snuffling for truffles. Papers flew in her wake. "Wait just a second! I've got it *right* here! Don't go anywhere! Don't move! Yeah-HA!" She hauled herself up the bed and dropped a saliva-covered pamphlet in my lap.

"Here!" she said triumphantly, paging to the back and pointing to an advertisement.

I picked it up and read:

SQUIRREL EXTERMINATOR NEEDED
⋈ Flamethrower Experience a MUST!!! ⋈
DEMOLITIONS EXPERTISE A PLUS!
Applications accepted at the Mermaid Lakeside Theatre ticket office.

"No! No! No! The one below that! Here!"

"Wait, have you heard about this Mermaid Lakeside Theatre?"

"Yes, yes, yes. It's an all-cat repertory company. I understand they're performing Shakespeare's *Merchant of Venice* next. I'm considering auditioning for the role of Portia. But that's not important right now."

"You act?"

"All cats act. We were born for the stage. How else do you think we could fool you monkeys so thoroughly?"

"Fool us?"

"Into being our slaves!" Grayson glanced away, suddenly angry with herself. "Slavery is such a harsh word," she added, recovering her composure. "Look, all I'm saying is that through history, behind every great playwright, you'll find a cat . . . whispering plotlines in the dead of night."

I probably should have been angry, but all I could think about was Grayson dressed in period costume performing the Bard's work. "If you get the part, can you get me tickets?"

"Yes, but don't come on Thursdays."

"I—I'm afraid to ask."

"Thursdays are when they allow the dogs in."

"Naturally."

Grayson thumped her paw on the advertisement below. "This one!"

Grimalkin's Curiosity Shop
Fine Feline Collectibles

Cashier needed. Must be able to speak dog and human. Additional languages a plus.

I let the pamphlet drop into my lap. "Now why would they

need you to speak dog?"

Grayson shrugged. "What's it matter? I speak thirty languages."

"Really!" I said, looking at her with renewed admiration. "But how would you get back and forth to work?" Grayson gazed at me apprehensively, her ears drooping. "Grayson?"

"It would only be temporary," she insisted. "Once we install the airship docking station, and I construct the KittyDirigy . . ."

I felt a chill grasp my heart. "You're moving out?"

"It would only be until—"

I stood up stiffly. My head nearly exploded with pain. "Oh, wow! Now *that's* a headache!" There was a big goose egg on the back of my head. "How did that—" and then I remembered everything. Falling off the ladder, Nimet flying through the air to my rescue. I felt for the Clockwerk cane in my pocket. It was there. I remembered telling Nimet I was fine, that it was just a bump. But Nimet had insisted her father check my eyes for signs of concussion. What was his name? Even his face evaded me. The last thing I remembered was us begging him not to tell my parents about it.

Grayson looked concerned. "Are you all right? When you came in last night you bumped into the sweater drawer. It took me half an hour to get it open. And by that time, you were out. And I mean out. In fact, if I didn't know better, I'd say you'd been drugged."

I sat back down again. That made my head hurt, too. "Listen, I'll be fine. Now about the parks, *I* can take you—" A lump formed in my throat. I wasn't ready for Grayson to go. My thoughts started tumbling out the way they do when I'm upset. "You said it yourself, Grandeur is full of parks. We could visit a new one every day and—"

"No," said Grayson softly. "I won't have you carrying me everywhere you go. I will *not* be a burden."

I picked up the advertisement again. "This ad looks like it was printed a hundred years ago. What makes you think this place is still in business?"

"It's just made to look old. And I don't think that's normal paper."

"What do you mean?"

"If you stare at the advertisements long enough, they change. If you had a microscope, I suspect you'd find those pages are actually paper-thin flexible computer displays."

I held the pamphlet up to my nose. It looked like regular paper to me. "It says Grimalkin's Curiosity Shop is in the Biowerks Burg. I'll take you there right after breakfast." Then I grabbed a towel and hurried out of the room so Grayson wouldn't see me cry.

At the table, I sized up my parents. They appeared to be doing awfully well for a couple starting their third day of forced imprisonment.

"Did you make these eggs, Dad?" I asked.

He had his nose in that book Mom had given him on our first day. "Yep, how could you tell?"

"Because they're edible," said Mom, smiling.

"You're not *that* bad!"

"You're very kind, dear. But I'm not ashamed to own my bad cooking."

"I was wondering if it would be okay if I took the Magnificent Lady Grayson to a park before Idiot school. It's just a couple blocks from here."

"I don't see why not," said Mom.

Dad turned a page. "Do you want company?"

I was afraid he might say that. "No thanks. I'm thinking Grayson and I need some good old-fashioned post-abduction bonding time."

It didn't take much effort on my part to give them a good chuckle. As parents go, I figured I had two of the best.

"Oh, Dad. I've been meaning to ask you." I pulled up the photo I'd taken of the pipes under Dr. Wudgepuddle's sink. "This make any sense to you?"

Dad closed his book.

"Now that's something you don't see every day."

"What is it?"

"Well, by the look of those chambers, I'd say you're looking at a system designed to insert something into a high-pressure water pipe. But I've never seen it done on pipes this small."

"Why would anyone want to do that?"

"Pipe inspection, maybe? Where did you take that photo?"

"A friend's house . . . under the bathroom sink."

"Willa, what were you doing poking around under their sink?"

Mom snorted. "Snooping, silly. Don't you know you should never leave a girl alone in a strange room?"

Saved by the Momster. Boy, she was just full of surprises lately.

After cleaning up the breakfast dishes, I gave big kisses all round. In my room, I tossed the Clockwerk Boy's memory book into Dad's empty tool bag and held it open to Grayson. She hopped right in.

Grandeurpedia placed Grimalkin's Curiosity Shop on an un-named alleyway off Tyrtamus Lane. The easiest way to get there took me through a beautiful park full of tall stately trees. They must have been hundreds of years old. Grayson sensed the park the minute I set foot in it.

"Please let me out! Please, please, please! I'll be good."

"Not a chance. There are squirrels all over the place."

"I will walk by your side—like a dog! I swear! Just while we walk through the park. Please, please, please."

I sighed. "You swear?"

"I swear on Bastet's tail!"

I unzipped the tool bag. Grayson leapt from the bag, chased a squirrel twice around a tree, and then shot up the trunk.

"Really?" I called. "Does Bastet even have a tail? Well, does she?"

I watched the squirrel race out onto a precarious limb, high above. It got thinner and thinner until the squirrel was forced to make a daring leap to a neighboring tree. A second later followed Grayson, claws out, tail streaming.

What can you do? I slowly made my way through the park. To Grayson's credit, she *seemed* to be making an effort to stay in my general vicinity. Near the far end of the park, I came upon some old stone benches and a statue ringed by cobblestones. The statue was of a robed man with curly hair and a beard, clutching a bou-quet of flowers. Engraved below him were the words:

Omne Initium Est Difficile

Theophrastus, traveling philosopher and botanist. (b. 371 BCE - d. 287 BCE) First to document plant reproduction, a discovery lost to Outside for nearly two thousand years before being rediscovered in 1682 by Nehemiah Grew.

I couldn't believe it. This dude Theophrastus made a discovery—a big honking scientific discovery—and it was lost for TWO THOUSAND YEARS? How did that happen? Why wasn't it rediscovered sooner?

I tapped my WatchitMapCallit and asked it to translate *Omne Initium Est Difficile*. It spoke back instantly. "Every beginning is difficult."

I about swooned. It got me wondering what else had been lost to time. The back of my knees bumped into one of the benches, and I sat down forcibly. Two thousand years of progress snuffed out. Think of all the foods that could be edible by now: beets, kale, artichokes—I mean, really, it has the word *choke* in it. But who am I kidding, it's going to take a lot more than two thousand years of improvement to keep me from spitting up kale.

A squirrel tail, minus the squirrel, fell out of the sky and landed next to me.

"Was he tasty?" I shouted to the branches above.

I stuffed the tail in my pocket. A little catnip, some string . . . I will drive her to the brink of madness.

I popped up a map on my WatchitMapCallit and got my bearings. Tyrtamus Lane was straight ahead. At the edge of the park,

CHAPTER NINETEEN

the Magnificent Lady Grayson leapt from a tree and sauntered toward me, her tail high, a smug look on her face.

"It should be right . . . over there," I told her.

We crossed the street, and I zoomed in on the map. It was showing an alleyway that wasn't there. I started walking, poking my hand periodically through a swath of ivy blanketing a wall: stone, stone, stone. Air! Walking a little farther, I found a passageway leading into the greenery. The way grew darker with each twist and turn. By the time I emerged into the alley itself, it was like stepping into a moonless night. Grayson brushed up against me. At least, I hoped it was Grayson.

"Keep close until your eyes adjust," she said. "Follow my voice."

Almost immediately a horrible face loomed out of the darkness. I sucked in a breath and was about to scream when I realized it was only a sign. The words *Grimalkin's Curiosity Shop: Fine Feline Collectibles* encircled the hideous, fanged head. Next to it was a recessed opening, and inside I saw cracks of light rimming an ill-fitted door.

I gulped. "Shall we?"

"Oh, don't be so dramatic," Grayson scolded, disappearing through a cat-sized door at my feet.

I was alone. Something between a *MEEP!* and an *EEK!* crossed my lips. I slapped my hand over my mouth. My heart pounded, and I couldn't pry my eyes away from the evil cat's eyes. Who would commission such a thing? Well . . . only one way to find out. I groped along the door until my hand closed around a cool metal knob.

A bell jingled above me. The light inside was dim, and the air smelled like old wood. The shop was long and narrow, bordered by display cabinets stacked one on top of the other. Behind the cabinets, cats in aprons and smocks worked busily. Some held little hammers in their paws, some had jeweler's loupes notched in one eye, and others stared through magnifying glasses on stands. All were hard at work, tinkering and polishing.

Grayson was a few feet in front of me, walking along an elevated catwalk. As I followed, I peered into the cabinets. The lower cases held jewelry, watches, and tool kits designed for paws. I saw opera glasses, violins, squirrel-fur riding breeches, miniature paintings, Turkish slippers, tea services, rubbings from Shakespeare's tomb, a bottle of water from the Dead Sea, Japanese kimonos—all sized for cats. Grayson strolled deeper into the store, her tail high, confident, unafraid.

At the back of the shop in a tall chair sat the largest and oldest cat I'd ever seen. He'd been white once, maybe. His ears were tattered and a single snaggletooth protruded past his raggedy cheek.

"What's this?" he asked in a gravelly voice.

"Grimalkin?" asked Grayson.

He grunted.

"I've come for the job," said Grayson.

"Name?"

"The Magnificent Lady Grayson of the Silky White Underbelly, or Just Grayson for Short."

"None of that here, little lady. What's your real name?"

Grayson hesitated, glancing briefly back at me. "Runa, daughter of Hrímhildr, of the clan Huldrekat."

Grimalkin gave Grayson a skeptical look. "Skills?" he asked.

"Chemist," answered Grayson, then added softly, "Mostly."

"Apothecary!" beamed Grimalkin, his eyebrows arching. Then he pounced forward and spat, "What are the six impossible ingredients of a Gleipnir chain?"

Grayson narrowed her eyes and swept back her ears. For a second, I thought she was going to spring forward, claws out. "The beard of a woman, the roots of a mountain, the sinews of a bear, the breath of a fish, the spit of a bird, and the sound of a cat walking. Now, do you want me in your employ or not?"

The ancient cat leaned back and gave the Magnificent Lady Grayson a good long look.

"You speak dog and human?" he asked.

"Of course. And I'll need a place to stay . . . short term."

Grimalkin opened a drawer and withdrew a single piece of paper. He smoothed it flat on the coun- ter with his big paws. It had writing on it in a language I'd never seen. He

pawed an uncorked ink bottle closer to Grayson. "The Scratching Post has inexpensive rooms. I can deduct the rent from your pay at a discount as long as you remain in good standing."

Grayson ran her eye down the form, dipped a claw in the ink—

"Wait!" I said. "How much will you give me for this?" I held up the Clockwerk cane.

Grimalkin furrowed his brow. "Is that . . . ?" He reached out. "May I?"

I handed it over.

"Luigi's ghost!" He inspected the buttons and gauges on the handle. "A very fine specimen. Don't see many by *this* maker nowadays, and never outside the Clockwerk Burg." He handed it back to me. "I'd have to put it up for auction."

My heart raced. "Would it fetch enough to buy the Magnificent Lady Grayson a new pair of vocal chords?" *With enough left over for an airship docking station and KittyDirigy?* I wondered.

Grimalkin eyed me carefully. "That and more. But since you're underage, I would require your sire or dam to vouch that it's yours. I run a respectable establishment."

What was I thinking? I couldn't sell it if I wanted to. It wasn't mine to sell.

"Of course," I said, unable to keep the disappointment from my voice.

"Thanks for the thought," said Grayson. Turning back to the contract, she wrote *Runa, daughter of Hrímhildr, of the clan Huldrekat*, in a flowing paw.

"Welcome to the Curiosity Shop," said Grimalkin, inspecting Grayson's signature before he placed the contract back in the drawer. "Has Runa been with you for long?"

"Three years now."

Grimalkin nodded. "Wait here a moment." He slipped his considerable bulk from the chair and silently vanished into the shadows.

"How long's that contract for?" I asked Grayson.

"Six months or two lives, whichever comes first. Sundays off, and my nights are my own. It's a generous contract."

Grayson had seen me through fourth and fifth grade. She curled up on my bed every night. Not that I think for a minute she stayed long once I fell asleep, but she was always back by morning. Tears welled up in my eyes. I was holding the empty tool bag in a death grip.

"So I guess this is it?" I said.

Grayson put a paw on my shoulder and head-butted me. "Take care of your dad. Keep both eyes on your mom. I'll write. Six months will go by faster than you think."

I kissed her on the forehead. "It'll feel like a million years to me."

Grimalkin grunted back into his chair and held out a plastic sleeve.

"Take it."

"What's this?"

"It's a token, a small piece of ephemera from my personal collection, for your three years' servitude."

I picked it up.

"It's the only copy I've ever seen that includes your model."

Inside the sleeve was a slim piece of folded paper. I thanked him quickly, then hurried out of the shop and sobbed against the wall in the alley for five full minutes before wiping away my tears and calling a Clockwerk cab. There were bigger things afoot than my eleven-year-old emotions. I had a memory book to deliver and a mystery to uncover.

I didn't have any problem finding the ladder Nimet and I had taken yesterday, but this time the long climb to the Clockwerk Boy's flat was a lonely one. At the entrance to his living room, I banged my fist on the underside of the floor.

"Hello," I shouted over the wind. "It's me, Willa."

Silence.

I stepped up a few rungs and popped my head into his room. The floor was littered with tools. The canvas on one of the paintings was torn. It looked like there'd been some kind of fight.

I found him laid out on his worktable. Someone had opened his chest and taken out his BrainBox. What remained was a lifeless metal corpse. It made me strangely ill to look at him.

Did he have a next of kin? Was I looking at a murder? What was I supposed to do, call the soothies? The idea made me shiver. I pulled the memory book from the tool bag, opened it, and held the first page in front of his eyes. I didn't expect it to do anything. It didn't. Someone had stolen his life, but I was now the keeper of his memories. Then I remembered the bookcase. The glass was smashed, but the books were intact. Whoever had done this must not have known what they represented.

He'd asked me last night if I thought he was in danger. I'd told him no. An upwelling of guilt and grief overtook me. I covered my face with my hands. This was my fault. How was I going to fix it?

Then I had a thought. If whoever did this didn't understand

the meaning of the books . . . I opened the small drawer in his chest. Was it still there? Yes! Inside was a thin volume, like the ones in the bookcase. The title on the spine read: *Evil Genius Under the Sun.* I opened it. The handwriting was of two different styles. The beginning was all in one hand, the rest another, both mechanical, both different.

I walked to one of the room's open edges. There were no guardrails. The builders of this place never intended for anyone to live here, human or Clockwerk. I sat down and dangled my legs. The park was far below. Off in the distance the three central towers rose up, up, up and disappeared into the clouds. Sunlight sparkled off thousands of bippy bots, and MiniDirigies glided over the city like bulbous puffer fish, dutifully moving people from one platform to the next.

Who could have done this? Even as I had the thought, something in the back of my mind nagged at me. Then it came rushing to the front. I knew exactly who wanted this very thing done. He might not have been the doer of the deed, but he had to be involved. *It was asking a lot of questions*, he'd said to Wyrmgear. *It was snooping*, he'd persisted. *I insist you destroy that BrainBox.* I hadn't seen his face, but I'd recognized his voice—Dr. Quimby Wudgepuddle. Heathcliff's dad.

I'd overheard those words on my first night in Grandeur, after Tuppence, posing as a plumbing dispatcher, sent my father to Gear Hall. Tuppence had even suggested he take someone along. She'd wanted me there.

More memories flashed into my mind. Nimet searching the crowd at the park last night. And later, Nimet checking behind us as we climbed to this very room. Had she seen someone following us?

The key had to be the memory books. What had the Clockwerk Boy overheard at Gear Hall the night of that party? What had he heard about me while he was working for the dragons? And what was the "evil under the sun" in the memory book I'd just found?

I needed the Clockwerk Boy whole again, and fast. But how? I knew what my dad would say. When solving a problem, start with a list of your assets and abilities.

I pulled out my notepad and untucked the gift Grimalkin had given me. I unzipped the plastic sleeve and slipped out the small piece of folded paper. One side was blank, and the other side simply said:

Luigi da Vinci e Figli
Fondata 1337

I used my WatchitMapCallit to translate: Luigi da Vinci and Sons, Established 1337. Carefully unfolding the paper, I discovered it was part advertisement, part instructions for a line of Clockwerk canes. I scanned past Danish, Dioula, Dutch, and Dzongkha before finding the English version.

The first on the list was a basic model, *The Courtier*; followed by the next model up, *The Baron*, and then *The Duke*. Each had more features than the last. I pulled the Clockwerk cane out of my pocket and pressed the button that made it telescope out to its full height. None of these models had as many buttons, gauges, and dials as mine. I was beginning to feel cheated when I turned the paper over and saw the entire back side was dedicated to a single model called *The Flying Time Traveler*.

I compared the handle in the illustration to mine. They were a perfect match. My eyes raced over the instructions for references to time travel, but it quickly became clear they weren't talking about transporting the cane's owner *through* time. Instead, they were talking about *saving* time by using a propeller blade feature for short hops. Sure, it wasn't as exciting as time travel, but I can't say I was the least bit disappointed. I mean, if this little Clockwerk cane was really made in the fourteenth century, it must have been one of the most advanced devices of its time, even for Grandeur. And yet, even with all its tricks, I didn't see how I could use it to help me with the Clockwerk Boy.

Obviously, the cane wasn't going to serve as a BrainBox. And given the Clockwerk Boy's weight, it probably couldn't safely fly us down to the ground either. And even if it could, I doubted whether half a winding could get us all the way back to White-haven Mansions. Wait a minute . . . half a winding? When did that happen? I didn't really have time to pursue this line of thought, but I jotted it down in my notepad. You never know when another clue might drop. Life is full of puzzles.

Right now I had a more important job, one for Idiots, and I knew just where to find them.

I folded up the instructions and stuffed them behind my notepad. Before I left, I filled the tool bag with as many memory books as it would hold.

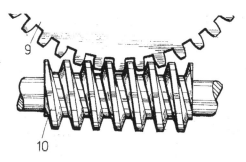

Pancakes Ahoy

I WAS glad to see that Ravenlock wasn't waiting outside the classroom door again. On the way to my seat, I gave Bertie a little wave and a smile. He grinned. Our adventures at the Blasted Dragon hadn't changed his mind about me. We were good. That made me surprisingly happy.

A few minutes later, Nimet and Ravenlock walked in together. Nimet looked frazzled. Had Ravenlock been harassing her? I shot an accusing look at him, but he just stared back at me, confused. Within seconds I felt that irritating flash of heat in my cheeks. I was about to look away when he seemed to get it. Motioning to Nimet, he shook his head and said, "Not a clue."

Nimet collapsed in her chair.

"What did you do?" I said, sounding more angry than I was.

Nimet startled. "I didn't kill anybody!" she said defensively.

Nimet's ability to surprise was quickly becoming her most endearing quality. "What?" I said, laughing.

She looked like she hadn't slept in days. "And you've no proof that I did . . . because . . . because there isn't any!" She seemed positively giddy about that last point.

"Ravenlock was waiting for you in the hallway, wasn't he? Did he threaten you?"

Nimet normally talks a little fast, but now it was like someone had set her playback speed on fast forward. "I spent the night at my house, by myself, all night, alone, reading a book if you must know."

"Are your parents . . . are they treating you okay?"

"No. I mean yes. I mean my parents are fine—they treat me fine. They didn't kill anybody either . . . that I know of. Why all the third degree?"

If I didn't know better, I'd have thought she and Ravenlock were up to something. But who was I kidding? Nimet and Ravenlock? That was almost as crazy as me and Ravenlock being up to something . . . together . . . hanging out. Telling each other our inner secrets. Baring our souls—

Professor Pedagogue's droning voice pulled me back to the classroom. Why hadn't Ravenlock shut him off? And why was Nimet avoiding my eyes? Had I pushed her too far too soon? I was her very first friend, after all. The problem was, I needed her now more than ever.

I pulled out my notepad, wrote what I'd seen at the Clockwerk Boy's flat, and tore out the page.

Her eyes got huge when she read it.

Snapping out of her funk, she jotted down something and passed the note back.

We have to find out what is in that memory book. I have an idea.

When class ended, Nimet was the first to stand up. She was out the door before I could get halfway across the room. I didn't catch up to her until we were out on the sidewalk.

"Nimet, why all the rush?"

"We need a team," she said, inspecting the students filing out of the building. "A good one."

She shouted to Rufus Feynman and CeeCee da Vinci. Rufus, who had been racing away on a low wall at breakneck speed making jet airplane noises, leapt off the wall and veered back like he'd hit the afterburners. CeeCee skipped over, ponytails bouncing.

"Where's Bertie Babbage?" Nimet asked. "We have to have Bertie Babbage."

"Good to feel wanted," said Bertie, stepping up from behind.

"Aren't Rufus and CeeCee a little young?" I asked.

"Rufus can talk his way out of anything, which is an extremely valuable skill. And don't judge CeeCee by her ponytails. She can play every instrument in an orchestra and she's already written three symphonies."

"What's going on?" asked Bertie.

"The Clockwerk Boy had his BrainBox stolen, and we're assembling a team to put him back together pronto."

Bertie looked stunned. "You're kidding."

"This is not a joke, Bertie Babbage. Are you in or not?"

"Count me in," said Bertie.

"What about Ian Tesla?" I suggested.

"Too dangerous," said Bertie. "Definitely an Idiot Genius in the making, if you ask me."

"But he *is* an Idiot, right? Like us?"

"Ian could easily go either way," said Bertie. "In fact, half the kids in our class are borderline Geniuses."

"Not me, though," I said with a snort of laughter.

"What do you mean?" asked Nimet.

"Me? I'm no Genius!"

"Are you in our class, Willa?" demanded Nimet.

"Well . . . yeah."

"Then case closed," she said with finality.

Nimet had to be wrong, of course.

"What about Kayla Hawking?" Bertie asked.

"That girl is trouble with a capital T," said Nimet.

"I can't believe I'm saying this, but what about Heathcliff?" Bertie asked.

"Too immature," Nimet and I said at the same time.

"What about Masa Mochi or Ji Taam?" I asked.

"Good choices both," said Bertie, "but their parents send them to special tutors after school, so their weekdays are pretty much shot."

Rufus, his arms swept back, aviator goggles in place and jet engines at full throttle, was now on a collision course.

At first, it seemed funny. But then . . .

"Why isn't he slowing down?" asked Nimet.

Right about the time I started to panic, Bertie stepped in front of us. "I got this." Gesturing with his arms, he guided Rufus in for a safe landing.

Rufus stored his wings and snapped his goggles onto his forehead. "What's up, Nimet?"

Nimet placed a finger over her lips. Once we were all gathered, she announced, "Willa has a mission—an Idiot mission."

Rufus's face turned serious. "And you want me and CeeCee

on your team?"

"Yes," I said.

CeeCee's eyes lit up. "I'm in! I'm in!"

"Hold on, CeeCee," interrupted Bertie protectively. "You haven't even heard the details yet."

I lowered my voice. "I don't feel comfortable talking about it in the open. Is there someplace quiet we can go, where no one can overhear us?"

"Hmm," said Nimet, her eyes darting around the group. "How about someplace noisy?"

Rufus fist-bumped Nimet. CeeCee actually jumped up and down, clapping her hands.

"Ever been to the *Jolly Rajah* on a Friday?" Nimet asked, a grin engulfing her face.

"You *know* I haven't," I said, now intensely curious.

"Well then," said Bertie, "there isn't a moment to lose."

A shadow passed over us, and Ravenlock Sward appeared from out of nowhere.

"Off to save Grandeur from a plague of evils?"

I started to speak up, but Nimet stepped on my toes. Ravenlock eyed the five of us for a long moment. "Call me if it gets serious." We all nodded. "Good day, my fine young Idiots."

The instant Ravenlock was out of earshot, Rufus looked at me. "Promise me we won't call him."

"Done," I said, staring at Ravenlock's back as he casually walked down the sidewalk, his eyes devouring the day. "This is *our* mission."

"Our mission!" echoed Rufus. "Whatever . . . it . . . is."

It was only my second time aboard the *Jolly Rajah*, yet it was already feeling a bit like a home away from home. As before, we entered through the gun deck, only the mood inside was different. Elefantkin milled around toting heavy boxes, placing braces of pistols next to every table. Powder monkeys, which were *real* monkeys dressed like pirates, hauled up sacks of black powder through the hatches. The deck rolled heavily, like we were already at sea. Waves pounded the ship, splashing—and occasionally pouring—through the open gunports. Between the creaking of the decks and the chattering customers, we had to shout to be heard.

I examined the cutlass I'd been given as we boarded. Everyone had one. It didn't weigh a whole lot, but it looked lethal enough. Gingerly, I tested its edge. It was as dull as a wooden ruler.

"Willa! You forgot your hat!" shouted Rufus. I turned around and was surprised to see that the opening I'd just walked through now looked as real and solid as any other part of the ship. A second later, Rufus appeared, running right through the solid wood. He jumped up and plunked a hat on my head. Now we all had 'em, big pirate hats with long feathers draping down our backs. *Arrr!*

I caught CeeCee's eye, hoping she might be the soft touch of the group. "So, CeeCee, what's going on here?"

She pulled out her cutlass and brandished it at me. "You'll get nothin' from me, you scurvy dog!" she said in her best pirate voice. My opinion of her instantly rose threefold.

We took a booth on the port side, right between two huge cannons. I knocked on the hull. Solid oak.

The elefantkin who weren't preparing for battle were singing and dancing, their arms laden with overflowing platters of food, their trunks pouring pitchers of syrup. In less than thirty seconds, our table was a treasure trove of pancakes, sausages, fried eggs, potatoes, and steaming tankards of hot chocolate topped with mountains of whipped cream. Only this time we had a new centerpiece: a black, dome-shaped device covered with dials and blinking lights. A short curlicue antenna rose from its top. All the tables had one.

I scanned the crowd. All the kids were dressed like pirates. There were a lot of parents dressed like pirates, too. But the adults without kids were clearly up to something, wearing dark hats pulled down low, sunglasses, and big nondescript coats with their collars turned up. A bunch of them were even wearing cheesy fake mustaches.

"What's this thing?" I shouted, pointing to the device in the center of the table.

"That's a muffilator," said Bertie. "Watch." He pressed a button and flipped some switches. The unit hummed to life. "First I'll set the size to encompass only our booth. Then . . . check this out." Adjusting a big dial like it was a volume-control knob, he turned down the sound of the room.

"That's amazing!" I said, way too loudly. "Does this mean no one can hear us now?"

A platter-bearing elefantkin leaned partway into the sphere of our muffilator and replaced the stack of pancakes Rufus had just wolfed down. It was Jaja Toosk. The jingling of his earrings sounded clear, but the background noise of the restaurant remained muffled. "CeeCee! Rufus! Bertie! Nimet! Willa!" he shouted. "Glad t' be havin' ye all aboard! Ready t' earn yer grog, I hope? 'Tis a hungry sea this day."

"Not as hungry as me!" shouted Rufus, stabbing the new stack of pancakes.

"Your first Friday aboard the *Jolly Rajah*," said Jaja, looking proudly at me. "Ready fer action?"

"Where are we, Jaja?" asked CeeCee, slathering butter on a stack she couldn't possibly eat in two sittings.

"Don't rightly know, CeeCee. We've been blown off course somethin' terrible. Lost our convoy in the night. And a fog has set in. Smugglin's a hard business, a hard business. Say now, in honor of it bein' Willa's first time and all, do ye be havin' any . . . preferences?"

Bertie wore a strange grin. "Jaja . . . did you know Willa's from Boston?"

"You don't say!" he said. "Ha! Imagine that! Well, I'll be. . . . I—I'll be right back." And he scurried off.

"Where's he going?" I asked, but they ignored me. "And how did you know I was from Boston?" I asked Bertie.

"Ravenlock said so, first day of school."

"And is Ravenlock always right?"

Bertie took a swig of hot chocolate. "Yes, he is. It's one of the things that makes him insufferable."

"Enough tongue waggin'," shouted CeeCee in her pirate voice. "Time we got down to business!"

I considered bartering for an explanation about why we were all wearing pirate hats and armed with cutlasses, but they seemed to be having so much fun keeping it a secret that I didn't have the heart. Besides, who doesn't like a mystery?

I put the Clockwerk Boy's memory book, the one he'd given me on the first day, on the table. "The way I see it, we have to accomplish one of two tasks. We either crack this code or find a new BrainBox so the Clockwerk Boy can read it to us."

"May I?" said Bertie, pointing to the book.

"By all means."

Bertie leafed through the pages.

Rufus whistled. "That's pictograph binary, that is."

Bertie nodded sadly. "We'd need to backwards engineer a mainspring-mechanical rotor cipher. And even then, we'll need the Clockwerk Boy's internal key."

"Nothing's uncrackable!" shouted CeeCee. "Arrr!" Bertie showed CeeCee a sample page from the book. "Except maybe that."

"I hate to say it . . ." began Bertie.

"Then don't," interrupted Nimet.

Bertie sighed. Diplomacy wasn't Nimet's strong suit.

"We should put everything on the table. Bertie, what's your idea?"

"Ravenlock might be able to—" The table shouted him down. "Or not. Do we have access to the . . . to the body?"

"Yes," I said. "It's in the Windwerks Burg, but I'm a little worried that whoever did this might come back for him."

Bertie nodded. "Then that should be our first order of business. The soup shop has a commercial dirigy we use for catering. We can attach a cable to him and fly him anywhere in the city. But where?"

"We could take him to my nonna Benedetta's villa in the Clockwerk Burg," offered CeeCee. "The da Vinci workshops are old school, but they're *really* well equipped. We could sneak him into one of the more . . . out-of-the-way shops."

Nonna, in case you don't know, means grandmother in Italian. The WatchitMapCallit's translation feature was becoming indispensable.

"Okay," I said, "so it sounds to me like all we need is a Brain-Box."

Rufus slapped his hands over his face. "Is that all?"

"I actually have an idea on that one," I said. Everyone turned to look at me. "Two nights ago my dad and I did a plumbing job at Gear Hall. I met this girl, Tiffany—" Now everyone turned to look at Bertie, who was groaning and making a face. "Wait, what's up?" I asked.

"Tiffany is Bertie's cousin is what's up," said Rufus.

"My very distant, very creepy cousin," corrected Bertie. "Look, my family hasn't lived in the Clockwerk Burg for a long time. Don't look to me for connections."

"But you're a Babbage," said Nimet. "You must know somebody who works at the Machinery."

"It's not like that," Bertie explained. "Not all Babbages are created equal. We own a soup shop! I was born in Greater Grandeur, not in one of the burgs."

"Is it possible your grandmother has a BrainBox, maybe in her attic?" asked Nimet.

"I mean, she might, but Babbage BrainBoxes are incompatible with Gear Hall BrainBoxes. Sure, they're very similar in what they do and how they do it—gears are gears, after all—but our boxes are square."

"The one we need is definitely long and rectangular. Bread loaf sized," I added.

"Maybe we could sneak into the Machinery one night and 'borrow' one," said CeeCee, rubbing her hands together, a maniacal gleam in her eye. CeeCee made me miss being eight.

A dark shadow momentarily appeared in the rolling cloud bank outside our open gunport. But when I bent my head for a closer look, all I could see was the roiling sea. I seemed to be the only one who noticed.

Bertie speared a newly cut tower of pancakes. "Not a chance, CeeCee. That place is crawling with WatchDogs, day and night. And it's not like they leave BrainBoxes lying around for people to steal."

CeeCee scrunched up her face and eyes until she looked like a cherubic mad scientist (which wasn't as big a stretch as you might think). "What if we posed as plumbers, snuck back into Gear Hall, smashed the glass case containing Torsicus Widderchine's Brain-Box, and stole *it*?"

We all laughed . . . then stared at each other.

"No!" I said, breaking the silence. "No! We're not thieves! Besides, it's probably not even glass, and I bet they have some wicked clever alarms." That's how we talk in Boston.

Suddenly the pancakes felt all heavy and gooey in my stomach. "There's something I haven't told you yet."

Bertie looked concerned. "What?"

"When my dad and I were at Gear Hall, I overheard a conversation between a Clockwerk named Wyrmgear"—Bertie shivered involuntarily—"and my neighbor across the hall."

"Dr. Wudgepuddle?" asked Nimet. And I could see her thinking about something.

"Yes! He said a free Clockwerk was snooping around at a party at Gear Hall. He told Wyrmgear he wanted that Clockwerk found and his BrainBox destroyed!"

"The Windwerks Burg was docked in the Clockwerk Burg last

week," said CeeCee.

Nimet gasped. "Willa, those books in the bookcase . . . do you remember the title of the last book?"

"I wrote them down." Taking out my notebook I read aloud, "*Peril at Gear Hall.*"

Rufus suddenly turned invisible, only to reappear a second later.

CeeCee, who noticed everyone staring disapprovingly at him, whispered, "It's okay, he thinks better when he's puttering."

Rufus looked up from his faulty invisibility device. "Do you think Heathcliff's dad has the BrainBox in his apartment?" he asked.

"No," I told him. "Wyrmgear offered to put the Clockwerk Boy's BrainBox in a vault and keep it there for a hundred years. I hate to say it, Bertie, but I think we need to talk to Tiffany."

"Willa," protested Bertie, "are you really sure you want one of her BrainBoxes? You've seen the—" He held up a hand with his ring finger bent down.

I'd've shivered even without the visual.

Bertie sighed. "Well, at least this Clockwerk is an old one. Did she tell you they won't let her near anything modern?"

"Yes," I said, "but maybe she can get into the vault. Wouldn't it be best to have the same one?"

Bertie chewed a sausage thoughtfully. "We can work around that. You see, Clockwerks are designed to be repaired and upgraded indefinitely. Gears break, spindles wear out, whole BrainBoxes can crack up into little bits. That's why the primary encryption code for every Clockwerk is buried deep inside its main chassis, not the BrainBox. Once we have him in a proper workshop, though, it won't be hard to get the code. Especially since his BrainBox has already been removed."

"So you're saying you'll talk to Tiffany?" I asked Bertie.

He gave me a *why me* face. "Oh, all right. We passed a bippy booth on the way in. I'll send her a message as soon as we're finished here. But remember I was against involving her. Don't look at me when things go barking mad."

"We will not hold you responsible, Bertie Babbage," said Nimet.

Something outside caught my eye again, past the cloud bank: a bit of rigging? This time, however, Rufus saw it, too. He leapt out of the booth, cupped his hands around his mouth, and yelled, "Beat to quarters!"

A steady drumroll sounded, muffled by the muffilator, but still loud. Elefantkin rushed into the room, heaved back the cannons from the gunports, and rammed sacks of black powder and cannonballs down their barrels. But before they could get off the first shot, the cloud bank erupted in fire.

Thumpa-thumpa-thumpa-thumpa-thumpa-thumpa-thumpa-thumpa!

There was a ship out there, laid aside at pistol shot. (That's about fifty feet, for you landlubbers out thar.) The side of the *Jolly Rajah* shook. Splinters sailed through the air like daggers. A cannonball burst into the room and ricocheted hard off the mainmast. I held up my arms, ducked my head, and screamed.

My tablemates laughed. I untucked slowly. My arms weren't covered with blood and splinters. But it had all looked so real!

"Holograms?" I asked.

They ignored me.

Now the *Jolly Rajah* returned fire, one cannon after the other, right down the line. *Thumpa-thumpa-thumpa-thumpa-thumpa-thumpa-thumpa-thumpa!* The sound overpowered the muffilator. The deck shook with the recoil of the great guns. The elefantkin's trumpets of delight quickly changed to shouts of dismay. "Shiver me timbers!" shouted one. "Her sides are made of iron!"

My Boston girl's ears perked up at that. "What did he say?"

"He said, 'her sides are made of iron!'" said CeeCee, giggling.

The cloud bank lit up a second time, twice as loud as before. A huge chunk of the hull next to our booth disintegrated, and large pieces of it seemed to pass right through our bodies with no ill effects. Even so, I couldn't stop myself from quickly examining my arms and legs. It seemed *that* real. We were unharmed. But I couldn't say the same for the *Jolly Rajah*. A massive gap had opened up, stretching gunport to gunport. A tall wave smashed against the hull, its top half sluicing foamy sea water onto our deck. I leaned out as far as I dared, shading my eyes from the howling wind. A 44-gun frigate, the only one I knew by sight, emerged from the cloud bank under full battle-sail.

"It's the USS *Constitution*!" I shouted. "We're goners! She's never lost a fight!" I'd always wondered what she might have looked like in her glory days. I'd just never imagined she'd be manned by . . . elefantkin? "She'll sink us for sure!"

"We're more valuable to her as a prize. She'll try and board us to take our cargo!" shouted Nimet.

We all pulled out our cutlasses and waved them over our heads, yelling like bloodthirsty pirates.

"How long before that happens?" I asked.

"Not long," said CeeCee. "They've got the weather gauge. All they have to do is come about again. Less than ten minutes, maybe? See there"—CeeCee pointed—"they're readying grappling hooks."

"I wish they wouldn't turn down the violence level so much," complained Rufus.

"What are you talking about?" I asked.

Rufus got an evil gleam in his eye. "If this was an evening battle for adults, there'd be bits of tusk and guts and blood all over the place!"

CeeCee hid a smile. Nimet and I stared at each other. "Boys!" we said at the same time. Bertie pushed his plate of food aside and placed a hand over his mouth.

"Well, if we have a few minutes, then can I ask, what is it about Ravenlock? Why's everyone so spooked by him?" The table went silent. "Who was Ravenlock's Idiot Genius ancestor?"

Bertie looked uncomfortable. "That—that's not the problem. Ravenlock's Idiot Genius ancestor entered Grandeur over a hundred years ago. Ravenlock's problems are more . . . immediate."

"But we don't have any proof," said CeeCee quietly.

"Yes, we do," said Rufus.

"No, we don't," said Nimet. "But it fits."

"What are you all talking about?" I asked.

Bertie looked at CeeCee, who'd tucked herself against my side and wrapped her arms around my middle. Rufus dove under the table and came up huddled on my other side.

"Tell her, Bertie," CeeCee's voice trembled. "She has to learn sometime."

"All right," said Bertie, putting on a brave face. "You already know about Idiots and Geniuses and Idiot Geniuses . . . but have you heard about anything else?"

"Well, the Black Fez told me there were three types of Idiots: Real, Stupid, and Complete."

"Actually, there's a fourth type, too: Quarks. Quarks are people who get Genius-like ideas from time to time, but don't have a Genius IQ. But I'm talking about the people grown-ups pretend don't exist, the ones too dangerous to keep in Grandeur."

I glanced at Nimet, but she averted her eyes. "Evil . . . Geniuses," I said, and a contagious wave of the willies went around the table. Twice.

"Right. Ever wonder what happens when the soothies find an Evil Genius?"

"No. But I am now," I said, my voice rising.

"The Evil Genius . . . disappears," whispered Bertie.

"But I thought nobody leaves Grandeur."

"Then where are Ravenlock's parents?" asked Bertie. "They used to be here. No one has seen them for years."

"They say his mother was as mad as a Clockwerk missing half its gears," said Nimet.

I felt Rufus trembling next to me. "At bedtime my brother tells me they're coming for me. He says locking the doors won't even slow them down."

"Ravenlock's parents? That's terrible!" I said, putting my arm around him.

"Actually, he just says the Evil Geniuses are coming for me. I never thought about them being Ravenlock's mom and dad," whispered Rufus, looking horrified. "I wouldn't want it to be them."

"Willa," said Bertie, "these are the most dangerous minds on the planet. Any one of them could destroy the world—or worse."

"There's something worse than destroying the world?"

"A highly contagious virus that renders the entire world blind," said CeeCee.

"Or one that extends life, but leaves you wracked in pain, like your flesh is on fire," suggested Rufus.

"A device that forms a black hole—sucking in the Earth, the moon, the planets, our sun, and half our galaxy." Everyone turned to look at Nimet. "What? Evil can't be suicidal?"

"Still waters run deep," said Bertie.

"That's enough," I said. "I've got the picture. So, Bertie, where are you thinking Ravenlock's parents are?"

"With all the other Evil Geniuses. In Delusionarium Sub Rosa, or, as people more commonly refer to it: Delusion." I started to reach for my WatchitMapCallit. "Don't bother. You won't find it in Grandeurpedia. Some say it's as big as Grandeur, only inside it's one giant raving-mad prison."

"I hope it's buried under miles of ice . . . in the center of Antarctica!" said Rufus.

The *Constitution* slammed against the *Jolly Rajah*. Elefantkin on both ships fired their guns simultaneously, ripping gigantic holes in both hulls. We leapt from the booth, seizing the single-shot pistols left for us by the elefantkin. Aiming carefully into the newly created opening, we fired, tossed the guns aside, and drew our cutlasses. Whooping, cheering, and swearing hearty pirate oaths, we all followed Rufus into the breach.

I couldn't remember the last time I'd had that much fun. After all, it's not every day you get to board and capture the most celebrated American frigate in all of U.S. naval history. Twice.

After it was all over, Jaja couldn't stop laughing about his little surprise. We couldn't even understand half the things he said, but it didn't matter. After the second battle, as a reward, he invited us up to the quarterdeck. But we had a Clockwerk Boy to put back together, and with great regret, we left the *Jolly Rajah*. But take it from me, if you ever make it to Grandeur, put Fighting Fridays at Jolly Rajah Man-o'-War o' Pancakes high up on your list.

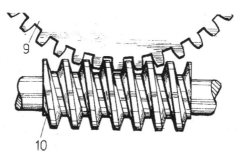

Villa da Vinci

TRUE to his word, Bertie wrote a note to his cousin Tiffany. We all stared silently as the bippy, not much larger than a baseball, lifted off and zoomed away, making little *bip-bip-bip* noises as it went.

Then we split up. Rufus and Nimet set off for the Clockwerk Boy's room in the Windwerks Burg. Bertie headed for Babbage's Bouillon, Bisque & Bean to get the catering dirigy. CeeCee and I jumped into a Clockwerk cab.

"Village Tourbillon," shouted CeeCee to the Clockwerk sitting atop the cab. And off we went.

I pointed at the flowers in the vase hanging inside the cab. "What kind of flower do you suppose that is?" I asked.

Without a moment's thought, CeeCee said, "Japanese anemone."

I knew Nimet had said CeeCee was brilliant, but seeing is believing.

"That's it? Just . . . Japanese anemone?"

CeeCee considered the flowers again. "Um, well. They're

commonly known as windflowers, although they don't do so well in the wind. They're not even native to Japan; they come from China."

Now that was more like it. "Anything else?"

CeeCee frowned at me, like she knew I was testing her, but not why. "Anemone comes from the Greek. It means daughter of the wind."

Yep. She was the real deal all right. At the age of eight, she'd probably stuffed more things into her brain than I would by my fifties.

The cab rolled along. "CeeCee . . . when I was in Gear Hall I heard Tiffany refer to Wyrmgear as—"

"Her GrandClock?" I nodded. CeeCee tilted back her head and gave me a look like she was channeling a sixty-year-old psychiatrist. "And that disturbs you," she stated. She was spot on, but reflexively I tried to wiggle out of it.

"I'm not sure *disturb* is the—"

CeeCee grinned. "It's all right. Sentient Clockwerks are few and far between Outside. You grew up with what? Four grandparents?"

"Actually, only the two, on my dad's side. On my mom's side . . ." *On my mom's side . . . were Mom's even alive? How could I not know that? And did CeeCee just say there were sentient Clockwerks Outside?*

"I have two bisnonni, four nonni, and twenty-two Grand-Clocks."

"Hold on. There are sentient Clockwerks . . . Outside?"

"My GrandClock Turcuccio spent over a hundred years Outside, traveling all over Europe and North America playing chess.

He beat lots of famous people."

"Anyone I might have heard of?"

"Napoleon Bonaparte?"

"No way!"

"It's true. And Catherine the Great." I was speechless. CeeCee clapped her hands in delight. "She tried to cheat, more than once."

"Who else?"

"Well, while in Paris, he played Benjamin Franklin."

"And the Black Fez just let this happen?"

CeeCee lowered her voice. "It was the Black Fez that put him up to it. They were trying to catch an Idiot Genius Clockwerk maker who was stirring up trouble back in the 1730s. But even then, Grandeur's Clockwerks would've stood out. What they needed was an *old* Clockwerk design. So they asked Turcuccio to play the part because he was set in motion back in the year 1352."

"Weren't they afraid somebody might steal him and get a hold of something they shouldn't have?"

"I'm sure some people believed he was real, but the clever ones were certain he was a trick. The Black Fez encouraged it. They kept him half-stuffed in a cabinet, and before every match, they'd make a big deal of opening all the doors in the exact same order. One particularly suspicious journalist, a young Genius named Poe, claimed—"

"Edgar Allan Poe?" I nearly shouted.

"Yes. That was during the American tour, in a city named Richmond, I think. I forget the year, but Turcuccio would be happy to tell you everything. He has it all written down in a memory book. He works in Nonna's library. I'll introduce you some time. Anyway, Poe wrote a very detailed article. In it, he described how he thought a man hidden inside the cabinet operated the automaton, by pushing and pulling levers. The article was reprinted up and down the East Coast. It was quite the sensation. People have written whole books about my GrandClock Turcuccio. He called himself the Turk."

"Poe," I repeated, and the name felt powerful in my mouth. "There's a name I'd expect to hear in Grandeur."

CeeCee cocked her head and furrowed her brow. "I don't—I don't remember ever hearing it. In Grandeur, I mean," she added quickly. "Ask Grandeurpedia?" I glanced at CeeCee's wrist, where I thought her WatchitMapCallit should be. She tapped her wrist and nothing happened. "It's in my backpack. I'm not allowed to use it in the burg, and we're almost there."

"But I'm allowed to use mine?"

"Not exactly. But you won't get in big trouble for it. And I don't think anyone will notice in the cab."

Remembering something I'd seen in one of the tutorials, I glanced at my WatchitMapCallit and quickly said, "Remain cloaked." It did. "Grandeurpedia, how many people are there in Grandeur with the last name of Poe?"

"There are no people with the last name of Poe currently living in Grandeur," it said.

"That might not be true," said CeeCee.

"What do you mean?"

"Well, Grandeurpedia wouldn't count the Black Fez or the soothies. Or for that matter . . . anyone in Delusion."

"Great. But Delusion is far away, right?"

"Two miles under the ice of Greenland, if we're lucky."

"CeeCee, how is it you know how thick the ice of Greenland

is?"

She held out her arms and shrugged her shoulders. "I don't know. How is it you don't?"

It was all too much, and something told me the day was just getting cranked up. I glanced out the window and realized I'd lost track of where we were. Happily, all the different architecture and clothing styles zooming past made for a welcome distraction. Apparently, no fashion had ever gone out of style in Grandeur.

Unlike when I'd crossed into the Biowerks Burg, there was no missing the dividing line between Greater Grandeur and the Clockwerk Burg. One moment I was in a modern city; the next moment I was on a rough, narrow road, speeding toward a village surrounded by thick woods. Village Tourbillon was surrounded by a feudal-looking stone wall, and as we passed through its gate, the coachman announced our arrival.

CeeCee leaned out the window and shouted, "Clockwerk Couture, Thread Street, please."

I tilted my head quizzically.

"It'll be a while before they can get the Clockwerk Boy airborne," explained CeeCee. "So I thought we could kill some time shopping!"

She must have read the look on my face, because the next thing she said was, "Don't worry, I know you don't have any dolleurs yet. Consider this . . . a welcoming gift from the family da Vinci."

Thread Street teemed with humans and Clockwerks. The humans were dressed in the latest Clockpunk fashions, the Clockwerks clad in metal and paint. The houses and shops grew closer as they got taller, propped up with wooden buttresses to keep the jutting upper stories level. Some of the highest balconies drew so close that neighbors could shake hands. Flying bippy bots whizzed above the crowd.

The coachman let us out two blocks from the store.

"What's it like . . . Outside?" asked CeeCee. "Is it true you can go anywhere you like?"

"Yes, you can pretty much go anywhere."

"Even the Grand Canyon?"

"Yes."

"Have you been?"

"No." The idea that now I'd never be going hit me unexpectedly hard.

"Have you seen a glacier? Or a real volcano?"

"Neither, but I've seen snow," I offered.

"I've skied!" said CeeCee, her eyes lighting up.

"In Grandeur? Where?"

"Inside Winterland, near the lake. Mondays are the Swiss Alps. Have you been to the moon? People Outside go to the moon, right?"

"No."

CeeCee looked at me disappointedly. "Oh. So where have you been?"

"Well, I've been on the real *Constitution*."

"Really?" I had her attention again.

"Yep. It was a sleepover. I was a powder monkey, and my Dad was a gunner."

"THAT'S SO COOL! No wonder you recognized her so fast."

Clockwerk Couture was a hive of activity. We weren't there for more than a minute when CeeCee began talking to a smartly dressed but severe-looking older woman. The conversation heated up, with lots of wild hand gestures and arm waving on both sides. I have no idea what they were saying—it was all in Italian—but CeeCee kept firing right back at the lady. In the end, the severe woman threw her hands in the air and stalked off.

CeeCee said, "She loves me."

We climbed a staircase to what I guessed was the teens department on the third floor, where CeeCee started grabbing things from racks and holding them up to me for size. When we had a pile, she pushed me into a dressing room.

"CeeCee," I protested, "I don't want to get you into any trouble."

"Stop worrying," she said.

I stood in front of a mirror and held up the cutest dress—covered with bronze- and gold-colored clocks, watches, chains, and so on. It was short in the front with a billowy train. I'd never worn anything billowy before.

"CeeCee, how am I ever going to repay you?"

"Just put something on!"

I tugged on a pair of leggings, followed by a pair of Victorian high-button two-tone leather boots with matching leather gloves. I could feel resolve fading fast. The sleeves of the dress were opaque netting, with small ruffles at the elbows.

"Come out and let me see!"

When I opened the door, CeeCee squealed. From behind her back she produced a Clockwerk tiara, which she placed on my head, and a small purse.

"There now," she said. "No one would know you hadn't been born here."

CeeCee turned suddenly to the staircase. "My Aunt Mila," whispered CeeCee.

"Really? I don't hear any—"

CeeCee's aunt glided up the staircase on high heels and circled me like a predatory animal, staring at me with narrowed eyes.

"I'm—I'm—"

"No talking," she said in English.

So that was embarrassing.

"CeeCee," she snapped, "do we have this one in red?"

"I think so."

"Get it, and bring me the black leggings." Then, to me, "It will go better with your pasty complexion."

They pushed me back into the changing room. How did I get myself into this mess? More importantly, how would I get out?

"I don't have all day!" barked Aunt Mila.

I finished changing as fast as I could and opened the door. CeeCee gasped. Aunt Mila tilted her head at me.

"Come," she demanded.

I stepped forward. She spun me around, pulling and tugging roughly at the dress.

"It could be worse," she concluded. "Downstairs I have a lovely choker that would go perfectly with . . ."—she waved a hand at me with an air of general distaste—"this."

She pointed at my old clothes. For a second, I thought she was going to say something like *Burn them*. But instead she said, "Bring *those* down when you're ready to leave. We'll have them sent to your home by parcel." Then she stomped down the stairs and was gone.

I felt terrible. "CeeCee! What are you getting me into?"

"She likes you."

"She does not!"

"Does too. Now let's go out and show you off."

"One second." I ducked into the dressing room, emptied the pockets of my old clothes, grabbed the tool bag full of the Clockwerk Boy's memory books, and activated the Clockwerk cane as I stepped back out. "What do you think?"

CeeCee's eyes filled with wonder. "The Flying Time Traveler. Where did you find it?"

"The Clockwerk Boy gave it to me." I held it out, and CeeCee cradled it in her hands like the cane was a jeweled scepter.

"It could use a winding."

"Yeah, about that. I could've sworn it was fully wound yesterday. Do these things wind down on their own?"

"The internal clock uses some spring power, but you'd never notice it, even after a year."

"So half a winding—"

"Willa, have you been flying around?"

"No."

"Are you sure?"

CHAPTER TWENTY-ONE

"I think I'd remember that." It didn't make any sense. "How do you wind them back up?"

"Well, bringing it to the Clockwerk Burg is a good start. We could use a public station here in the village, but the ones at my nonna's are faster. I'll show you. It's easy. But don't flash it around. It'll attract too much attention."

I stuffed the cane in my purse. I felt conspicuous enough already.

Downstairs, Mila was waiting with a black velvet choker. Its heart-shaped timepiece was just darling. Once on the street, I felt deliciously in tune with everyone else. Like I belonged here. That's when I first wondered if I was falling in love with this place, falling in love with Grandeur. Had life in Cambridge, with the river and the bay and all the history that comes with it, ever seemed this real, this exciting? A little warning siren started wailing in the back of my head. It said *Careful what you fall in love with, Willa Snap*. But I wasn't listening.

I have no idea how long we spent in Village Tourbillon (which is a difficult thing to pull off when everywhere you look is one type of clock or another, from a small timepiece embedded in a door handle to a five-story clock tower). We were in something like a soda shop, about to inhale some ice cream floats, when a bippy circled us, took a good look at me, and then hovered expectantly. This bippy was different from the others I'd seen. It had propellers and made whirring sounds, as if somewhere inside it a powerful spring was slowly winding down.

"Put your hand out," CeeCee told me.

I held out my palm, and instantly the propeller blades slowed. Tiny landing gear popped out from the bottom. Inside the bippy's belly compartment was a note.

> *Willa,*
> *Operation Delivery Man a success.*
> *We're waiting on you now.*
>
> > *Bertie*

I showed the note to CeeCee.

"About time. Let's get going."

"Should I reply?"

"Give it here."

CeeCee jotted down something on the back, put the note into the bippy, and whispered a name I didn't catch. The propellers spun up, and the landing gear retracted. Rotating, the bippy tilted sideways and bipped out a window.

I gave CeeCee a questioning look.

"We'll need a co-conspirator. In case we're caught."

"Right. Got someone in mind?"

"My bisnonno. He just had his ninety-second birthday."

"And we can trust him?"

"He's more of a little boy than Rufus. And pure Idiot. Oh, and you might want to show him that Clockwerk cane."

CeeCee flagged down a cab. We leapt in, and CeeCee shouted, "1369 Sforza Court!"

With all its twists and turns, Village Tourbillon felt larger than it really was—not an uncommon illusion when visiting a burg. In fact, Grandeur often seems more like a vast theme park than a hidden city filled with Idiot Geniuses (who, if let loose, would surely destroy the world). With a bump we passed under a stone archway and onto a gravel road. Almost immediately, the cab pitched gently backward.

"The Hill da Vinci," announced the coachman.

"It's the tallest hill in Grandeur," said CeeCee proudly.

The view was tremendous. The forest and village behind us already looked quite small. As we got higher, I could see the sprawl of Greater Grandeur. At the top of the hill we entered a grand courtyard encircling a marble fountain. Its gushing water added a coolness to the light breeze.

"Welcome to Villa da Vinci!" said CeeCee.

The grounds were charming. The villa blanketed the hill with red terra-cotta roofs, courtyards, stucco walls, and terraced gardens. From somewhere in the center, a tall square tower rose high into the blue sky.

"It's beautiful!" I said. "So where do we go?"

CeeCee went into stealth mode. At each corner and at the top or bottom of every flight of stairs, we stopped and peeked around before proceeding. She was clearly enjoying sneaking around. At the entrance to one particular tree-filled courtyard, she squeezed my hand and pointed to two huge wooden doors on the opposite side.

"That's Luigi's old workshop."

As we dashed from tree trunk to tree trunk, our footsteps seemed impossibly loud on the old cobblestones. But eventually, we reached a set of worn marble steps. A lion's face was carved in the center of each door. CeeCee flew up the steps and grasped the big brass ring in one set of jaws.

"Pull!" she grunted.

I heaved on the other ring, and the doors slowly creaked open. Inside, the workshop managed to seem both old and eternal, as if there had never been a time when it wasn't in use. Shafts of sunlight slanted through a bank of windows overlooking the hillside and illuminated motes of dust hanging in the air. Racks of gears and tools covered every bit of wall. Tables and benches piled high with works in progress ran the length of the room. Wings of all shapes and sizes hung from the ceiling. Wings! Ones that actually worked, too. (Not that I would know firsthand, of course. I mean, if you were to sneak into the place in the dead of night and strap on a pair of those bad boys before leaping off da Vinci Hill . . . then you might know . . . for certain . . . that they worked. Although you might want to master steering first, so you don't end up hanging by the minute hand of the tallest clock tower in Village Tourbillon, screaming bloody murder at three in the morning. Because . . . that kind of thing isn't as far-fetched as it might sound. Not that I would know anything about it.)

CeeCee and I snaked around the worktables until somewhere near the center, we found Bertie, Rufus, Nimet, and a very old man: CeeCee's bisnonno. Nimet and Rufus, legs dangling, sat on one of the worktables. Bertie and the old man hovered over the Clockwerk Boy. Bertie had changed into a T-shirt that said *Got Gear?* He was twirling a spanner over the open cavity in the Clockwerk Boy's chest. When he saw me, he fumbled the spanner. It narrowly missed clipping Rufus's ear before spinning out of sight.

"You look smart," he said.

I played it cool.

Bertie picked up another spanner.

"Bisnonno," said CeeCee, "this is my friend Willa Snap, newly arrived from Outside."

Bisnonno was short, even standing up straight. His face, weathered by age, was a kind one. Wispy hair floated around the tops of his ears. When we shook hands, his grip was frail. His eyes, however, were as clear and sharp as a kid's.

"Please, call me Bisnonno," he said in a thick Italian accent. "CeeCee tells me this Clockwerk has something to do with you?"

"He sought me out the day I arrived. He said my timeline was in danger and that I was somehow tied to the fate of the dragons. But he wound down before he could tell me anything more."

CeeCee's great-grandfather patted the Clockwerk Boy. "This is original work. It belongs in a museum. Do you know who did this?"

"I have some ideas. I think the thief took his original Brain-Box to Gear Hall and placed it inside—"

"Wyrmgear's private vault," finished Tiffany, stepping out of the shadows.

Bertie, who was closest to her, started so violently he tripped over a toolbox and tumbled to the floor.

"Gears and spindles, Tiffany!" Bertie cried, leaping to his feet. "When did you get here?"

"About the same time I did," said Bisnonno. "If I'm not mistaken."

Tiffany wheeled a long wooden box into our circle. I couldn't be positive, but I thought Tiffany and Bisnonno shared a small private smile as she upended the narrow dolly and undid its straps. For the first thirty seconds or so, Tiffany radiated a self-assuredness I hadn't seen before. But I quickly got the feeling her new-found confidence was on a timer—one about to run out.

"Bisnonno," said CeeCee, "this is—"

"No need, my dear. I know Ms. Widderchine." Bisnonno took Tiffany's hand and gave it a pat. "You look more like Mother every day."

"Lucky me," said Tiffany, but she didn't sound like she felt lucky. In fact, she looked downright spooked. "I—I've brought a BrainBox," she said. "I couldn't get the original, but this one should do the trick."

Bertie shivered, like someone had drawn an ice cube down his spine.

Tiffany's eyes fell hungrily on the Clockwerk Boy.

We all turned, which I suppose was Tiffany's design, because when we turned back, she and the dolly were gone.

Bertie spun around in place. "What the–where did she–she's always doing that!"

Bisnonno handed Bertie a crowbar and pointed at the box. "It's time for us to get to work."

Bertie pried off the lid. "Rufus, Nimet, we'll need your help." CeeCee and I took their places on the worktable.

"All right, now," said Bisnonno, "let's try and get this right the first time."

Bertie aimed a flashlight into the deepest recesses of the Clockwerk's torso and called out a series of numbers. Bisnonno patiently entered them on a row of corresponding click-wheels embedded in the BrainBox, repeating each one for good measure.

That done, Bisnonno extended two guide rails and held them in place while Rufus and Nimet lined up the BrainBox's bolt holes just so.

Bertie kept his voice calm and reassuring as he threaded bolt after bolt. "Once all the bolts are in place, you can let go, Nimet. But not before, okay?"

Nimet nodded.

"And if you'll just step to the side, Rufus," said the old man. "Hold steady, Ms. Simit." I could see Nimet's fingers trembling.

Bertie's spanner spun again and again. "Almost there," said Bertie.

Nimet's hands shook. "It's too heavy!" said Nimet, a trickle of sweat curving around her lip. I could see my friend was in a swivet. (Proving the Yanks aren't without their share of cool-sounding words! "In a swivet," if perchance you don't live with a Genius, means FREAKING OUT.)

Bertie popped on another bolt.

"Losing my grip!" cried Nimet.

"Clear!" yelled Bertie.

Nimet let go and the BrainBox slid into the empty cavity with a satisfying click. Bertie raised his arms in victory.

Most superheroes need something extraordinary in order to transform: radioactive arachnids, magic rings, phone booths. All Bertie Babbage needed was a spanner.

"Really?" said Nimet, astonished. "We did it?"

"Molto bene!" shouted CeeCee's great-grandfather, looking pleased. "Everyone stand back."

Bisnonno's hands flew over the Clockwerk Boy, turning dials, flipping catches, tightening screws. Bertie peered over the old man's shoulder with great interest.

Finally, he closed a panel and locked it in place. "Meraviglioso!" He patted the Clockwerk Boy lovingly. "Good as new," he said, smiling like an Idiot.

"You have steady hands, young man," Bisnonno told Bertie. "You may apprentice for me anytime you like."

Bertie's jaw fell open. "Are you serious? At the da Vinci workshop?" Bertie turned to CeeCee. "Is he serious?"

"Officially, I'm no longer responsible for any of the da Vinci workshops," said Bisnonno. "But I can teach anyone I like in this one. Age has its privileges."

Bisnonno pulled a lever, and the top of the worktable tilted until the Clockwerk Boy's feet were on the ground. CeeCee loosened the pair of heavy leather straps holding him in place, then Bertie and Nimet teetered the lifeless form side to side, walking the Clockwerk Boy several feet from the table. I stepped around and read the dials on his back. His memory counter was a row of zeros; his mainspring was above three-quarters capacity.

"His memory's zeroed," I observed.

"Yes," said Bisnonno. "When this Clockwerk wakes up, it will not know where it is. It could get flighty. A new memory cycle is a little like being born. Its internal programs will attempt to assess the situation, but it may try and return home. Now, Rufus, thread those chains on the floor through the loops on the backs of its feet. Before we turn it on, I want to hear the BrainBox spin up to confirm that all is well."

He opened a small access panel and flipped some switches. "Bertie, hand me that rod, if you will."

Bertie picked up a metal rod about two feet long. "This one?"

"The very same." Even though the BrainBox was now secured within the Clockwerk Boy's chest, portions were still visible
through all the gears, springs, and framework. Bisnonno threaded
one end of the rod through an opening until it touched a corner of
the BrainBox's outer casing. Then he held the other end up to his
ear. "Nimet, if you would please turn the black knob in the access
panel clockwise two clicks."

A *whirrrrr* filled the workshop. Moving quickly, the old man
touched one end of the rod to several different places, listening
to the other end each time. After a few minutes, he put down the
rod, spun down the BrainBox, and closed things up. He seemed
satisfied but uneasy.

"What is it?" CeeCee asked her great-grandfather.

"All is as it should be," he said quickly. "Let's begin."

"Bisnonno," CeeCee hissed, while eyeing him as though she
expected better.

"Ah, yes. I forget myself." Clasping his hands to his chest and
bowing his head, he said, "Buon seme dà buoni frutti."

CeeCee's face darkened. "What?" Bisnonno protested.
"'Good tree makes good fruit,'" he said, trying to sound offended.
But the smile on his lips betrayed him.

"Bisnonno!" CeeCee stomped her foot.

Bisnonno nodded, and this time there was no hiding the pride
he felt for his great-granddaughter. We all clasped our hands to our
chests and bowed our heads.

"Metal or flesh, heart or wheel, we are all measured by our
gifts and our deeds. Today we seek to set a fortunate whirlwind in
motion. And above all, may it be clock wise . . ."

"And a quarter turn foolish," finished CeeCee and Bertie,

grinning.

Were they saying they wanted him to be a Clockwerk . . . Idiot?

Nimet's finger hovered over the *on* button. "Willa, memory book?"

I dug it out of the tool bag. "Got it!" Nimet jabbed the button and stepped quickly aside.

This time the Clockwerk Boy came to life, gears whirring and bellows puffing. The lenses in his eyes shifted, adjusting to the light, and he made a noise like clearing his throat. The instant he saw the book, his eyes locked onto it. I handed it to him and he rapidly turned the pages. The old man signaled to Rufus to undo the chains. After turning the final page, the Clockwerk closed the book. "Look at me," I said to him.

The Clockwerk Boy's eyes locked onto my face. "Are you Willa Snap?" he piped.

"Yes."

"Quickly! What day is this?"

I told him. There was something slightly different in his voice. I couldn't put my finger on it, but something had changed.

"Did you meet . . . ?" The Clockwerk Boy scanned all the new faces in the room.

"The dragons? I did."

"Did they send you?"

"No. I decided not to go."

"Did they tell you whom you were to save?"

"No, but they said if I traveled through time . . . I'd die."

"That is not *exactly* what they said."

I thought for a moment. "They said . . . my body . . . would 'not come back alive.' How is that any different?"

"Understanding a dragon augury is a tricky business, Willa Snap. I was there the night Meerax first spoke of you. *I* know whom you are to save."

"The dragons said their timeline would end for certain if they told me."

"Ah! And therein lies the rub. The augury was very clear that a *dragon* could not tell you. But *I* am no dragon."

I took a step back. "The dragon Vapherra said if I knew who I needed to save, I'd definitely want to go. But now that the time machine is destroyed . . . I—I—don't think I want to know."

The Clockwerk Boy nodded. "I will respect your decision, of course. But I don't agree with it."

I glanced at Bertie and Nimet. "Maybe you didn't understand. The time for me to save them has passed. The dragons smashed their time machine to smithereens so the soothies wouldn't find it."

"I understand you perfectly, Willa Snap."

I took the Clockwerk cane from my purse. "I suppose you'll be wanting this back?"

"Luigi's ghost!" breathed Bisnonno.

The Clockwerk reached out and carefully closed my fingers around it.

"I give this to you," he said. "Keep it wound, and may it serve you well."

"I couldn't! It's too nice a gift—"

"Then consider it . . . an exchange," he said.

"For what?"

The Clockwerk Boy tapped his chest where the BrainBox had

been installed. "For what you have given me." He turned to face each one of us, as if he were recording the moment. "Thank you all."

"Clockwerk Boy," I said, "do you know who it was that attacked you and removed your BrainBox?"

"No. I'm afraid that information lies in my original Brain-Box."

"Where will you go?"

"I must retrieve the rest of my memory books and find a safer location."

"Wait!" I reached into the tool bag again. "I took as many as I could carry, for safekeeping."

He took the books and thanked me before disappearing between the worktables and shadows. All the while, something tugged at the core of my being. Off in the distance, above the piled-high worktables, the shop doors swung open.

"Clockwerk Boy!" I shouted. "Who was I supposed to save?"

The doors froze. Light streamed in from the courtyard.

"The augury called her . . . Ms. Snap."

"You mean"—the door creaked shut with a thud—"my mom?" I turned around slowly. Everyone was staring at me.

Rufus broke the silence. "Bumm-errr."

Bertie swallowed hard. "That could happen . . . fifty years from now."

"Yeah, or tomorrow," said Rufus.

Nimet shushed him. "Ms. Snap doesn't have to mean your mother," she said, trying to sound hopeful. "It could mean your father's mother."

"And that makes it better how?" I asked.

"Ooh! It could mean you!" Nimet's face fell as she realized what she was saying.

CeeCee rushed forward and wrapped her arms around me tight. "I don't want you to die!" she wailed.

But for all the sad faces, I couldn't join them. Why, you ask? Because I smelled adventure.

"Why are you smiling, you crazy girl?" asked Nimet.

I pulled out the notepad Tuppence had given me and retrieved a card. I must've looked smug as I held it out. "I know where there's another time machine!"

With the compliments of

THE WONDROUS

Professor

Vander Graaff Farsical

the 24th

401 W. Firebox Lane, Steamwerks Burg, near The Ghost Factory

Bertie took the card from me and read it out loud. "Willa," he said, "I can guarantee this guy doesn't have a time machine."

"But he does! He told me so the day I arrived. He's the one who told me about the reverse time-eddies."

"The Ghost Factory," said Nimet, her voice hollow.

"The Ghost Factory is abandoned," said Bisnonno, straining to revive an old memory. "But there used to be a row of shops on Firebox Lane that ran alongside it."

CeeCee tilted her head up at me. "Can I come?"

Bisnonno gently detached his great-granddaughter's arms from around my waist. "No, CeeCee," he said softly. "Another time."

Bertie handed Professor Farsical's calling card back to me. "You're serious about this?"

"How else can I save my mom?"

"He *won't* have a working time machine," Bertie told me. "You've seen how large they are. It takes a small army to build and maintain one. And the soothies would be all over him if he tried so much as to test it."

"I have to find out."

"She'll need a Steamwerks outfit," said Nimet.

Bertie sighed. "That's right. Nimet, do you know anyone Willa's size?"

Nimet frowned. "She could wear mine."

"*You* have a Steamwerks outfit?" said Bertie, shocked.

Nimet smiled nervously. "Doesn't everybody?"

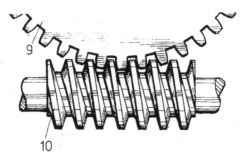

Professor Farsical's Ghost Story

I TURNED in the mirror. "Oh, snap!"

Nimet pulled the corset tighter. "Why do you keep saying that?"

"Tighter," I wheezed.

"If I tighten it any more, you'll suffocate."

"I . . . don't . . . care."

Nimet tied the laces fast. "That's as tight as they go."

I couldn't stop staring at myself in the mirror. "Nimet, look! I've got—I've got—"

Nimet rolled her eyes. "In your dreams, crazy girl."

I adjusted my hat. It had a big lens resting above the brim, and a smaller one called an oculus tucked underneath. I swung the oculus around and centered it in front of my left eye, then pressed one of the buttons on my sleeve. Nothing.

"Oh, snap."

"What is the problem now?"

"Um, which button did you say activated the spectral detection lens on my hat?"

Nimet jumped to her feet, fully alert. "Don't tell me you pressed another button!"

I pointed to my sleeve, third button from the cuff. "I think it was that one."

Little wisps of smoke came out of Nimet's ears. Okay, I made that up. But I think that's where she was headed.

"Hey, did you bring the guns for these holsters?"

Nimet pointed a finger at me. "What did I tell you, Willa Snap?"

I stared down at my feet. "To behave."

"And are you behaving?"

I clenched my teeth and blew air through them. "Nooooo."

Nimet reached into a box and pulled out two wicked-looking steam-compression guns. "Now these are just for show! You're *not* to pull these out for *any* reason. Do you understand?"

I nodded and tried not to smile like an Idiot, but it was hopeless. "Hey, can this skirt go any lower?"

Nimet stood back and sighed. "I'm afraid not. Short skirts are all the rage in the Steamwerks Burg these days. But I might have a cloak."

"A cloak?" I placed my hands on the skirt. "Then who's gonna see these hips, sister?"

Nimet fell on the floor laughing.

"Finally, you've been so formal ever since—"

She stopped laughing and jumped to her feet, sober as a soothie. "We have to get you to the Steamwerks Burg."

"Is something wrong, Nimet?"

"What do you mean?"

"Ever since that first visit to the Clockwerk Boy, you've been very . . . quiet." *Strange would be more like it,* I thought.

Nimet busied herself by nesting the boxes and wrapping paper she'd packed her outfit in. She looked scared.

I tried to fill in the silence. "Listen, forget I said anything. Can you check the living room and make sure the coast is clear? Because there's no *way* my parents would let me go out dressed like this."

At the agreed-upon time, I took a Clockwerk cab to a part of Greater Grandeur that was decidedly ungrand. And ungreat, too. Empty rundown warehouses and vacant lots lined the streets. A perpetual cloud of steam drifting from the Steamwerks Burg spat dirty rain into dark puddles and mysterious industrial pools. We were right on the border.

Bertie was late. I was beginning to regret not listening to Nimet, who had begged to ride along, when I heard the sound of wheels rolling down the street.

I ducked under an overhang and disappeared into the shadows.

Another Clockwerk cab rolled to the edge of the Steamwerks Burg and stopped.

I waited. One minute. Two. Five. The Clockwerk cab turned around and stopped again. The doors bloomed open, and out stepped a man, a devilishly handsome man—oh, wait, nope, it was just Bertie.

His outfit was as outlandish as mine. Black velvet bowler with goggles, check. Double-breasted paisley vest with brass buttons, check. Gleaming pistol grips poking from holsters sewn into his breeches, check. Funky brass-headed cane and knee-length boots with too many buckles, check. And to top it all off, a velvet-trimmed Regency tailcoat in a shade of burgundy so deep it was nearly black.

I stepped out of the shadows, and Bertie started.

"Willa? Is that you?"

I smiled. I had never looked so—

One of my high heels plunged deep into a puddle. I pitched forward, my arms pinwheeling. I was going down—*MAYDAY! MAYDAY!* And then Bertie was there, pulling me upright just before splashdown.

"Watch your step there," he said. And then there was an awkward moment where I slapped him away from me. I may have even said a few unladylike things, but eventually that passed, too.

After the Clockwerk cab pulled away, we were alone on the street.

"So . . . what do we do now?" I asked.

"Well . . ."

We both felt it at the same time. A vibration in the street. *DUM-DUM DUM-DUM DUM-DUM.* And it was getting louder. We turned toward the Steamwerks Burg just in time to see it round the corner: an enormous steel-plated steam-powered rhinoceros. The second it saw us, it ducked its head and started to pick up, well, steam.

I whipped out both my compression guns—*KABLAM! ZA-PHOOM! KLACKA-KLACKA-KLACKA!*—I was making all these sounds with my mouth, mind you, because the only sounds coming out of the guns were anemic clicks—*BLAMMO! . . . BLAM!*

. . . BLAM!

I snuck a look at Bertie. He was slowly shaking his head and pinching the bridge of his nose like he had a headache.

"What? It's not like you're doing anything to rescue us!"

The rhinoceros was nearly on us, white steam jetting from its horn, black smoke billowing from twin rump-mounted smokestacks. Bertie didn't seem worried. I didn't figure out why until the rhino slowed and showed us its flank. A door in its side opened, and steps folded down.

"Oh," I said.

Bertie waved a hand. "Our ride."

I twirled my guns around on my fingers and holstered them, polishing the gleaming handles with the palms of my hands.

"Someday these will be real."

"God help us," prayed Bertie.

I slapped Bertie's hand away when he tried to help me up the stairs. Some guys are slow learners. Inside, the seats were covered in crushed red velvet.

"401 West Firebox Lane," I said in a raised voice.

The rhino snorted. Steam billowed out of its horn and drifted into our faces as it picked up speed. We donned our goggles and thudded toward our date with a time machine located next to an abandoned ghost factory. Yep, just another regular night on the town in Grandeur.

"You could have warned me," I said a little testily.

Bertie considered this. "You don't have rhino cabs Outside?" The hint of a smile quivered at the corner of his lips.

I gritted my teeth. "Not that I ever saw."

"I see. Well . . . I'll keep that in mind if I ever order us a steam-powered tarantula cab."

"Totally bean! Could we take one of those on the way back?"

"Hey, did you know we have a soup named that?"

"You have a soup named Steam-Powered Tarantula?"

"No, Totally Bean!" Bertie scratched his chin. "Although I bet Steam-Powered Tarantula would sell a few bowls."

"What would you put in it?"

"Hairy crab legs, I imagine."

I tried not to grimace, but it wasn't easy.

A short time later, our rhino cab turned a corner, and the streets became bleaker, if that was possible.

"So what's a Ghost Factory?" I asked.

Bertie squirmed in his chair. "A hundred years ago, Edison—"

"Wait, you mean Thomas Edison, the inventor of the light bulb?"

"The very one. So, a hundred years ago, he built a machine he called a ghost portal that earned him a visit from the Black Fez. You see, Edison believed that life is indestructible. And that inside everyone are trillions and trillions of tiny *life entities*, that our bodies are just vessels to hold them in place and give them a voice. He designed the ghost portal to try and hold them together at the time of death. Only it didn't turn out quite the way he'd hoped."

"So why didn't the Black Fez bring him to Grandeur?"

"Because Edison understood the dangerous nature of his machine. He agreed to destroy both it and the plans. Of course, the Black Fez don't destroy technology. They collect it. So they brought everything back to Arkheia Tower."

"Is that one of the skyscrapers?"

"Yes. The other two are IOI Tower, which houses the soothies and the Institute of Intellect, and the Lab, where your mother works. But Arkheia Tower is mostly a museum, run by the Black Fez. We take field trips to it all the time in Idiot School. They've got working copies in there of every significant invention, good or bad, that humans have ever made."

"*Ever?* How's that even possible? It would have to go—"

"All the way to the top, and they aren't skinny little towers like you see Outside." Bertie let that sink in.

"And the dome is how high again?" I asked.

"Almost four miles. You could fit entire cities into one of those buildings. In Arkheia Tower, the inventions are laid out chronologically, with the first floor starting around 5,000 BCE."

"What could they possibly have from then, a club?"

"Don't laugh. The idea of a club, one used on people, would have been considered a very dangerous idea 7,000 years ago."

"Yeah, well, that one got out. Didn't it?"

"It happens. The Black Fez can't catch *everything*. Nor can every dangerous invention be contained. And I'm not sure that's a bad thing."

"Bertie, are you an anarchist?" That's a person with tidiness issues.

Turning onto Firebox Lane, I spied my first working gas lamp, hissing and sputtering away. Bertie pointed to the hulking silhouette of what I figured must be the Ghost Factory. It squatted a hundred feet back from the lane, like a mountain of night surrounded by a swampy ditch. The rhino cab pulled up to a row of dimly lit shops. The doors opened, and steps unfolded just short of the slick cobblestones below.

We sat perfectly still and stared.

A large lopsided sign read WARD'S LOCKS AND CLOCK REPAIR, and below that, in smaller type, *401 Firebox Lane.*

"Well," Bertie finally said, "let's get this over with, shall we?"

The dark flagstones leading to the door were cracked and uneven. The only light flickered from a porch two doors down. The entryway was black with soot. I reached to knock, and the door creaked inward. Inside stood Professor Farsical, holding his cane at arm's length and pointing it at me. The cane top was in its expanded, concave dish form. The pale green light coming from the brass porthole in his forehead darkened the rest of his face, making his expression hard to read.

With a bounce of his cane, the top collapsed in on itself. "Please, come in. I've been expecting you."

The building had seen better days. The walls and counters were covered with samples of keys, locks, and clocks. Pushing through some thick curtains in the back, we entered his living quarters. Here it was warmer. A fire crackled in the fireplace. The professor removed his coat and draped it over a stand specially crafted to hold it.

"I trust you've come to use my time machine?"

I nodded. Bertie frowned. I didn't have to ask the professor how he knew. It was clear he'd been tracking my time eddies all the way to his doorstep.

"Quickly," he said, "follow me. There's very little time."

We exited the back of the house through a stout door, where a raised covered walkway vanished into the night. Our only light came from the pale green porthole in the professor's forehead.

"Excuse me, Professor," I said, "but about that time machine—"

"No doubt young Mr. Babbage has told you it doesn't exist. I don't blame you, Bertie, I would feel the same way myself."

I looked at Bertie. "You know him?"

Bertie shook his head. "I've never set eyes on him—"

Professor Farsical spun around, finger raised. "That's where you're wrong, Mr. Babbage. You *have* seen me, many times. You just don't remember. But I remember you. Oh, yes. The dragons' darling. Impressing them daily with your feats of prestidigitation."

The light from the professor's porthole reflected off us just enough to illuminate his dancing eyes.

Bertie squinted. "You were a chimp twist!"

Professor Farsical smiled, turned on his heel, and resumed his rapid pace. "It was *my* last year, and *your* first," he called over his shoulder.

Bertie placed a hand on my arm, letting the professor get a little bit ahead of us. "Willa, you understand where we're going, don't you?"

I looked around, not having really paid attention. "To his time machine, I hope."

"That's not what I meant."

I tried to get my bearings. "Well, we left from the back of his house, and we've been going straight as an arrow ever since. So we're headed for—"

"The Ghost Factory."

"Come, come," pressed Professor Farsical. "Very little time."

I dragged Bertie forward. "Bertie, aren't laboratories illegal in Grandeur?"

"For Geniuses and Idiot Geniuses they're a serious offense. They don't care so much about us Idiots, but time machines . . .

only the dragons get away with that one."

"So constructing his lab in the Ghost Factory is actually kind of clever. I mean, no one in her right mind would set foot in the place."

"Especially after dark," added Bertie.

"Right. Or with a potential Idiot Genius."

"Excellent point."

We hurried on. The walkway ended in a stand of stunted trees. We were in the factory's shadow now. Professor Farsical was nowhere to be seen.

"Do you think we can risk a little light?" I asked.

Bertie put his goggles on and turned a dial. "Set your oculus for infrared." He fooled with some buttons, and suddenly, looking through my oculus, it was like the tip of his cane had become a powerful flashlight.

I followed Bertie along a path that led to an abandoned loading dock. We stepped inside the factory, and the temperature must have dropped twenty degrees. A ways ahead of us, lights were coming on. I parked my oculus, and Bertie removed his goggles. After a short trek, we came to a high-ceilinged room with an exact replica of the dragon's time machine, only this one was about fifteen feet tall. On either side stood sheet-covered lumps.

"You're insane," Bertie told the professor. "It's much too small. You couldn't send an ant to Tuesday with this thing."

Professor Farsical considered this. "Actually, I think I could send an ant, and perhaps as far as Friday."

"You know what I mean!" said Bertie, getting mad. "It's too small to send a person!"

I stepped forward. "Professor, why have you brought us here?"

"You came to see me because you were ready to travel through time," said the professor matter-of-factly. He began flipping switches. Gears groaned. The twin iron rings encircling the time machine's central tower slowly began spinning in opposite directions.

I looked at Bertie. He shook his head.

"And how are you going to make that happen?"

Professor Farsical tore away one of the sheets, revealing yet another machine. "With this!" he cried.

Bertie gasped. "That looks like a ghost portal! Willa, this is a one-way ticket to Delusion. We've got to get out of here. Now!"

Bertie grabbed my hand, and for once I didn't smack it away.

"Wait!" yelled the professor. "Bertie is correct in one respect.

It does *look* like a ghost portal. But I can assure you this is no bridge to those in the afterlife. This is a spectral duplication device. Look." He produced a piece of paper from inside his jacket. "I have a license to operate it." He handed the piece of paper to Bertie. "Approved by the Institute. The soothies have been here. They've deemed it harmless."

"Well?" I said, after a moment.

Bertie handed it back. "He's telling the truth, but it's a provisional license. Tell me, professor, what did the soothies think of your time machine?"

"They laughed, much as you did."

"And with good reason. You *can't* change the laws of physics! Willa's mass far exceeds the amount of energy you can create with this. . . ." Bertie waved at the pint-sized time machine. "You couldn't send Willa's shoelaces to ten seconds ago!"

Professor Farsical nodded. "Ah! But I'm not going to send her shoelaces. . . . I'm going to send her ghost!"

"My what?"

Bertie stepped in front of me. "He's mad, Willa."

I squirmed past him. It was chivalric and all, but it was *my* ghost we were talking about here. "Just a minute, Bertie. Professor, I have a ghost?"

"We'll get to that. The spectral energy of a ghost is infinitesimal compared to solid mass. My time machine may be small, but I can send a ghost to the ends of time."

I turned to Bertie. "Do you remember what the dragons said—that my body would not come back alive?"

Bertie still wasn't convinced.

"Oh, don't be that way, Bertie. Ghosts are terribly misunderstood creatures, you know," said Professor Farsical. "The idea that they're all dead people . . . it's nonsense. Ghosts form all the time. In nature, they're created by intense magnetic spikes emanating from the Earth's core. They're a kind of *recording*—if you will—of our life force. And when conditions are exactly right, those *recordings* can . . . play back. They're not inherently dangerous. They think just as you and I do. They have memories. What they don't know is what happened to them. And that's only because no one has ever told them what they are. Willa Snap—*your* ghost will be the first to know!"

"You're saying ghosts have free will?" I asked.

"Absolutely."

"How long will my ghost . . . remain . . . ghostly?"

"That's a good question. The spectral cohesion of a ghost created by the Earth can last centuries, reappearing again and again as the right conditions repeat themselves. But if my calculations are correct, the spectral cohesion of *my* ghosts will last about thirty minutes, give or take ten."

"And what happens then?"

"They . . . cease to exist."

"You mean die."

Professor Farsical gave this some thought. "I suppose . . . in their way. Yes. It would be like dying."

"Bertie," I said, "don't you see? It all makes sense now. Meerax said I must sacrifice my 'self' to right the wrong. But she wasn't talking about sacrificing my body. She was talking about sacrificing my ghost!"

Bertie looked at the spectral duplication machine. I could see he was thinking about my safety. It was kind of nice in a way. But

I wasn't happy about it. Worrying about me was *my* job.

To my surprise, though, Bertie let it go.

"Professor," he said, "exactly how does this work?"

Professor Farsical tore the sheet off the other machine, revealing a chair inside a cage, the whole thing surrounded by wires and glass tubes. "Willa will sit in here, where her spectral energy will be recorded. Her ghost will form in the spectral duplication device. Freshly made ghosts are naturally attracted to those they're made from. So it will be drawn to Willa but never reach her."

"Why?" I asked.

"Because when the ghost reaches *this* platform," Bertie explained, pointing to a two-by-two-foot square next to the central tower, "a time vortex will open and send it on its way."

Professor Farsical's eyes lit up. "Precisely!"

"But Professor," said Bertie, "won't you need to know *when* to send her ghost to?"

"That's easy," he said. "I'll send it to the end of her timeline."

"Where I must right the wrong," I said.

Bertie looked directly into my eyes. "Are you sure you want to do this?"

"What choice do I have? How else do I save . . . Ms. Snap?"

"Whatever that means," said Bertie.

"Yes . . . whatever that means," I echoed. Bertie kept looking into my eyes. We were standing really close, too close. Feynman's bongos! Was he thinking about kissing me? I'd always wondered how my first kiss would be, a hundred years from now, on a windswept beach at sunset, the horses cooling their hooves until I galloped off, tears streaming down my face, leaving behind the only man who ever understood me.

"Professor," said Bertie, walking away, "how fast do you need to get the outer wheels spinning for primary ignition?"

"42,000 rpm should do it."

My eyes fluttered open. What just happened? Hey, it's not like I *wanted* to be kissed. Nooo! Ew! Yuck!

Bertie whistled. "You've tested it?"

"This will be its fourth run."

Bertie pointed to an auxiliary control board next to a rack of tools at the foot of the time machine's central tower. "You have a chimp twist to run that board?"

"No. I run things from out here."

Bertie looked alarmed. "How do you compensate for temporal disturbances?"

"I approximate."

Bertie stripped off his jacket, doffed his bowler, and rolled up his sleeves. "I'll be your chimp twist on this one."

Professor Farsical opened the door to the caged seat and motioned for me to enter. "See? You couldn't be in safer hands."

I stomped over and sat down roughly on the chair. "It's not his hands I'm worried about. It's his pea-sized brain."

"Try and stay as still as possible," continued the professor, ignoring my complaints. "You can hold onto this bar in front if you like, but don't touch anything else during the recording process." He closed the door and with a key from his pocket locked me in.

"What's the lock for?" I asked, putting the drama queen routine on pause—just for a second, mind you. Drama is all well and fine, but I didn't see any reason to let it jeopardize the experiment.

"Consider it a precaution. Nothing to worry about."

"Why does Bertie need to be in there?"

"That's a bit technical," he said too quickly.

"Humor me."

"Well, in the final stages, the temporal wave fluctuations pouring off the central core will render *my* control board slightly out of phase. I had estimations planned, but Bertie is quite right. Having a chimp twist inside is the best way to go. He'll be in no danger." He smiled placatingly.

It was one thing to be locked in a cage, but to be patronized while locked in that cage? It made me want to wrench the door off its hinges and breathe fire.

"And the temporal wave fluctuations won't hurt him?" I asked, trying not to sound worried.

"Not in a lasting way. Listen, all you need to do is sit still and wait for the temporal vortex to open. The rest depends entirely on your ghost's actions. Yours is not the only timeline in danger tonight."

"You mean the dragons?"

"I don't give a Higgs boson about the dragons, Willa."

"But then who—" But he'd turned his back on me and returned to his control board.

I watched the jerk-head chimp twist, and by that I mean Bertie, step through the slowly spinning iron rings. I watched him through slitted eyes as he flipped switches, tapped a dial, and rearranged the tools next to him, picking up a spanner and twirling it like a baton.

"You ready?" he asked me.

I gave him a false smile through clenched teeth. "Whatever," I grumbled.

He gave me a puzzled look.

"Fire it up, chimp boy!" I said.

Bertie gave Professor Farsical the thumbs up sign, and the rings encircling the time machine sped up.

"You sure you're going to be okay in there?" I asked, instantly regretting how concerned I sounded.

He gave me a devil-may-care smile and said, "As long as this contraption can get up to speed without blowing apart, I'll be fine."

Good for you, Bertie Babbage, I thought. I figured I had a good twenty minutes of pique left in me.

"Willa Snap," yelled Professor Farsical. "I'm going to engage the spectral duplication device. Brace yourself."

The tubes outside my cage lit up, and a humming noise filled my mind. A wave of vertigo passed through me, and it felt like the world was suddenly spinning out of control. I clutched the metal bar in front of me in a death grip. Then, all at once, it was like something inside of me wrenched free. The dizziness vanished, but I still felt light, like my body would have floated to the top of the cage if I'd let go of the bar.

Now that the time machine's central tower was turning, I could see through it like the blades of a spinning fan. In the machine opposite me, a ghost shimmered into existence. It—or I, or whatever you want to call it—had its eyes closed, like it was sleeping.

"Professor," yelled Bertie, "I'm getting a bit of shimmy on the temporal harmonizer."

The professor checked his control board. "It's within operational parameters. Don't worry about it."

Bertie picked up a different spanner. "I'd feel better if I stabilized it."

"No, it's spinning too fast, and we don't have the time to slow it down."

Bertie laughed. "You call this fast? Give me thirty seconds." He gave a tiny twist to each of a half dozen bolts as they spun past him. I wouldn't have thought anyone could move his hands that fast. But there he was, doing it like it was nothing special.

Bertie held up his spanner and shouted, "Clear."

"Well done, Mr. Babbage," shouted the professor. "Engaging primary temporal ignition."

All at once the time machine sped up like a helicopter taking off.

My ghost began drifting toward me. An uneasiness stirred in the pit of my stomach. I didn't know why, but I didn't like the idea of it getting closer.

All of a sudden, a spray of sparks flashed out of the time machine's core. Bertie shifted the pair of safety goggles from his forehead to his eyes and, leaning forward, stared intently into the spinning metal.

"Cracked bearing, Professor," yelled Bertie. "We've dropped down to 39,000 rpm. I'm going to shut it down—"

"No! Don't!"

Bertie's hands hovered over the controls. "Professor, if the rest of these bearings go, they'll ricochet around in here like superheated pinball-size bullets."

Professor Farsical left his station and stood just outside the spinning rings. "We *must* send the ghost now!"

"The what?" Bertie looked up and noticed my ghost for the first time.

Professor Farsical cupped his hands. "A ghost is never more dangerous than when it's first called into existence. To reassimilate a newly formed ghost into living flesh . . . Bertie, people don't die of fright . . . they die of ectoplasmic overload to their central nervous systems."

Bertie instantly turned to me, his face deadly serious.

"Shut it down," I mouthed. "I'll be fine."

Red lights started flashing on Bertie's control board. Without taking his eyes off me, he said, "Professor, we're going to need a whole lot more power."

Professor Farsical ripped open a panel on the floor and began flipping switches. "Bringing auxiliary generators online!"

"No!" I demanded.

"40,000," announced Bertie, "41,000 . . . more juice, Professor!"

"That's all we've got!"

Bertie returned his attention to the time machine's central core. "Professor, if I could wedge a spanner between the decoupler rings, it would reduce the load on the remaining bearings."

"You don't have the time!" shouted Professor Farsical. "Prepare to send the ghost!"

Bertie traded out his spanner for a much larger one, then faced the rotating tower. It was going way too fast. He made an unsure stab, then pulled back.

My ghost was now passing through the central tower. "Willa!" I screamed to it. Its eyes opened, and my mind immediately filled with its confused thoughts. At first, I felt like they'd overwhelm me, but I forced myself to focus. Then I had an idea. If I could hear my ghost's thoughts, maybe it could hear mine.

Bertie needs time! I thought. *Can you slow yourself down?*

I pointed to the platform where the time vortex was forming.

Bertie stabbed the spanner into the tower. It bounced off and came flying right back. The recoil spun him around, and he lost his footing. As he tried to catch his balance, he stumbled head first toward the spinning iron rings. At the last possible second, he fell to his knees and slid to a stop, his face inches from the blurring tons of metal.

"Bertie!" I yelled.

He acted like he didn't fully understand his danger. And I could see blood. One of his fingers was pointing at an odd angle. He forced it back into place with a grimace and got to his feet. When he approached the tower for the second time, he looked wobbly.

"Nooooooo!" I screamed, climbing out of my seat and shaking the cage.

"Babbage," screamed Professor Farsical. "The ghost is in position!"

My ghost was struggling to stay on the platform, flailing her arms, trying to step back, but I couldn't tell if it was having any effect. The spray of sparks coming out of the central tower was like a ring of fire now. Bits of hot metal were shooting out like tracer bullets. As Bertie lined himself up for another go, a wave of distortion billowed out of the tower and, just for a second, Bertie looked like a toddler. A few seconds later, he looked like an old man.

As if things couldn't get any worse, the ghost's thoughts were now twisting into my mind like a hot hive of bees.

Bertie swayed backward and shook his head like he was trying to clear it. He pointed the spanner at the tower, but he couldn't find his timing.

CHAPTER TWENTY-TWO

The whole platform was beginning to shake.

"Just send it!" roared the professor. "Send it anywhere!"

And then Bertie did something that really scared me. He closed his eyes.

"My God, man!" screamed the professor. "Have you lost your mind?"

But suddenly I knew exactly what he was doing. He was seeing without his eyes. He was listening without his ears. He was finding his timing.

Bertie raised the spanner up in the air like a spear and jabbed.

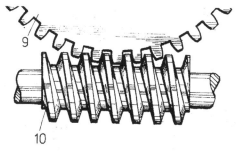

The Kiss

I DON'T mean to burst any bubbles or anything, but being a ghost sucks. First off, there's no instruction manual, so good luck trying to figure out how to float around. Second, expect confusion, because seeing your living body doing and saying things on its own isn't exactly going to clear anything up. Third, if you don't have a time machine on hand to whisk you away from your living body, then be ready to lose whatever mind you have left.

Here's what I know. One second I was floating in front of my living self, who was screaming something about giving Bertie time by slowing myself down, and the next second it was like I'd fallen down the deepest well ever dug.

I should mention one other thing. During that brief moment I was still in the Ghost Factory, I could feel and hear others, *lots* of others, all through the building. It was terrifying.

Professor Farsical had said I'd have very little time as a ghost, so I'd have to make the most of it. That meant learning about myself and my surroundings as fast as I could. At first it was dark and quiet, but that was changing—quickly. Four dim lights—people-shaped lights—formed off to my right. Their speech was muffled. A street lamp reflected off puddles of standing water. We were in a street—no, an alleyway.

It was while looking around that I first noticed my body was a no-show. I wasn't ready for that. I was used to having a body.

I took a sniff. Nothing. I waved my hands before my face. Nothing. In fact, it felt like my hands were passing through each other. I concentrated on where my body should be and tried to will it into existence. That seemed to help, because suddenly I could understand the people talking next to me. The world felt more real, though the living gave off an aura that was painful to me.

"We're not supposed to kill her," said a man. He was a soothie, and his name was Frank. I don't know how I knew that, but there it was.

"Hold her still," a woman said. She was a soothie, too. Her name was Vera, and she was dangerous.

Frank and another soothie were holding a teenage girl by the arms. Her light was the brightest of all.

Vera pinched the girl's chin with one hand and showed her the device she was holding in the other. It was a sifting rod. "Tell me where the dragons have sent the Nano Prince, and I'll let you live," said Vera softly.

"B-b-bugger off!" said the girl. Her mind was a puzzle to me. All I could sense from her were long lists of catalogued words. But there was something else—something that made my new-found ghost nerves jangle.

I tried to step closer, but my feet didn't work that way.

"You can't sift what's not there to begin with," said Frank.

"Oh, it's in there," said Vera, adjusting the device in her hand. "And I'll get it!"

Vera planted the sifting rod on the teen's forehead, lighting up the flesh where it touched and causing the girl's body to convulse. Something about the way she moved sent a shock through me. I *knew* that body. It was my mother's! She was younger, for sure, but there was no mistaking it. This whole time I'd been thinking I was going to be sent forward in time, but I'd been sent backward!

Leave her alone! I yelled, but nothing audible came out of my mouth.

Vera wrenched the device free, glanced at it, and cursed. "Where is the prince?" she screamed.

Drool dripped from the corner of Mom's mouth. "T-t-t-too late—" Her eyes rolled back in her head.

"No!" screamed Vera. She gave the sifting rod a wicked twist. Its tip glowed bright red. "I will sift you. One way or the other, I WILL SIFT—"

Vera plunged the device into my mother's forehead at the exact same time I noticed a shiny object fly seemingly out of my own head and bury itself in Vera's wrist. Vera screamed, dropping the sifting rod and clutching her wounded arm. A large shadow passed through my body, and suddenly the soothies were fielding blows from all directions.

To my ghostly senses, the shadow was a kicking and jabbing blur. In seconds the soothies were down. Then I sensed others arriving from behind me. A man ran past and caught my mother before her head smashed to the ground. He knelt down and cradled her head on his lap. He was panting as though from a long run.

"My God! What have they done?"

A third presence entered the alleyway, this one swooping down from above. I looked up and saw the glint of two eyes inside a dark sphere. "Are we too late?" it purred. "Can you save her?"

"Tell us what to do!" said the person who'd knocked out the soothies.

The man's hand trembled as he ran it over my mother's face. "I'll need . . . I'll need someplace quiet to work. And access to electricity."

"On it." The woman kicked down the closest door and disappeared into one of the buildings.

What was my mother, as a teenager, doing in Grandeur?

"Can you unsift her?" came the voice from above.

The man threw back the hood of his cloak. His long dark hair whipped back and forth as he frantically searched the ground. "Give me light," he demanded.

A tiny spotlight blazed down from the floating sphere, which I could see now was some kind of little flying saucer with propellers.

A glint of light flashed on the ground. It was Vera's sifting rod. The man snatched it up and quickly read something off the side.

The woman leapt out from a broken doorway. "Kill that damn light! Do you want this whole alley full of soothies?" The spotlight went dark.

"How many times?" asked the voice from above.

There was a long pause before the man whispered, "Six."

The woman ripped off her black hood, exposing flaming red hair. "What's the most you've unsifted?"

"Four," said the man, "but the others . . . they trusted me."

"Willa will never trust you, Ravenlock."

Ravenlock glanced up at the kitty-sized MiniDirigy hovering above us. "Grayson, do you have a potion to make Willa trust me?"

"I'm an apothecary, Ravenlock, not a wizard."

"Then you're no good to me down here. Get some altitude and let Nimet know where they're coming from."

"Will do," she purred, vanishing upward with the sound of whirling propellers.

To say I was stunned didn't begin to cover it. The body I'd thought was my mother was . . . a teenage me!

Ravenlock picked up my seemingly dead body from the alleyway.

"Show me what you've got, Nimet. We've very little time."

"It's not much," said Nimet, walking through the doorway. "Watch your step. The floor's caving in in spots."

I stared down at the three fallen soothies. Nimet had bound and gagged them at the same time she was beating them up. Where'd she learn how to do that? Something told me I didn't want to know. What I really wanted to know was what was going on in that abandoned building. But how could I get in there? I closed my ghost eyes, which doesn't really work when you're a ghost, and made little ghost fists . . . which also did nothing. What was I supposed to do?

I could still sense the three of them moving away from me through the building. I willed myself to latch onto Nimet. But her mind squiggled away from me, like an eel into a forest of kelp. I tried for Willa, but her jumbled thoughts evaded me. Then I reached out for Ravenlock, and it was like I'd plunged a harpoon into a breaching whale. I shot through a wall and into the building.

I whooshed through furniture, safes, piles of rotting clothes. I flew through the ceiling and reeled toward them until, passing through an old boiler, I found them.

Ravenlock had laid Willa on the floor and was unclipping a string of small devices from a harness on his chest. Nimet pulled an electrical wire out of the wall and spliced it together with a tiny kit she'd removed from her fez.

Since when did Nimet have mad electrical skills?

"Try not to overload these, all right?" she told Ravenlock. "I have no idea where the breaker box is in this place."

Ravenlock took the wires from Nimet. He attached them to one of his devices, and the whole string lit up. He stabbed the sifting rod into the top of the largest mechanism, a box. On its face, a row of numbers and letters began tumbling like the symbols on a slot machine. Nimet started to stand, and Ravenlock grabbed her hand.

"Nimet, whatever happens—" he choked. "Whatever—I want you to know I'll never forget what you've done for me."

Nimet patted Ravenlock's hand. "Oh, sweetie . . . I wouldn't be too sure about that." Ravenlock studied her warily. "Listen," she said, "you just bring our girl home."

Ravenlock glanced down at Willa's limp form, and in the blink of an eye, Nimet flashed out of the room before he could look back again.

When did Nimet get super speed?

Ravenlock gently lifted Willa's head and began attaching electrodes to it.

"Six," he said to himself, his voice breaking. "Oh, God, six!"

Ravenlock bowed his head, and a tear fell from his cheek and landed on hers. Now he was connecting electrodes to his own head.

"Don't leave me alone in this place, Willa. We have a job to do, you and I. Heathcliff is still out there. We've got to stop him. You were right about the BrainRents. I know that now. I was arrogant to think I could beat him at his own game. He was always one step ahead. I just didn't know it."

Ravenlock adjusted some of the dials on his machinery. There was something similar about his equipment and the sifting rod—like they'd been made by the same people.

"There's just one thing, Willa," he said. "You have to trust me. You have to let me inside so I can try and undo what they've done."

Just then a number flashed into place on one of Ravenlock's boxes. Willa made a noise and grimaced. Ravenlock reacted too, echoing the pain in her face.

A new light entered the room, a bluish green one. Ravenlock noticed it, too. Then I realized he was looking directly at me. I held up a glowing hand. My ghost self was finally becoming visible.

Ravenlock stared at me. "Franklin's fire! What new horror is this?"

A second number froze into place. Willa writhed in pain and, a second later, Ravenlock did the same. In Willa's mind, I sensed some of Vera's sifting give way.

"She doesn't trust you," I said, and I could hear my voice whisper into the room like dead leaves brushing across the floor.

Ravenlock continued to stare at my ghostly form. "You're not—real," he told me. "You're a false memory, a trap placed into my brain by Heathcliff to trip me up."

"You think I'm a phantom placed in your brain by that little snot Wudgepuddle?"

"What else would you be?"

"What else? I'll tell you what else. I'm a ghost, made by Professor Farsical's spectral duplication device, sent forward through time. I've been sent here to try and repair the dragons' timeline, and mine, too. So if you could stop wallowing in self-pity and doubt for just long enough to help, I'd really appreciate it!"

"Professor Farsical sent you?"

"Yes! With Bertie's help. Who may or may not even be alive." Ravenlock cast his eyes down. "Wait a minute! This is the future. That means you know if Bertie's alive!"

"The less information you bring back from the future, the better."

"But I'm not going back."

"How's that?"

"This is a one-way trip for me. My ghost dies *here*, in your present."

Ravenlock stared at the face in his lap and smiled. "So . . . whatever I say to you . . . it's kind of like I'm saying it to her."

"Right. Only she's fifteen-year-old me."

"Sixteen, actually," interjected Ravenlock.

"Whatever. I'm eleven-year-old me."

"Bertie still lives," said Ravenlock. "In fact, the two of you are quite the thing."

I threw my hands up. "Whoa! Too much information! TOO MUCH INFORMATION!" We stared at each other for a moment. "So . . . why isn't Bertie here saving me?"

"It's probably best I don't tell you that."

"What's it matter? You can't save her." I pointed to Willa. "She doesn't trust you. *I* don't trust you. And if she doesn't trust you, then you have no way of unsifting her. Am I right?"

"Actually, I *can* unsift her by force . . . but there's a price."

A third number froze into place. My teenage body cried out, its eyes fluttering open just for a second. But I don't think Ravenlock noticed, because he was convulsing in pain himself.

"You told Nimet your limit was four, but Willa here—" I pointed. Boy, it was weird referring to myself in the third person. "—has been sifted six times. This is *exactly* the reason we'll never trust you. You're a liar!" But even as I said it, I knew what I was saying was, itself, a lie. The fact was, I'd always known why I didn't trust Ravenlock. The truth blazed in my memory like an immutable law. He was broken inside, he couldn't feel love, and, even if he *could* feel love, I'd be the last person on Earth he'd share it with. If I'd had more time to think, maybe I'd've figured out how foolish that sounded, but things were moving too fast. "So what's the price?"

Ravenlock was losing his breath, like he was running a race and it was slowly getting away from him. "I've . . . I've survived as many as four," he said. "But six—"

The fourth number froze into place. Ravenlock's eyes closed and his mouth opened, but no noise came out. He'd stopped breathing. The glowing light that surrounded his body faded. Then, with a jerk, he started breathing again. The glow came back, but less brightly.

Sixteen-year-old me opened her eyes. I could hear the thoughts in her mind more clearly now. She seemed to know where she was, but not much else. Seeing Ravenlock, she tried to reach up to his face.

"Noooo," Willa said weakly, and a love and longing surged through my ghostly being, consuming everything I was until it subsided, like a tide receding into the sea. And when it was finally gone, all that existed was distrust. Alternating waves of love and distrust. There was nothing else.

As my living self fell into something like a restless sleep, Ravenlock's eyes opened.

I pulled myself closer to him and I tried to tear one of the electrodes off his head, but the wire barely jiggled. That seemed to make him happy.

"What's the price?" I demanded.

"It's . . . a small thing," he said. "But well . . . worth it."

"A minute ago you said we still had a job to do, that Heathcliff was still out there, and something about BrainRents. What was that all about?"

Ravenlock blinked his eyes like he was having trouble getting them to focus. "Heathcliff's been using the BrainRents to hack into our brains and mess with our memories. I think he's been doing it since the first day we met. In the beginning, he only had access to the unused parts of our brains, limiting the damage he could do. But he's smarter than he appears, much smarter. In time, he began branching out . . . into our permanent memories. For me, he filled my head with irritability toward you. His little gift to *you* was distrust of me."

"That meddling weasel!"

Ravenlock looked at his device. Four numbers were in place. The fifth was a blur, but I knew it could freeze into place at any moment.

Suddenly, I understood what he was doing. He was letting himself die so I might live. "Ravenlock, what you're doing isn't a *small thing*. Don't you dare sacrifice yourself for me."

He slumped backward. His face seemed less pained. "It's better this way," he whispered.

I felt the distrust that Heathcliff had planted in my head shatter and break apart.

"Ravenlock! I understand! I trust you now!" I said. "And since eleven-year-old me trusts you, doesn't that mean sixteen-year-old me will too?"

"I'm afraid not," he croaked.

"Why?"

"You said it yourself. Your ghost dies here, and your thoughts will die with you. Sixteen-year-old you will never have your memories."

I looked at my teenage face. Ravenlock was right. This living me wouldn't know a thing.

Unless . . .

I let go of my hold on Ravenlock. Instantly, I felt a tug from my living self. It was like the pull I'd felt from eleven-year-old me when I was trapped in Professor Farsical's cage, only weaker.

As I drew closer to my living body, my ghost body flared brighter. As we touched, I felt the steely connection of Ravenlock's devices. They were building up to unlocking the fifth number, and that would be the end of Ravenlock. I willed my ghostly self into my living self. The sound of angry bees buzzed in my head.

You must sacrifice yourself to right the wrong. This was the moment the Clockwerk Boy had been talking about. *This* was my sacrifice.

Trust, I thought. *Trust Ravenlock.*

And then I was part of sixteen-year-old Willa. I felt our arms reach up. I felt our fingers dig into Ravenlock's . . . raven locks. I felt our lips touch his lips.

Ew, yuck! What did I tell you? Being a ghost sucks!

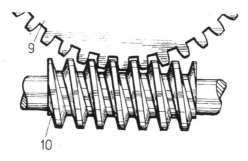

Furturum Tempestas

M Y ghost self vanished. Bertie shut down the time machine. Professor Farsical unlocked the cage I was in, and when the iron rings slowed down enough, Bertie stepped safely out.

I'd never hugged someone so hard in all my life. "I thought you were a dead man, Bertie Babbage!"

"Thought crossed my mind, once or twice."

He tried to let go, but I held on for another full minute before I let him get out of my grip.

"How's the finger?"

"Ah, comes with the territory. It'll be fine."

"Good." Then I called him a jerk-head and smacked him so hard he went down like a fifty-pound sack of wheat.

I wheeled around and advanced on the Professor. "Lock *me* in a cage, will you?" He ran off into the darkness.

Bertie didn't catch up to me until I was back on Firebox Lane, where he circled me from a safe distance.

I tapped my WatchitMapCallit, and Bertie said, "Cab's already on the way."

"Maybe I don't want to ride in a cab with you. Ever think of that?" I paced like a lion. "Did you at least send my ghost to the right place?" I asked.

Bertie smiled. "Yeah. She got where she needed to go. Can you . . . feel anything?"

"You mean from my ghost self?"

"Yeah."

"I could hear her thoughts before she vanished. After that, nothing."

Bertie looked down at his feet. "Well, for what it's worth, I'm betting on you."

A clanking-thudding filled the street. A moment later, a giant steam-powered tarantula cab turned the corner and started bearing down on us. This time, I left my guns in their holsters.

"Aw! You remembered to get the tarantula."

My last bit of anger faded. I put my arm through Bertie's and leaned my head against his shoulder. He flinched a little. I couldn't really blame him.

Twice he tried to talk while the tarantula cab thudded back to Greater Grandeur. Twice I told him to shut up, and twice he listened.

That was going to get old fast.

From the edge of the Steamwerks Burg, we switched to a Clockwerk cab. Apparently, the steam-powered creature cabs weren't allowed in Greater Grandeur. As planned what seemed like five years ago, Nimet met me in the Whitehaven lobby with a change of clothes. I used the bathroom to don my English-cousin-of-Nancy-Drew outfit. Adjusting my cloche hat in the mirror, I was surprised at how happy I was to be wearing it again.

"Everything go as planned?" asked Nimet. She was nervous. Jumpy even, like she was afraid of what I might say next.

"I *think* so. But I'm naturally optimistic, so who really knows."

"Professor Farsical might be able to learn something from your time eddies."

"Yeah, well . . . it may be a little while until I see Professor Farsical again."

In the hall outside my apartment, I eyed Heathcliff Wudge-puddle's door suspiciously.

"What's up?" asked Nimet.

"I have a feeling we aren't finished with him. We need to know what's in the box under that sink and what those weird pipes do."

Nimet nodded. "Agreed. But that's for another day, right?"

"Yeppers." We said our goodnights and retired to our apartments. I chatted with Mom and Dad, who were cuddling on the couch in the living room, watching some gritty detective show that took place in the Steamwerks Burg. Mom paused it when I walked in. She already knew how to work all the gadgets in the place, like she'd been here forever. Dad said he'd gotten another plumbing job. Mom was dutifully proud. It was crazy how normal it all felt. I mean, if you didn't count the time machine . . . and the spectral duplication device. But I was beginning to imagine a future when those might seem normal, too.

In my room, Grayson was stretched out on my bed, eyes half-open, tracking the occasional bippy bot whizzing by our window. She looked quite relaxed, even comfortable.

"How did you get in?"

"Climbed up the wall and picked the lock on the window," she said through the little speaker on her BrainRent.

Right! The BrainRent! I'd taken the thing off before going into the Steamwerks Burg. I fished mine off my desk and clipped it to my ear.

Grayson swished her tail at me. "I wish you wouldn't wear that thing."

"Don't be such a worrywart. It's just until we have enough dolleurs to buy you some vocal cords."

"And the KittyDirigy with the docking station," she added. "Don't forget that."

I rolled my eyes. "Like I could ever forget that."

I took a quick shower and changed into my pajamas. Once I was under the covers, Grayson tucked into the curve of my legs.

"Is Grimalkin treating you well at the Curiosity Shop?" I whispered.

"I'm a little rusty on the apothecary business, but it'll come back. I'll probably even learn a few things."

"When do you have to be at work?"

"Before first light. Don't worry. I'll let myself out. You been up to much?"

"More than I even know."

"How's that?"

I told her everything I'd done after dropping her off earlier in the day.

"Little different from Cambridge," she said after I finished.

"Little bit."

It was probably foolish of me to go to the Blasted Dragon alone. But I didn't feel unsafe, not with the Clockwerk cane in my pocket. And I needed to think. Something about the Clockwerk

Boy was still bothering me, but I couldn't put my finger on it.

The dragon statues rumbled as I ran up the stairs, their smoking jaws erupting into flame as I leapt through the opening.

The crowd was more unruly this time. Lots of shoving. A chair flew past my head. I gripped the Clockwerk cane tightly in my pocket. I was thinking about turning around and making a run for it, but then I saw Morgan, the black unicorn, tending bar.

I chose my steps carefully, but I couldn't keep a hyena-like creature from bumping into me accidentally on purpose. Its paw slipped into my pocket and relieved me of my notebook. I pulled out the cane, expanded it to its full size, and pressed a button. It made an unwinding sound, and the tip sparked with electricity.

"I'd give that back, if I were you," I said in my most menacing voice, which had sounded much more menacing in my head than when I actually said it.

The hyena eyed the tip of my cane fearfully. "You mean this?" he said, holding up my notebook.

I snatched it from his paw. He bared his fangs, and I swung the cane between us.

"Riven!" shouted Morgan. "Step away, you Idiot, before she shocks you into the next burg."

Riven growled and faded into the crowd.

"You're . . . Bertie Babbage's little friend," said Morgan, filling a pint for a tipsy elefantkin.

"Yes. My name is Ms. Snap."

"Well, how about you leave my bar, Ms. Snap. This is not a place for someone like you."

"I need to talk to Meerax or Vapherra."

Morgan leaned over the bar, putting her horsey teeth in my

face and coming pretty close to poking my eye out with that stub of broken horn. I made a mental note to cross unicorns off my list of imaginary beasts. "Don't know anyone by those names, Ms. Snap," she hissed. "And even if I did, I'd never speak 'em out loud, if you understand my meaning."

"I still need to talk with them."

"And what makes you so special?"

The room got quieter.

This was the moment I'd imagined, and I had only one card to play. I just hoped it would be enough.

"I've recently traveled through time," I said, "and I thought they might like to talk to me about it."

The room erupted in laughter. Everyone except Morgan. She vaulted over the bar in one go and whisked me off to a private room filled with billiard tables.

"When?"

"Last night."

"Where?"

"That's between me and the dragons."

Morgan's big eyes darted around the room. "Vapherra said you might come back."

"So you know them?"

"Officially, Ms. Snap, the dragons exist *only* as legend." *Like unicorns,* I thought.

"But everyone knows about them."

"There's a big difference between *thinking* and *knowing*. And it often involves *seeing*, which very few actually get to do."

"So what do we do now?"

Morgan shivered. "I'll take you to Meerax's chambers."

We got into an elevator, and as we descended, Morgan's tremors increased.

"Are you all right?" I asked.

"Dr-r-r-r-agons," she whinnied in a high voice.

"And horses are terrified of dragons."

Morgan nodded stiffly.

"But you're a unicorn—"

"What of it?" she snapped.

"Well, unicorns are . . ."

"Are what?"

"Um, magical?" I said, feeling stupid as the word left my mouth. I believed in magic about as much as I believed in the tooth fairy.

Morgan's eyes rested briefly on the broken tip of her horn. "Magic is the stuff of bedtime tales, Ms. Snap. You would do well never to forget that."

We traveled in silence for a time.

"Do you need to . . . call ahead or something? To let them know I'm here?"

Morgan looked at me nervously. "Have you truly traveled through time?"

"Yes." *In a way.*

"Then they'll be expecting you."

The elevator emptied into a normal-sized hallway. With each step Morgan became more skittish. By the time we reached the door, she was breathing heavily through her flaring nostrils.

"Do you think you can find your way out?" she asked.

"Yes."

"Good." And she galloped back the way we'd come.

CHAPTER TWENTY-FOUR

The door opened onto a balcony overlooking a warm cavern. Meerax—at least I thought it was Meerax—was curled up in the corner. Vapherra was reclining on a mound of rock that served as a sort of chair and kept her green, spiky head level with the balcony.

"Ms. Snap," said Vapherra. "You've been busy."

"Did I succeed?"

Vapherra narrowed her eyes at me. "How can you not know?"

The last thing I wanted to do was tell her about Bertie, Professor Farsical, and my ghost.

"Did I succeed?" I asked again.

"Meerax sensed a disturbance in our mutual timelines last night."

"And?"

"*Futurum Tempestas.*"

"In English?"

"She encountered an impenetrable maelstrom."

"What does that mean for us?"

"It means that our timelines are uncertain. And until the temporal storm clears, we'll know no more than we did before."

"How long will it take to clear?"

"There's no knowing, I'm afraid. But how did you do it? We would have detected the operation of another time machine capable of sending you away—as would the soothies have. As a creature of scientific thought, Ms. Snap, I'm confounded when patently impossible tasks are undeniably accomplished. I have, in fact, spent all this last night in contemplation of how you could possibly have managed it, and for all my energies, I've only been able to concoct a single possibility."

I steeled myself. "And that is?"

"That you've been to the fabled Nano Empire and gained access to the very thing soothies fear most: a time machine so small as to be undetectable."

Or one small enough to send a ghost, I thought. I couldn't decide what to say. If I set Vapherra straight, she'd no doubt spend more time trying to figure out how I'd done it. If I told her she was right, it would be a big fat lie. Which led me to a third course of action: to claim neither.

"Why fabled?"

"Because the location of their burg is unknown."

"How could you not know where an entire burg is?"

Vapherra gave me a look as though she thought I might be playing her.

"Because the Nanowerks Burg, which is believed to be populated by millions, is said to be no larger than one of Ceolwulf's silver pennies. Well, *that's* going to date me," she added with a grumble.

"Oh."

Vapherra stared at me intently. "I must caution you, Ms. Snap. If you are indeed in league with the Nano Empire, then you would do well to keep it secret. If the soothies thought, even for a second, that you knew the whereabouts of the Nanowerks Burg, they would stop at nothing to find it. Nothing. Do I make myself clear?"

"You aren't suggesting they'd sift me, are you? I mean, a mettle man told me the soothies were forbidden to sift a developing mind."

Vapherra's jaw dropped open in wonder. "You've met a mettle man? My, my, you have been very busy indeed! While it's true that a soothie is forbidden to sift a developing mind, it's also true that you won't be eleven forever. The soothies are nothing if not patient."

I was getting the feeling I'd learned all I could from this meeting. At this point, I couldn't see any good coming from hanging around. I stepped away from the balcony. "Well . . . I'm sorry about the maelstrom and all."

"Ms. Snap, you have no need to—"

I fumbled with the door knob. "I didn't mean to hurt Meerax."

"Willa!" I froze in place. "You have surpassed our wildest dreams."

"But I may have done nothing."

"And you may have done everything. For that, you have our deepest gratitude, and we are in your debt. We will not forget your efforts on our behalf. I'd be very surprised if our paths don't one day cross again."

When I passed through Morgan's bar on the way out, she motioned to me.

"A woman was in here looking for you."

"Did she give her name?"

"She said her name was Tuppence."

"Really! Is she still here? What did she say?"

Morgan nodded to the front doors. "She's waiting for you in a Clockwerk cab."

I dashed through the gaping stone jaws, the fire nearly singeing my dress.

Tuppence, the rather plain-faced mettle man, waved to me from the window. She was wearing the same beautiful pale-green chiffon party dress I'd first seen her in.

"Where may I drop you?" she asked, as I sat down.

"Home, I suppose."

"Whitehaven Mansions," cried Tuppence out the window, and the Clockwerk cab lurched forward. "Can I trust you're finished playing with the dragons? Are you ready to get down to the serious business of saving Grandeur?"

I thought about Heathcliff Wudgepuddle. "*You* put us in 56B, didn't you?"

"Very good."

"You think the Wudgepuddles are up to something."

"It's more complicated than you know. And if Dr. Wudgepuddle thinks a mettle man is sniffing around—"

"It'll be that much harder to catch him."

Tuppence stared at me for a long time. We were nearly halfway home before she spoke again. "What can you tell me . . . about that Clockwerk?"

And suddenly, I understood many things. "Ah! You were surprised that day in the MiniDirigy, when the Clockwerk Boy came aboard!"

"It's not every day a Clockwerk runs down in Greater Grandeur," she explained, lifting her eyebrows.

"No," I said, my voice rising. "It wasn't that. You were surprised because . . . you *knew* him."

Tuppence smiled. "Now what makes you say that?"

"You want to know where he is right now."

Tuppence said nothing.

"You've been to his house. I bet it was empty. And you're asking me about him now because you want to know where he's gone."

Tuppence's eyes flashed. "And why would I want to know that?"

"Because you have a new memory book to give him. I bet it's in your purse right now." Tuppence looked down at her purse. "The Clockwerk Boy doesn't know, does he?"

Tuppence shifted in her seat. "Doesn't know what?"

"That you're his handler. That he's your operative. That his memory books are missions written by you! That's why the handwriting at the beginning of the books doesn't match his. It's yours. But now he's gone. And you don't know where. I bet he took his books with him, too."

"What you are suggesting is beyond his capabilities. He's an old Clockwerk, and a rather simple one at that."

I smiled. "Not anymore."

"Oh, really? Care to enlighten me?"

"The week before my family was abducted, the Windwerks Burg was docked over the Clockwerk Burg. The memory book the Clockwerk Boy was carrying then was *Peril at Gear Hall*. On that mission, he attended a party as hired help. While snooping, he learned that Dr. Wudgepuddle had been using BrainRents to gather information on incoming Idiot Geniuses. That's how the Clockwerk Boy knew exactly when the Black Fez were bringing my family to Grandeur. What he didn't know was that Wudgepuddle was onto him and wanted his BrainBox destroyed. After the Windwerks Burg moved to the Biowerks Burg, Wudgepuddle lost the scent.

"You then sent him on a new mission—to nose around the time-traveling dragons. But something unexpected happened. He learned that my timeline was in danger. It might have ended there, since Meerax wasn't about to tell the other dragons when I'd be arriving. But lucky for me, the Clockwerk Boy already had that information. And since a Clockwerk's deep programming won't allow a human to come to harm—he felt compelled to try and save me. Only in his haste he wound himself down before he could tell me the whole story.

"I knew where to find him because he left a message for me in his memory book. But *I* wasn't the only one looking for him. And that's when I made a terrible mistake. You see, the night you sent me to Gear Hall for that little plumbing job, I thought I'd made a clean escape. But Wudgepuddle must have seen me because the next day, while Nimet and I were tracking the Clockwerk Boy to the Windwerks burg, Wudgepuddle was tracking *us*. We led Wudgepuddle straight to him. We're the reason his BrainBox was stolen!"

Tuppence held up a hand. "Wait! Wait! His BrainBox was stolen?"

"Yes. We had to find him a new one."

"Oh no," said Tuppence. "Don't tell me you contacted Tiffany Widderchine."

"Er, we did."

"I asked you not to tell me that."

"CeeCee da Vinci's bisnonno thought something was odd about Tiffany's BrainBox." And then I remembered how the Clockwerk Boy's *voice* had seemed different, too. "I don't think Tiffany gave us an ordinary antique BrainBox."

"Tiffany Widderchine," said Tuppence, "heir apparent to the great Thiphania Widderchine." Tuppence whistled. "Willamina Snap, not even *I* saw this one coming."

"And that's another thing. Why's everyone so worried about Tiffany?"

"Oh, that's easy. No one wants another Torsicus Widderchine."

Torsicus. I'd seen that name, but where? Then I remembered. "He designed the BrainBox on display at Gear Hall!"

"No. He *is* the BrainBox. Thiphania considered him her crowning achievement. She even gave him her last name. Torsicus was a new idea: a sentient Clockwerk designed to think for *itself* first and humans second. His arrival sparked the great Clockwerk uprising of 1219. You can read about it in Grandeurpedia. But I must warn you it's a sad tale.

"Don't ever underestimate the significance of a new idea, Willa. Unpredictable, powerful . . . a single idea can save the world—or destroy it. Grandeur was conceived to stamp out dangerous ideas before they could do any real damage. But even the Black Fez can't be everywhere at once. When a particularly unfortunate idea gets past them, it's up to Grandeur to add something back—to balance the scales. It's not an easy job. We don't always get it right."

"And when something tips the balance here in Grandeur, the soothies deal with it?"

"Correct, although sometimes the cure is worse than the disease." Tuppence picked a piece of holographic lint from her dress and released it into the air. A few inches from her hand, it winked out of existence. "The mettle men are a more recent addition. Our arrival dates to 1926." Tuppence looked at me to see if I was listening. I was. "It's not in my power to directly interfere with the soothies, Willa. If you run afoul of them, I can't help you."

"Who do the mettle men serve?"

"Why, Grandeur, of course. Grandeur above all else."

We pulled up in front of Whitehaven Mansions.

"The Clockwerk Boy is going to be a problem, isn't he?"

"That remains to be seen."

"What are you going to do now?"

Tuppence opened her purse and pulled out a little memory book. I quickly glanced at the spine: *The Boffin in the Library*. "Whatever I do, I won't be needing this."

I left her staring at the book.

On Sunday, Dad decided we needed a day out, so we wandered into Theophrastus Park and found a lovely spot under a tree. I'd invited the Magnificent Lady Grayson. Dad brought his binoculars, and Mom pulled the picnic basket from her purse when she thought no one was looking.

It will never take the place of Squirrel Brand Park, which holds so many of my earliest memories. But that didn't stop us from giving it the honorary name of Skíouros Márka Párko.

At one point, I wandered down to a little duck pond and tossed in the bread scraps from our sandwiches. It was then that I spotted him: Ravenlock Sward. The sight of him sent a flutter through my stomach. It only got worse after he noticed my parents. A smile flashed across his lips and he increased his speed. I mouthed *NO!* to him, but he ignored me. By the time I got there he'd already introduced himself to Mom and was shaking my father's hand while saying something about Idiot school.

He couldn't have looked or sounded more charming. My mother couldn't stop fawning over him, trying to offer him a bowl of strawberries. My father looked impressed, too.

Ravenlock may have been the most handsome boy I'd ever set an eye to, but there was something wrong inside his head. Something inside *my* head told me he didn't care about people, least of all me. And deep, deep down, I knew I could never trust him. He was nothing like Bertie. Bertie actually liked me.

"Ah, here she is," said Ravenlock, acting as though he was seeing me for the first time.

I fumed, answering in terse, one-syllable grunts. My mother tried to give me one of her private *Smile and be polite, dear* looks. I ignored her. I had absolutely no intention of saying or doing anything that would extend this chance meeting. Have I stated this strongly enough? Ravenlock = ugh.

Eventually, he turned to me and asked, "Walk with me for a moment?"

I turned sharply on my heel and strode away, a little faster than I meant to. Ravenlock had to use his long legs to catch up.

"Willa, slow down—" he began.

"Slow down?" I craned my neck to look him in the eye. "Why are you introducing yourself to my parents? What do you want? Why are you here?"

"I wanted—I mean, I understand you've made the acquaintance of . . . a certain professor."

I couldn't believe what I was hearing. "You've been following me?"

"No. Listen. I . . . know of him. He's dangerous, Willa. You shouldn't have anything more to do with him."

I was seething now. "I'll make my own decisions, thank you very much." The irrational part of my brain began concocting reasons to revisit the Ghost Factory, but each reason was crazier than the last. There was something incredibly creepy about that place, like things were watching us . . . dead things. Still, I wasn't going to tell *him* that.

Ravenlock's face hardened. "Don't be stupid. I can assure you he doesn't have your best interests at heart. He's *obsessed* with his experiments. They're *all* he cares about!"

"Oh! And *you* have my best interests at heart? That's a laugh! And for your information, Professor Farsical may have saved not only my life, but the lives of all the dragons! So how about you just keep your big nose out of my life—and stay away from me!" I turned to leave, but he sidestepped and got in my face.

"You're not unlike him, you know. You're both reckless."

"I'm eleven," I said.

"Oh, is that your excuse, you're eleven? Well then, I guess we'll all just have to wait for you to grow up. I hope Grandeur can withstand the wait."

"What are you going on about? What does Grandeur need from me?"

"There's an evil coming to Grandeur, Willa Snap. I can feel it."

Tuppence had said something just like that, on my first day in Grandeur. She'd said something else, too.

"'The soothies are restless,'" I said.

"Yes," hissed Ravenlock. "Yes, they are. And if you don't want to find yourself sifted,"—he touched his finger to my forehead—"you might want to consider carefully the type of people you call friend." And with that said, Ravenlock strode away. Leaving me without a snappy reply. I hate it when that happens.

Early the next morning, I went to the Jolly Rajah Man-o'-War o' Pancakes to talk to one Jajanana Toosk, elefantkin and waiter.

"Willa Snap!" he exclaimed. "Back in port so soon? What can I do for ye?"

"Actually, I was looking for you."

"Really, now. An' how may I be of service?"

"I don't know that you can. You see, I need to talk to a certain Black Fez."

Jaja tweaked the gold ball on his short tusk. "The Black Fez, ye say. Nae an easy squadron t' approach."

"You ever see any in here?"

"Aye, that I 'ave. After a voyage they like t' entertain on the fo'c'sle, where you can see the stars. They can be a bit of a rowdy bunch."

"Do you know Heather Peaceout?"

"Aye, that I do. But thar's no knowin' where she be."

"Why's that?"

"It's common knowledge, Willa. The Black Fez don't live in Grandeur. They don't even 'ave addresses. And as you know, sea dogs an' landlubbers alike be billed by the'r addresses."

My hopes plunged.

"If you don't know their addresses, how do they pay you?"

"The Black Fez never pay fer anythin'. I submit the'r bills directly t' Source. I suppose the Institute o' Intellect takes care of it. What's this all about?"

Then I had an idea. Even if the members of the Black Fez didn't *live* in Grandeur, surely there must be times when they had to stay overnight.

"Jaja, you're an Idiot, right?"

"Through an' through twice over, lassie. Now get on with it."

"I need a favor."

"Name it."

"I want you to imagine Heather's face—just her face—as perfectly as you can. Can you do that?"

Jaja closed his eyes. "Aye, that I can."

"Good. Now take off her fez and hair."

Jaja nodded. "Aye, fez and hair gone."

"Now, imagine her with every style and color of hair that you've ever seen." Jaja scrunched up his face and ground his teeth, concentrating. "Come on, Jaja. . . . You *never* forget a face."

The elefantkin's eyes sprang open. "Why, blow me down! Emilie Sauveterre, 46B Whitehaven Mansions."

"Thanks, Jaja."

"Blimey! Did I say that out loud?"

Except for the color of the carpet, the fourth floor of Whitehaven Mansions was a mirror image of the floor above—my floor—making the walk to 46B a surreal one.

I knocked on the door.

The woman who opened it had long black hair, nothing like Heather's, but I'd expected that. She seemed thinner, less athletic looking. I hadn't expected *that*. And the way she held her arms and body didn't seem right either. On her head sat a small pink fez, pinned into her hair at a jaunty angle.

"Qu'est-ce que je peux faire pour vous?" she asked in a heavy French accent.

Foreign language? *That* I had a plan for. I summoned my WatchitMapCallit and activated the conversation demon.

What can I do for you? read the screen.

"Ms. Sauveterre?"

"Oui?" *Yes.*

"I have a message for Heather Peaceout. Can you deliver it for me?"

While I waited for the WatchitMapCallit to translate my English into French, she rolled her eyes and motioned with her hands for me to get on with it. If she was Heather, she was *very* convincing.

"Well, can you?" I asked.

"Quel est le message, petite fille confuse?" *What is the message, you confused little girl?*

Emilie sighed and started to close the door. I planted my foot in front of it. I was still unsure. Then she stared down at me with her sky blue eyes, and I knew.

"Please tell her," I said, "that I'm tired of being eleven."

Don't miss Willa Snap's
second highly illegal memoir:

This book was independently published by a small band of Idiots who have yet to master the concept of regular paychecks. As a result, the success or failure of Willa Snap is in your hands! RATE THIS BOOK on Amazon, Barnes & Noble, iTunes, or Goodreads. Give us a shoutout on your favorite social media site (booktubers: I'm talkin' to you!). Join our email list. Visit WillaSnap.com for promos, events, giveaways, helpful tips on how to eradicate your local infestation of demonic squirrels, stuff like that. Order your flamethrower kit while supplies last!

Fun things you may enjoy searching on the internet, or in an ancient, smelly fire hazard of a book:

Agatha Christie (may I suggest starting with her mysterious disappearance in 1926?). Buckminster Fuller sphere. Cloche hat. The Turk. Thomas Edison's ghost portal. Charles Babbage's difference engine. John Ericsson's marine screw propeller and the *Robert F. Stockton* (Ericsson's more famous ship being the USS *Monitor*). TI's DLP projector. Theophrastus. Saint Nicholas's bones (they really are in Bari and Venice). The Flying Wallendas. Gleipnir chain. USS *Constitution*. Baba Kharak Singh Marg (great place to grab a bite next time you find yourself in Delhi). Stephen Biesty's *Cross-Sections: Man-of-War* (that's a book I can't stop looking at). Art Deco. Worm gear. Blockhouse #1, which is located in Central Park . . . hold on—that's in the second book! Don't look that up! Ninjutsu. Bastet. Leonardo da Vinci. Franklin's fire (electricity). And the Hall of Speculative Science at MIT, which is available strictly by invitation. Don't bother asking the administration about it. They'll just deny it exists. I'd suggest a ton of others, but you'd have to be somewhere other than Outside to research them.

Lastly, a bunch of long-dead—and a few not-so-long-dead—authors you should really read before picking up another one of my books. In alphabetical order: Jane Austen. Mildred Augustine Wirt Benson (you might know her better as Carolyn Keene; Mildred wrote or contributed to the first twenty-three Nancy Drew novels). The Brontë sisters (Charlotte, Emily, and the oft-omitted Anne). Agatha Christie (you might want to start with the Tommy and Tuppence novels). Wilkie Collins (*The Woman in White*). Sir Arthur Conan Doyle (give his Brigadier Gerard a go; there's more to Doyle than that guy with the pipe and funny hat). William Pène du Bois (particularly *The Twenty-One Balloons*—Yes!—read that one immediately! you won't regret it). Lord Dunsany (I'm particularly fond of his short story "The Three Sailors' Gambit"). Astrid Lindgren. E. Nesbit (I recommend starting with *The House of Arden*). Edgar Allan Poe ("The Gold-Bug" is some of the earliest American detective fiction, complete with cryptograms—it's great fun). And P.G. Wodehouse (because I said so).

Richard Due

I write books featuring bioengineered pygmy elefantkin short-order cooks. Yep—that's a thing I do. Also, I see moons.

And when not shifting unpredictably into third person, Richard lives with his wife, two lovely daughters, some cats, and three ducks, in a magical bookstore that is—quite frankly—the only thing that stands between you and raging hordes of zombies who haven't read a good book in, like, forever.

Carolyn Arcabascio

is a writer and illustrator. She began her career in the educational textbook market doing visual development and academic illustration. Her editorial and kidlit illustrations can now be seen in various consumer and trade publications.

Carolyn coaches writers and painters at The Oatley Academy of Visual Storytelling. She lives in New Hampshire with her husband and two high-maintenance terriers.

Made in the USA
Middletown, DE
21 April 2018